The
Proposal

Center Point
Large Print

Also by Jasmine Guillory and available from Center Point Large Print:

The Wedding Date

The
Proposal

A Novel

Jasmine Guillory

CENTER POINT LARGE PRINT
THORNDIKE, MAINE

This Center Point Large Print edition
is published in the year 2018 by arrangement with
Berkley, an imprint of Penguin Publishing Group,
a division of Penguin Random House LLC.

The text of this Large Print edition is unabridged.
In other aspects, this book may vary
from the original edition.
Printed in the United States of America
on permanent paper.
Set in 16-point Times New Roman type.

ISBN: 978-1-68324-944-3

Library of Congress Cataloging-in-Publication Data

Names: Guillory, Jasmine, author.
Title: The proposal / Jasmine Guillory.
Description: Center Point Large Print edition. | Thorndike, Maine :
    Center Point Large Print, 2018.
Identifiers: LCCN 2018035793 | ISBN 9781683249443
    (hardcover : alk. paper)
Subjects: LCSH: Large type books. | GSAFD: Love stories.
Classification: LCC PS3607.U48553 P76 2018b | DDC 813/.6—dc23
LC record available at https://lccn.loc.gov/2018035793

To my dad, Paul Guillory.
You have always believed in me.
Thanks for raising me to believe in myself.

Acknowledgments

Throughout this publishing process, I've been overwhelmed with gratitude for so many people and their kindness, generosity, and willingness to help. I've gotten advice, assistance, and support from countless people, without whom this book wouldn't exist.

I couldn't have dreamed of finding as wonderful a publishing home as Berkley. Cindy Hwang, thank you for being a fantastic editor and champion. Kristine Swartz, Megha Jain, Jessica Brock, Fareeda Bullert, Jin Yu, Erin Galloway— thank you for everything you've done for me and my books. I'm grateful for you every day. Marianne Grace, Emma Reh, Vikki Chu, and Rita Frangie, thank you for making sure my books look amazing, inside and out. Lauren Monaco, Andrew Dudley, and the entire Berkley Sales team, you're all superstars. I'm thrilled to work with all of you.

Everyone should be so lucky as to have an agent as good as Holly Root. Thank you so much to you and everyone at Root Literary.

So many writers have shared their time and

knowledge with me. Amy Spalding and Akilah Brown, your guidance has been invaluable to me. Thank you for responding to all of the texts and IMs and emails, for talking me down and for pumping me up. I will forever be grateful for Roxane Gay, Heather Cocks, Jessica Morgan, Ruby Lang, Sara Zarr, Melissa Baumgart, Tayari Jones, Robin Benway, Caitlin Cruz, Nicole Cliffe, Daniel Ortberg, Laura Turner, Jami Attenberg, Stephanie Lucianovic, Samantha Powell, Nicole Chung, Rainbow Rowell, and Alexis Coe. All of you have helped me in countless ways.

Rachel Fershleiser and Margaret H. Willison, your enthusiasm for books in general, and my books in particular, is the absolute best. Thank you for being you.

My friends are the most wonderful people in the world. Janet Goode, I love you so much. Melissa Sladden and Jina Kim, thank goodness we found each other. Simi Patnaik and Nicole Clouse, I have no idea what I would do without you both. So many others have loved and supported me in so many ways: Jill, Katie, and Sally Vizas, Lisa McIntire, Sarah Mackey, Julian Davis Mortenson, Nathan Cortez, Kyle Wong, Ryan Gallagher, Sarah Tiedeman, Toby Rugger, Leslie Gross, Kate Leos, Lyette Mercier, Joy Alferness, Nanita Cranford, and Laurie Baker.

I owe so many thanks to Wellesley College and the entire Wellesley community, but especially to Colleen Richards Powell, Korrie Xavier, and Marthine Satris.

I would be nothing without my family. My parents, Paul and Donna Guillory, filled our home with books and taught me by example the joy of reading. My sister, Sasha Guillory, who I read to and who read to me. My grandparents, aunts, uncles, and cousins, who love me to pieces. Thank you for everything.

Natalie Stewart Cortez, I hate that you aren't here to read this book, but I try every day to live up to your memory. You found joy and laughter in life, even during the hard times, you fought for what you believed in, and most of all, you loved and loved and loved. May we all have people to love us as much as the world loved you.

Chapter One

● ● ● ● ● ●

Nik Paterson looked around at the perfect Los Angeles day: clear blue sky, bright green baseball field, warm sun shining down on the thousands of people with her at Dodger Stadium. There was only one thought on her mind: *when can I get out of here?*

Fisher was next to her, his blond man bun golden in the sun, laughing as he drank warm beer to celebrate his birthday. He and his buddies were talking about lifting, or their latest auditions, or their upcoming car purchases—all of the things his friends always talked about, all of the things Nik couldn't care less about. If she'd known this birthday outing was going to include a bunch of Fisher's friends, she would have at least gotten one of her girlfriends to come along so she would have someone to talk to.

Although to be fair, it was possible Fisher had told her his friends were coming and she hadn't been paying attention. She tended not to pay that much attention when Fisher talked, but then, she hadn't been dating him for the past five months for his conversational skills.

Nik looked back up at the scoreboard and sighed. It was still only the fifth inning; she probably had at least an hour, maybe an hour and a half, more of this.

She didn't have anything against baseball, exactly. It was just that she'd rather be spending this beautiful spring day at home with her laptop and a glass of bourbon on the rocks than outside at a baseball stadium with a warm beer. But when the hot dude you were sleeping with wanted to go to a Dodgers game for his birthday, you sucked it up and went along with him and his bros.

She sighed again and reached for her phone. Maybe she could get some work done as she sat there.

Just as she was starting to make some actual progress on a draft of an article, Fisher nudged her hard.

"Nik! Put your phone down, you can't miss this!" He threw his arm around her and kissed her on the cheek. She pressed save and tucked her phone back in her pocket. His favorite baseball player must be coming up to bat or something.

She looked down at the field, but nothing was going on there. She followed Fisher's pointed finger and looked up at the scoreboard, just in time to see on the screen:

NICOLE: I LOVE YOU. WILL YOU MARRY ME? FISHER.

She turned to Fisher, her mouth wide open.

"What the hell is going on?"

To her horror, he dropped down onto one knee, on top of the peanut shells that carpeted the concrete, dangerously close to the puddle of spilled beer.

Oh God. He had a ring box in his hand.

"Nikole." He tucked a strand of hair behind his ear and opened the ring box. She averted her eyes. "Will you make me the happiest man in the world?"

Was she asleep? This definitely felt like a nightmare.

They'd only been dating for five months! That he loved her was news to her—he'd certainly never said *that* before—but a proposal? He didn't even know how to spell her name!

She tried to put on a smile, but she'd never had the best poker face—except, strangely, when she was actually playing poker. Not even his best friends would call Fisher perceptive, but even he could tell something was off with his happy moment.

"Nik, did you hear me? You're just standing there. You haven't even put the ring on!"

"I don't . . ." She cleared her throat and tried to talk in a low voice, so the whole damn stadium couldn't tell what was going on. "It's just that we've never discussed this. We aren't really in a place to . . . I didn't . . . I just wish you'd brought this up before . . . before now."

13

"Are you saying no?"

He was still on one knee, good God.

"I'm saying this isn't really the place to have this conversation."

He just stared at her, wide-eyed.

"Are you saying no?" he repeated.

She took a deep breath.

"I'm trying not to say that out loud so everyone can hear me."

She was still hoping this was some sort of a joke. That any minute, he would reveal this was for a commercial or a reality show or something, and they would all laugh and go back to not paying attention to the game.

"Come *on,* Nik," Fisher said. Why wouldn't he stand up? "We're great together! Live a little! Give us a shot!"

Live a little??? Was he approaching marriage like he would a spontaneous trip to Palm Springs for the weekend?

"Fisher. Don't do this."

"I can't believe *you're* doing this to *me.*" He snapped the ring box closed, stood up, and tossed his head. The head toss didn't work as well when his hair was in the bun. "Rejecting me in public! On my birthday! What kind of a person are you?"

He stormed off and ran up the stadium stairs. So she guessed this wasn't a joke then.

She looked at his bros, and his bros looked

at her. They shook their heads like they were disappointed in her, turned, and filed out of the row after him.

Which left Nik alone to face the forty-five thousand pairs of eyes on her.

Carlos nudged his sister Angela as the blond dude and his bros stalked up the stairs and out of the stadium.

"Now I know what to tell your boyfriend not to do."

Angela rolled her eyes.

"Nice try, but I don't have a boyfriend."

Damn. She consistently refused to let him meet guys she was dating, so he was reduced to trying to trick her into admitting she had a boyfriend. Either he never managed to catch her off guard enough to admit it, or she'd never had a boyfriend since he started trying this. He was betting on the former.

Granted, he never told Angie anything about the women he went out with, either, but that was different. He hadn't dated anyone seriously in years, and none of the women he had minor interludes with these days mattered enough to meet his sister.

"You have one good point," Angela said. "Anyone dating me should definitely not do that." Angela's hand gestures got bigger as she talked. "She said they hadn't discussed it. Who proposes to someone if they haven't discussed it? Especially in public?"

He looked back down at the woman—Nicole—now alone in her row. She'd sat back down and was typing something on her phone. The sun picked out the golden highlights in her dark curly hair. She was doing a very good job of pretending the whole stadium wasn't talking about her.

"I feel so bad for her." He couldn't believe she hadn't jumped up to flee the building. The game had started back up again, but no one was watching. Everyone was looking at her. Including Carlos.

"So do I," Angela said.

Nicole twirled one of her curls around her finger and pretended to watch the game. Carlos realized he was staring at her and forced himself to look away.

He turned to Angela and shook his head.

"I get trying to make a big romantic gesture and all, and wanting a surprise, but . . ."

"Deciding to spend your life together shouldn't be a surprise," Angela said. "It should be something the two of you talk about first!"

"Oh, hey, speaking of," he said. "Did I tell you Drew proposed to his girlfriend a few days ago?"

She laughed.

"Really? That's fantastic. I never would have thought a year ago that your friend Drew would be engaged." She looked up at the JumboTron, and then at Carlos. "She did say yes, right?"

He laughed.

"She did. But then, they'd talked about it first."

Carlos looked back at the woman two rows down, who had *not* said yes. She was aggressively not looking at anyone around her. Her hair moved in the breeze that blew through the stadium, and her dark brown skin glowed in the sun. He'd only seen her face briefly up on the JumboTron, until he'd realized that this real-life drama was going on just ten feet below him, but he'd seen a striking face, with big dark eyes and bright red lips. He wondered how long she was going to stay at her seat. She probably hadn't wanted to leave right away for fear of running into the man-bun guy, which made sense. But if he knew anything about the way things happened in L.A., if she sat here too long, she was in danger of . . .

Yep, there it was. The camera crew.

He poked his sister. She looked down and saw the problem immediately.

"Oh my God, what a nightmare," she said.

"We've got to save her," he said.

"How do you propose to do that? Pun not intended."

"Follow my lead." He stood up and made his way out of their row, Angie right behind him.

He walked down the wide stadium stairs, his

17

eyes on the field. When he got two rows down, he paused and glanced to the side. *I hope this works,* he thought, before he went in.

"Nicole? Nicole, it is you!" he said, loud enough that not only she and the entire camera crew heard but also the other rows around them all turned to look. "Angela, look, it's Nicole! We haven't seen you for . . . my God, how many years has it been?"

Angela took up his prompt as Carlos pushed the camera crew aside to get to Nicole.

"At least five years, Carlos, it's got to be? Nicole, how are you?" His sister threw her arms around the grinning woman, and whispered something in her ear before the embrace ended.

"It's so great to see you after all this time!" Angela said. She looked around with a huge smile on her face, and appeared to notice the camera crew for the first time. "Oh my goodness, are we interrupting something? I am so sorry, guys!" She smiled at the three men who had surrounded Nicole up until about thirty seconds before, with that wide-eyed look that had never failed to make men fall at her feet. "We haven't seen each other for so long, imagine running into you here."

"Oh wow, how do you know each—"

Carlos stepped in front of the guy with the camera. If the dude got aggressive, well, Carlos was pretty sure he had at least four inches and thirty pounds on him.

"We were just heading to get more beer and Dodger Dogs, want to come with?"

Want to come with? He sounded like one of his sixteen-year-old patients.

"Great idea, I'm starving." Nicole wiggled past the cameraman. "Chat with you guys later!" she called back to them, as she, Carlos, and Angie raced up the stairs.

Hmmm, apparently, sounding like your sixteen-year-old patients was a way to not seem suspicious.

They kept up the pretense on their way up the stairs, all saying things like "Wow, it's been so long!" and "Fancy meeting you here!" and "I couldn't believe my eyes that it was you!" over and over. When they finally got all the way up the stairs and inside, the three of them all leaned against the nearest wall and erupted with laughter.

"Thank you guys SO MUCH for saving me," Nicole said when she finally stopped laughing. "I was in the middle of trying to remember the martial arts moves I learned twenty years ago, but you rescued me without me having to knock someone down or, more likely, embarrass myself."

"You're not saved yet," Carlos said. He put his hand on her back and grabbed his sister by the arm. "We've got to get you out of this stadium. They'll find you again if you stick around."

19

"Oh, I can find my own way out. I'm sure you want to get back to the game." She stood up straight and smiled at them. "But thank you again, I really appreciate it."

He was about to say good-bye when he thought of something.

"Did you drive here? Or was your . . . or did you get a ride?"

She shrugged.

"My ride seems to be long gone, but I'm sure there's another way to get back to Silver Lake from here. Isn't there a shuttle or something? Or I can get a ride. I have all of those apps."

He and Angie exchanged glances. He envisioned her waiting in the parking lot at Dodger Stadium for a ride and getting ambushed again. He bet Angie did, too.

"Silver Lake is in our direction," he said. "We can give you a ride back." He could miss the rest of the game. It wasn't like they were playing the Giants or anything.

She raised her eyebrows at him and turned to Angela to shake her head.

"No, seriously, that's okay. You don't have to give up the rest of the game for me; you don't even know me. Plus, you two probably have better things to do than drive a stranger around Los Angeles."

Angela looked confused and then laughed.

"Oh wait, did you think we were on a date?

Ugh, no, he's my brother. Trust me, I'd rather be driving you around L.A. than watching baseball with him."

Nicole looked at Carlos.

"Are you sure? You really don't have to."

He grinned and threw his arm around both women.

"Call it my good deed for the week," he said. "Come on, let's go before those vultures follow you."

Chapter Two

• • • • • •

Nik walked across the parking lot with Carlos and Angela. She was grateful the exodus from the game hadn't started yet, so they didn't have to wade through crowds of people. The few they did see gave her dirty looks. That's right, she was the bitch who broke the pretty blond boy's heart, live on the JumboTron.

She shook her head. That really had happened. She had really been proposed to, and then abandoned, in front of the world.

She could not believe Fisher had done that to her. Just that he'd proposed to her in the first place was shocking—she would have been certain neither of them thought their relationship was heading toward marriage. She didn't think either of them *wanted* their relationship to head toward marriage. But not only did he do it, he did it in public. At a *baseball* game? Good God, she was furious at him.

She also felt like a huge asshole. She'd just refused her boyfriend's proposal in front of thousands of people. On his birthday. All of the people giving her dirty looks hated her for a good reason. She hadn't meant to hurt Fisher! He was a perfectly nice, incredibly boring guy. She probably could have found a nicer way to respond to the proposal, but she was so stunned she couldn't think straight. Plus, diplomacy had never been her strong point.

Thank God she'd gotten rescued by the Wonder Twins here. She should probably be wary of getting in a car with two strangers who had picked her up at a baseball stadium at a low moment in her life, but she didn't have the energy. She should especially be wary of this guy, who seemed way too attractive for his own good, with his tousled dark brown hair, big brown eyes, and that slight Saturday scruff on his cheeks. Normal Nik wouldn't have trusted this guy for a second. Dazed by the JumboTron, Nik had told him where she lived. But at this point, she didn't have the strength to do anything but be relieved she was no longer inside the stadium.

"Thanks again for getting me out of there. I was just sitting there texting my girlfriends about this fiasco and trying to figure out how I was going to get home when the camera crew showed up. I still can't believe any of this happened."

Carlos unlocked his car, one of the fancy red sports cars she was used to seeing around L.A. Ah, yes, of course the kind of guy who would almost knock down the cameraman and smile while he did it would have a red sports car. He

23

opened the front passenger door for her. She shook her head.

"Oh no, I can get in the back."

Angela laughed and opened the back door.

"Don't worry about it, Nikole. I think you deserve shotgun today."

"Nik." She needed to make this one thing clear, even though she was only going to know these people for the length of the car ride to Silver Lake. "Everyone calls me Nik. My first name is Nikole, yes, but it's Nikole with a K."

Angela looked at Nik for a long beat, her hand still on the open back door.

"But didn't the screen spell it . . ."

"With a C? It sure did!"

She got into the passenger seat and put her seatbelt on, and Angela slid into the seat behind her.

"You do not mean to tell me he spelled your name wrong in his *proposal?*" Angela said.

"That's exactly what I'm telling you. Only one of the many things that stunned me about this afternoon." Her pocket buzzed. "Wait, hold that thought, I have to tell my friends my ride is taken care of."

She had forty-three new text messages.

"Shit."

She clicked on her messages and let out a deep breath. Okay, thirty-three of the messages were from the group chat with her girlfriends, first their reactions to her initial texts about the proposal and then their increasingly agitated texts asking her where the hell she was when she stopped responding.

Sorry sorry, camera crew was in my face, some strangers rescued me, getting a ride back to the eastside from them right now, long story. Meet me at the bar within the hour.

She scrolled to her other new messages. Two were work related, she would deal with those after she'd recovered from the hangover she had every intention of having tomorrow morning. Oh my God, three were from people she knew who had been at Dodger Stadium that afternoon and had seen her on the JumboTron. There were more than eighteen million people in the greater Los Angeles area, she knew no more than a few hundred of them, max, and three of those had just HAPPENED to be at Dodger Stadium the one time in her life she was there, just so they could see the craziest thing that had ever happened to her? This was like some sort of sick joke.

And the other five texts were from Fisher.

You fucking bitch, I can't believe

She turned the phone off and dropped it in her pocket. So Fisher wasn't a perfectly nice guy after all. She wasn't even going to think about looking at those texts until she had at least two or three shots of bourbon in her.

"Everything okay?" Carlos asked, glancing over from the driver's seat.

She laughed, even though none of this was really funny. Now she understood what hysterical laughter really meant.

"As okay as anything can get today, I guess. Sorry for zoning out like that, I had a bunch of texts. My friends are very relieved that I got out of there in one piece."

"God, me, too," Carlos said. "When we saw that camera crew coming for you, I was worried that you'd either punch them all and run or burst into tears."

"Believe me, I was contemplating both," Nik said. "Unfortunately, I don't exactly know how to land a punch, and I didn't really want to get filmed crying on top of everything else."

He grinned at her, and she grinned back. It was refreshing to be around a guy who would joke with her like this after months of Fisher, who would only look at her blankly.

"Where to?" Carlos asked. "Do you want us to drop you at home, or at a friend's house, or . . . ?"

She was glad that she'd already made plans to meet Courtney and Dana at the bar, otherwise Dazed-by-the-JumboTron Nik probably would have given the first guy she'd met in forever who had a sense of humor her home address.

"There's a bar on Sunset that has a bottle of bourbon with my name all over it. My friends

26

are meeting me there to hopefully get me drunk enough so that I forget this day ever happened."

"I cannot believe he spelled your name wrong," Angela muttered from the back seat.

"To be fair to him, we'd only been dating for five months, maybe he just hadn't absorbed that bit of knowledge about me yet."

"Wait, WHAT?" She'd thought that Angela was the loud one, but Carlos nearly shouted that. "You'd only been dating for five months, and he proposed? In public?"

If she had to pick a strange man to rescue her, at least it was one who was outraged by the right things.

"Exactly! We'd only been dating for five months, he proposed, in public. And I'm the bad guy for rejecting him on his birthday?"

"You are not the bad guy," Carlos said. "Trust me on this."

She was tempted to text Fisher back, curse him out from here to oblivion, and tell him what she really thought of his acting, but she restrained herself. Barely.

Angela piped up from the back seat. "So, how long have you lived in L.A., Nik?"

She was grateful for the opportunity to talk about something else.

"For about six years, but I've lived in California most of my life. What about you guys?"

"Born and raised on the Eastside," Carlos said.

"Don't let my big brother over here act like he's got Eastside cred; he's been living on the Westside for years and just moved back, thank goodness."

"Thank goodness?" Carlos said. "This is the first I've heard of my little sister being thankful that I'm back on the Eastside. Thank goodness for what, so you can have someone to come over to your house and kill spiders for you in the middle of the night?"

"Exactly!" Angela said. "That, and someone to build my IKEA furniture for me, and to dog sit for me when I go out of town."

Carlos somehow managed to roll his eyes while keeping both eyes on the road.

"You don't even have a dog!"

"But I might! Someday!"

The siblings' friendly bickering kept her entertained for the rest of the ride to the bar. And more importantly, it kept her distracted enough so she didn't text Fisher back.

By the time they pulled up to the Sanctuary, the bar that she and her girlfriends had been coming to for almost as long as she'd lived in L.A., she'd even managed to laugh a few times at the stories that Carlos and Angela told about each other.

"You guys are going to come in, right?" she asked them. "I owe you far more than a drink for what you did for me today, but we can start with that."

Carlos and Angela exchanged a quick glance. It was a look full of wordless communication, but she couldn't tell whether it was "This woman seems crazy, let's get the fuck out of here" or just "I was getting carsick in the back seat, let's get a drink."

"Sure," Carlos said. "I was about to get another beer anyway right when all the action started at the game."

She felt her shoulders relax as soon as the three of them walked inside the bar. The dark, cool interior was such a relief after the unrelenting bright sunlight that she'd been enduring all day. She pushed her sunglasses up to the top of her head, where they would undoubtedly get caught in her hair within minutes, and glanced toward the corner of the room. Her friends Courtney and Dana were right there, waiting for her in their favorite booth.

"I made it," she said as she walked up to them. "Where's my drink?"

"There." Dana pointed behind her. She turned around, and the bartender, who had been pouring them drinks at least twice a week for the past four years, handed her a glass of bourbon with one big ice cube. That was fast. Granted, they were regulars there, but this was a record. Courtney and Dana must have told Pete that something was up.

"Thanks, Pete. Get my friends here whatever they want, please? On me."

As Pete took their orders, she slid into the curved booth next to Courtney.

"Hey," Courtney said. "You okay?"

She leaned her head against Courtney's shoulder for the briefest of moments.

"I'm fine. Just kind of shell-shocked at what just happened, I think." She motioned for Carlos and Angela to join her in the booth.

"Dana and Courtney, meet Carlos and Angela. They saved me in about a dozen different ways this afternoon, and I will owe them far more than my firstborn child. Carlos and Angela, these are my friends Dana and Courtney, who were about to come to Dodger Stadium and carry me away from that godforsaken place, so it turns out you saved them, too."

Just then, the bartender brought two more drinks to the table.

"A toast!" Nik said when the drinks were on the table. "To friendship, both real and feigned."

They all clinked glasses, and Nik took a deep gulp of her bourbon.

"Okay," Courtney said. "We need details. What did that toast mean? He seriously proposed? For the record, I never liked Fisher. He was never nice to me—I don't think fat Korean women were in his target demographic. Where is he now? Did he cry? Tell us everything."

Nik took a deep breath. She still couldn't believe this had actually happened to her.

Dana patted her on the shoulder and shook her head at Courtney.

"Let her finish her drink first! You don't have to tell us the story right now. Are you hungry? Should we get pizza? What kind should we get?"

She definitely wasn't drunk yet, but pizza sounded incredible right now.

"Absolutely. Fisher hasn't eaten carbs in like two years, so pizza sounds fantastic. I don't care what's on it as long as it includes pepperoni and lots of cheese."

Dana pulled out her phone and opened a delivery app.

"Are you two in, too?" she asked Carlos and Angela. They both nodded.

After a few clicks, Dana looked up from her phone.

"Okay, it's on its way here. Where were we?"

She took another sip of her drink. Thank God for bourbon.

"I don't know where we were, but to tell the story backward, that toast was because these two pretended to be long-lost friends of mine to save me from a camera crew. God bless them."

"A camera crew?" Courtney stared at her, then at Carlos and Angela, Nik guessed to confirm she hadn't lost her mind.

"Yep." Carlos nodded. "We were sitting a few rows behind Nik and saw the whole proposal happen. And then when we saw the camera crew

31

walking toward her, we knew we had to do something."

"Where did you even come up with that idea? That was brilliant!" Dana said.

He nodded and lifted his glass.

"Thank you for that; I agree, it was brilliant." He grinned at Nik, and despite herself, she grinned back at him. "But I have to admit, the credit all goes to our cousin Jessie. She told me a story once about a woman in a parking lot doing that to her when there was a creepy guy following her, and I guess it stuck with me."

Angela laughed.

"I was going to let my brother take the credit for that idea, even though I knew he got it from Jessie. I'm just glad to know he pays attention to the women in his family."

Nik couldn't remember the last time she'd seen a man voluntarily give credit to a woman for an idea. That was one of the major reasons she'd gone freelance, all of the men talking over her and pretending they'd come up with her ideas, even when everyone had heard her say them out loud.

"Oh, please," Carlos said. "I pay probably too much attention to all of you."

Nik finished her drink, and within seconds another one showed up on the table in front of her.

"Thanks, Pete," she, Courtney, and Dana said in unison.

"You three must tip very well," Carlos said.

They all laughed.

"That, and Pete's had a crush on Dana for at least two years," Courtney said. Dana grinned and shrugged.

"Okay, okay." Nik took a sip of her new drink and set it down. "And now for my part of the story. Here is the most important thing: I had NO IDEA that anything like this was coming. I was racking my brain on the way here for where this came from, and I swear, I had no hints."

She'd actually started wondering within the last few weeks how much longer this Fisher thing would last. Not only did he bore her, but she didn't really think he was all that interested in her, either. She didn't look like the models his friends all dated, he didn't even pretend to be interested in her work, and she found his laughable. A great recipe for a marriage!

"Anyway. The game was whatever, fine, boring, sunny, et cetera. And then all of a sudden, Fisher told me to look at something. I thought it was some stupid baseball thing, so I looked at the field, but then he pointed toward the JumboTron. And up there, in twelve-foot-high letters, was something like 'I love you, will you marry me?' "

"You forgot the most important part," Angela said. "It said 'Nicole, I love you, will you marry me?' Nicole with a C!"

Dana and Courtney gasped in unison. The appropriate response.

"He spelled your name wrong in his proposal?" Courtney asked.

"Yes!" Nik said. "But wait, think about that part later, let me get the whole story out first. So when I saw the thing up on the screen, I thought it was some sort of joke or that he was just showing me because that's my name and it was someone else in the stadium, or something like that. He'd never even said I love you to me before—which, if he had, this whole nightmare today never would have happened, because I'd have cut that thing off in a heartbeat, but anyway. Wait, where was I?"

"You saw it up on the screen . . . ?" Dana prompted her.

"Oh, yeah. So I turned to him, and he was down on one knee. With a ring box in his hand!"

"What did the ring look like?" Courtney asked.

"The ring?" Nik paused. She'd been so freaked out at the time she hadn't even looked at it. "I have no idea. I don't think I even saw it. Hell, I don't even remember what I said to him, something about how we should have talked about this before, and then he said something like, 'Are you saying no?' and I told him I wasn't saying that out loud, and then he told me to just live a little. LIVE A LITTLE. Like deciding to get married on a whim is the thing all the cool girls are

34

doing these days. And when I again refused, he got furious and stood up and left and his friends followed him." She turned to Carlos. "Did I forget anything?"

Carlos made a face. Oh shit, what had she forgotten?

"Just that . . . just that there was a camera on you the whole time, so the entire thing was broadcast to the whole stadium. No one could hear what you were saying—I mean, we could, we were just a few rows behind you and your dude talked pretty loudly—but what was going on was probably pretty clear to everyone."

"Oh yeah, right. That part." Nik put her head down on the table. "I think I need to just stay here for the next few days. Throw a blanket over me and just leave me here in the bar, and for the love of God, take my phone with you. Maybe by the time I resurface, everyone will forget that any of this ever happened."

Dana patted Nik on the back and Courtney took the phone that Nik had tossed on the table and tucked it away in her pocket.

Someone pushed her drink against her hand. She grabbed it, lifted her head, took a sip, and put her head back down on the table. Thank God for bourbon.

"Did I forget anything else?" Nik sat up and pushed her hair back.

"I saw the ring," Angela said.

"WHAT?" the whole table said in unison.

Angela looked at Carlos.

"You didn't see it? Oh yeah. He opened the ring box when he first got down on one knee, and the camera zeroed in on the ring. I can't believe you didn't notice."

She knew there was a reason she'd wanted Carlos and Angela to stay.

"Well?" Nik asked. "Don't keep me in suspense. What did it look like? Please tell me you remember."

Angela paused.

"Okay, you know the Kate Middleton ring, right? The Princess Diana one? With the huge sapphire in the middle and diamonds all around it? It looked just like that. Except smaller."

Nik banged her drink down on the table. It sloshed everywhere, but she was past the point of caring.

"Does he think he's some kind of a prince?" She took a deep breath. "Wait, that sounded mean. That was mean, I guess. But . . ."

"But you are not a princess ring kind of person," Courtney finished.

"But I am not a princess ring kind of person!" Nik said. "Nothing against princess rings, but IF I wanted an engagement ring from him—which I absolutely did not—it wouldn't have been a replica of a princess ring. He obviously doesn't know me that well; I'm not a baseball-game

36

proposal kind of person, either. But seriously, a princess ring? For ME?"

"You did get up at four a.m. to watch Harry and Meghan's wedding though," Dana said.

"That was different," Nik said. "Anyway, is there anything else I missed about the proposal?" she asked Carlos and Angela. "Am I remembering the forlorn look on Fisher's face correctly?"

Carlos shrugged. "He looked more outraged than forlorn, really. Like a kid having a tantrum."

Yeah . . . that sounded like Fisher, unfortunately. She mopped up her spilled drink with some of the extra napkins Pete had left on the table.

"Carlos is right," Angela said. "No offense, but he seemed like kind of a baby."

Nik shrugged and sighed. Fisher had been kind of a baby. A baby with beautiful blond hair he constantly admired in the mirror and great abs. So yeah, it made sense that he would yell and storm off when she'd publicly rejected his proposal.

"None taken. He was kind of a baby. But babies can be pretty great sometimes—isn't that why people like them?"

Carlos cleared his throat.

"As a professional baby expert: people like babies because they're cute, they have big heads, and because they're pretty helpless without us. They can scream really loudly, though."

Courtney nodded.

"Yep, that sounds like Fisher. Down to the big—"

"COURTNEY!"

Dana and Courtney giggled and high-fived, and Nik tried and failed to suppress her laughter.

"You two are the worst friends in the history of the world, do you know that?"

They nodded, still laughing.

"We know," Dana said.

Carlos coughed. Maybe they needed a reminder that there was a guy at the table with them?

Nope, that just made all four women, his little sister included, glance his way and laugh harder. Excellent. He looked at Nik, who was looking back at him. She winked at him. He grinned and winked back.

One of the friends' phone buzzed. Dana, right? She was the black one who looked like a model. Courtney was the Korean one with pink lipstick on.

"Pizza's here!" she said. A few minutes later, a huge pizza box covered their table, and they all had big pieces of pizza in their hands, the pepperoni oil dripping onto more napkins that the bartender had thrown onto their table.

"I didn't even ask if anyone was a vegetarian or gluten-free or anything," Dana said. He and Angela both shook their heads.

"This is a Los Angeles rarity, to have five

people at a table all dig into a cheese-covered, two-meat, gluten-filled pizza without hesitating."

Nik lifted her almost empty glass.

"To new friends and gluten!"

They all toasted and stuffed pizza into their mouths.

"Wait." Nik looked up at him and started to say something, but stopped to finish chewing her bite of pizza. "Did you say a few minutes ago that you're a baby expert?"

His sister just shook her head.

"My brother. Always with the delusions of grandeur."

He had the opportunity to impress three attractive women with his degrees and knowledge— could his sister at least try to be a good wingman here?

"I'm a pediatrician, but to be perfectly honest, I don't see a lot of babies anymore. I'm the assistant director of the teen clinic at Eastside Medical Center."

"Oh." Nik put her pizza down and reached for a napkin. "You're a doctor."

Okay, he'd never had a woman with that look on her face when he'd said he was a doctor. Like she'd smelled something bad.

"Oooh, you brought us a doctor?" Courtney poked Nik.

Nik looked at Dana and rolled her eyes.

"A doctor," Courtney said, presumably to

the table at large. "That's a normal job. I didn't think people in L.A. had normal jobs anymore. All of the jobs here are, like, writer, magician, fit model, actor, cupcake baker, dog walker, social media manager, juice shop cashier, and nonsense like that."

"Well, what do you all do?" he asked Nik and her friends.

"Writer," Nik said.

"Cupcake baker," Courtney said.

"Actor," Dana said.

He and Angela both laughed, but they didn't.

"Oh wait. You're serious?"

Nik nodded and sipped at the dregs of her drink.

"It's true. We're a parody of L.A. sitting right here." She turned to Angela. "What about you? You are also probably something normal, like a teacher or a social worker or an accountant."

"Marketing, for one of the studios," Angie said. "I'm also a parody. Granted, I got my MBA first, so I could have done a normal job, but no, I went straight for the L.A. stereotype."

"What kind of stuff do you write?" Carlos asked Nik.

"Lots of entertainment and celebrity-related stuff, and some more newsy journalism occasionally."

"What about Fisher?" Carlos couldn't keep himself from asking. "Was he also an L.A. stereo-

40

type, or was he a lawyer or trader or some-thing?"

Nik shook her head. "Actor! I should have known! Never date an actor; you get proposed to in public with a fucking princess ring." She took another bite of pizza and swallowed it. "Sorry, Dana. No offense."

"None taken," Dana said.

Nik sighed.

"Speaking of Fisher . . . he sent me some texts after he left the game. I only saw a glimpse of one of them, but . . . it wasn't so great. I guess I probably need to read the rest, right?"

Ahh, that's probably what she had been looking at when her face shuttered when they were in the car. She probably didn't want to talk about this with strangers around. Carlos caught Angela's eye, and she nodded.

"Ladies, my sister and I should take off. We have a family event that we have to get to and we can't be late."

"Oh!" Nik looked up. Was it just his imagi-nation that her face fell? "If you have to go, I understand. But you guys, I can't thank you enough for today; you two saved me on what was maybe one of the weirdest days of my life."

Angela stood up, and all of the women followed her out of the booth.

"It was our pleasure," she said. Nik threw her arms around Angie and whispered something

41

in her ear that made her laugh. Then she moved over to Carlos.

"Carlos, thank you so much." She gave him a tight hug and a kiss on the cheek. He almost kissed her back, but stopped himself just in time. She'd probably had enough out of men today.

"Glad we could help."

Dana and Courtney both hugged him, too.

"Thanks for taking care of our girl until she could get back to us. *You* are the prince of the day," Dana said.

He and Angie left Nik and her friends to dissect the texts, something he knew women loved to do.

"That was nice of him, to leave just then," Dana said, after the three of them sat back down in their booth alone.

"What do you mean?" Nik said as she reached for another piece of pizza. "They said they had a family thing."

Dana rolled her eyes.

"Sure they did. He wanted to let you show us Fisher's texts without him around, so he made up some reason to leave." She took a sip of her drink. "I don't often say this about men, but I liked him."

Courtney nodded.

"I liked him, too. You know what I think?"

Oh God. Whenever Courtney asked that question, either something great or something terrible was on its way. Sometimes it was a little bit of both.

Nik rested her chin on her hand and closed her eyes.

"What do you think?"

"I think Carlos should be your rebound."

This time it was just terrible.

"Dana, talk some sense into her, please." Nik looked from Dana to Courtney. "Number one, Fisher and I broke up, like two hours ago. Number two, Carlos seems like a very nice guy, but he's a doctor, come on."

Dana looked at her blankly.

"And?"

What was wrong with them?

"*And* Justin was a doctor, remember?"

Dana and Courtney looked at each other, then back at her.

"Yes, Justin was a doctor," Dana said, in her most patient voice. Nik hated that voice. "That doesn't mean that all doctors are assholes."

That's not what she meant and they knew it.

Well, okay. That was kind of what she meant. But still.

"Justin was a surgeon." Courtney took a gulp of her drink and slammed the empty glass onto the table. "That's different than a pediatrician."

Not that different. She hadn't seen or talked to Justin in years, but she remembered him and his God complex all too well.

"Plus," Courtney said, "Carlos is hot. I would go for him myself, but he was staring at you all night."

Nik rolled her eyes and drained her glass.

"That is not true."

"Oh, come on," Dana said. "Even I think he was hot, and I'm a lesbian."

Nik shook her head.

"I'm not arguing that point. Of course he's hot, did you see those forearms? I meant it's not true that he was staring at me all night."

Courtney and Dana looked at each other and laughed. There was no point in arguing with them about this. Especially since she wasn't even sure if she was right.

"You have a rebound with Carlos if you want," she said to Courtney. "I'm taking a vow of celibacy. Men are clearly not for me at this point in my life."

Dana and Courtney dissolved into laughter.

"No really, you guys. I mean it!"

Their heads were down on the table. Courtney's face was possibly buried in a slice of pizza? It apparently didn't matter, they were still laughing.

"I'm not joking! I need a break. Once you find yourself on the JumboTron with a guy kneeling at your feet with a princess ring in his hand, you start to reevaluate your life, okay?"

Courtney sat up, a piece of pepperoni in her

bangs. After that performance, Nik wasn't going to tell her it was there.

Dana gulped down the rest of her drink and waved Pete over for more drinks.

"A pitcher of water, too, please," Nik said to him. "I want to be able to at least somewhat function tomorrow."

As soon as he walked away, Dana turned to her.

"If we say we believe you and your vow of celibacy, can we get back to Fisher's texts?"

"We believe you, we believe you," Courtney said, the pepperoni bobbing up and down as she nodded her head.

They did not actually believe her, she knew that, but there was no point in arguing with them right now. They'd see. She took her phone back from Courtney.

"Here." Nik unlocked the phone and pushed it across the table. "After the glimpse that I saw, I don't know if I want to see the rest."

Dana picked up the phone and Courtney looked over her shoulder. Nik looked at their faces as they scrolled through the messages. After about two seconds, they both looked ready to kill.

"That bad, huh?" she asked.

Courtney's eyes narrowed at the phone. Oh no, it was even worse than she'd thought.

"Okay. What do they say?"

Dana cleared her throat. Thank God neither

of them offered to just delete them for her. Her friends knew her far too well for that.

" *'You fucking bitch, I can't believe you did that to me on my birthday.'* That was the first one," Dana said.

" *'I can't believe you would be that stupid. I was the best thing that ever happened to you.'* " Dana looked up from the phone. Nik nodded for her to continue. " *'You're such a'*—I'm not saying that word—*'my friends always said so. I saw your potential when no one else did. You were lucky to be with me, you're never going to get the chance again. No one else will ever love an unfeeling bitch like you.'* "

Well, at least she didn't need to feel guilty about hurting him anymore.

"I don't *want* anyone else to ever love this unfeeling bitch. Something terrible always happens when a man says 'I love you.' First, Justin said it and then he tried to sabotage my career, then Fisher said it and I get put on a big screen and he texts insults to me. If that's what love means, no thank you."

Dana took a sip of her drink and kept reading.

" *'You're going to die alone, and you could have been my princess.'* There are five exclamation points at the end of the word princess. FYI."

At least that made her laugh. Thank God for unnecessary exclamation points.

"Okay, and here's the pièce de résistance."

46

Dana pushed the phone over to her, and she looked at the picture that filled the screen: Fisher, Dodgers cap on backward, middle finger in the air, with the princess engagement ring on said finger.

"OH MY GOD."

Dana and Courtney exploded with laughter. Courtney's head shook so much that the pepperoni finally fell onto the table and she didn't even notice. Nik laughed until tears streamed out of her eyes. They collapsed against the booth cushions, laughing so much and so loudly that even the too-cool-for-school dudes at the end of the bar turned and stared.

"Are you KIDDING me? Is this some collective hallucination? What was IN those drinks that Pete brought us? Since when is Fisher Vanilla freaking Ice?"

"Well." Nik managed to stop laughing and reached for what was definitely her final drink. "I feel better already."

Chapter Three

• • • • • •

On Monday morning, Nik stared at her laptop from the other side of the room. It wouldn't stop pinging at her. She'd turned the sound off, she'd moved over to the couch, but she knew it was still happening. It had been almost forty-eight hours since the nightmare proposal, and she was getting hundreds of messages in a constant stream through every possible avenue. She'd had so many texts when she'd woken up the day before that she'd thought her phone had malfunctioned.

Apparently, her JumboTron moment had been on SportsCenter on Saturday night. And then again on Sunday. She'd had no idea that she knew so many people who regularly watched SportsCenter.

To make things even worse, some enterprising person had tagged her on Twitter with the video of the proposal, so she was getting thousands of tweets about it. The bulk of them ranged from insulting to abusive, with a lot of just plain mean thrown in for kicks. A lot of men out there seemed personally insulted that she, a black woman, had rejected a white man. Most of their messages to her used either her least favorite insult for women or her least favorite insult for black people and, in many cases, both.

Until she'd blocked Fisher's number, he'd also kept sending her messages, and most of them weren't as unintentionally funny as the Vanilla Ice picture. The last few had been kind of scary, and she didn't scare easily.

The whole time she had to keep tweeting her way through it, because she used Twitter professionally, and she refused to let on that any of these assholes were upsetting her. Plus, that was her "brand" and all—that kind of sarcastic, witty, tough-skinned woman who nothing could bother. She had to pretend to be laughing with the rest of the world about what a bitch she was, retweet a few stupid memes with her face on them, and make a joke on Facebook about her relationship status changing, when she felt overwhelmed and outnumbered the whole time.

At least she hadn't seen any footage of Carlos and Angela posted anywhere. They'd probably jumped in before that camera crew had gotten anything worth posting. Whatever it was, she was grateful for it. She wouldn't have wanted them to get dragged into this chaos or to get punished by the whole world for their good deed.

Good deeds—plural. Not only had they pulled her away from the camera crew, gotten her away from the stadium of doom, and delivered her to her friends, but as she'd discovered on Saturday night after winning the fight with Dana and Courtney to pay their bar tab, Carlos had already paid for it. And she didn't even know his last name, or how to get in touch with him to thank him.

"Wait a minute, Nikole," she said out loud. She talked to herself a lot when she was alone in her apartment, which was frequently. "You are a journalist. You should be able to find this man in less than five minutes."

It took her about a minute and a half. There he was, Carlos Ibarra, picture and all, on the website of his hospital. Thank God the bourbon on Saturday hadn't dulled her memory. There was no email address listed, but she clicked around the hospital website to see what the other email addresses at his hospital looked like. She jumped over to her email account, opened the "compose" pane, and tried to ignore the dozens of new emails that had come in since she'd last looked.

To: Carlos_Ibarra@
eastsidemedicalcenter.com
From: Nikole@NikoleDPaterson.com
Subject: Thanks again

Hi! It's me, your friendly non-princess from Saturday. I just wanted to a) thank

you again for everything you did, and
b) yell at you for not letting me buy you
the drink I owed you afterward. I don't
know if you saw, but the whole proposal
has kind of gone viral, which . . . is an
experience, that's for sure. Anyway, I
hope you're well, and thank your sister
for me, too!

Nik

She typed the email in a hurry and pressed send
before she could reconsider. Her friends would
be so triumphant if they knew she'd emailed him.
They would think she bought into their stupid
rebound idea, when that wasn't at all the case.
Obviously she found him attractive—she wasn't
made of stone—but just as obviously, it was the
wrong time to get involved with anyone. She just
wanted to thank him again for saving her, that
was all.

Of course it wasn't until after she'd hit send
that she thought about the major downside of
actually sending an email right now—she'd have
to look at her incoming messages to see if he
responded.

She couldn't even get any work done. The story
she'd been working on at the baseball game was
still stuck in the same place it had been when
Fisher had told her to look at the JumboTron

screen. She'd been halfway through a sentence, and now she had no idea how the sentence was supposed to end. She probably had important work-related emails, but she'd have to wade through the hundreds of other messages to find them. She threw her arms in the air, went into her bedroom, put on the first real clothes she found, and left to go for a walk. Without her phone.

By the time she'd walked the thirty minutes to Courtney's cupcake shop, she felt a little better. Despite herself, the fresh air and the blue sky made her relax, and the physical activity even cheered her up a little. When she walked into Cupcake Park, she didn't quite have a smile on her face, but at least she could tell the scowl had gone away.

"Hey!" Courtney was alone in the shop when she came in, wearing her trademark pink lipstick and a pink polka-dot apron. "You haven't been answering your phone. Dana and I have both been trying to call. How are you doing?"

She groaned and leaned against the counter. Courtney's brightly colored cupcakes, all decorated with frosting flowers or trees, stared back up at her from the other side.

"Coffee, please?" She shouldn't have even bothered to ask. Courtney had already poured cups full for both of them and set one of each of her favorite cupcake flavors in front of her. "You're the best, thanks."

"We both know that," Courtney said. The bell rang, and Nik stepped aside so that the three teenage girls who came in could see and debate their cupcake choices. By the time they left five minutes later, Nik had finished her lemon cupcake and most of her coffee. Courtney poured her a new cup.

"How did business go today?"

Courtney had opened her cupcake shop just under a year ago, and there had been a number of touch-and-go moments with it, but lately business looked like it was picking up.

"It was great. There was a line out the door for like half the day, and I just got two big orders, including one for a wedding." Courtney looked hard at Nik. "But I know you didn't walk all the way over here to find out how my business is going. How are you? How bad is it?"

Nik groaned.

"It's so bad." She took a sip of coffee and reconsidered. "I mean, I'm not dying or anything, and this should all fade away within a few days. But God, it doesn't feel like that right now. I'm not answering my phone because I had to turn the sound and the vibrate off, and then put it in my refrigerator to chill out, because it feels like the whole world is calling me or texting me. I needed a break."

She could *not* tell Courtney that she'd emailed Carlos. She would do her "I told you so" dance around the whole cupcake shop. Had Carlos replied to her email yet? Ugh, she wished she'd brought her phone, just so she'd know.

Courtney checked the time and walked over to flip the sign on the door from OPEN to CLOSED.

"Do you think all of the proposal brouhaha will blow over?"

Nik grabbed a broom to help Courtney do her end-of-the-day cleaning of the shop.

"I'm sure it will. I just hope it blows over *soon.* The only email I responded to so far today was from the *TODAY* show, telling them no, I would not come on the show to talk about the proposal. I'm kind of worried that Fisher will say yes to them or someone like them, but there's nothing I can do to stop that, and I feel like reaching out to him at this point is a very bad idea."

"Have you heard anything more from him?" Courtney tossed Nik a cloth to wipe down the countertops while she packed away the rest of the cupcakes.

"Unfortunately, yes. I've blocked him every-where, which probably means he's saying all sorts of shit about me that I can't see, but at this point, that's better than the alternative."

Courtney turned on Missy Elliott to keep them company as they cleaned up.

"Oh, I'll find out what he's saying about you, don't worry about that." Courtney had an evil grin on her face that Nik decided not to ask about.

It was probably better that she be ignorant of whatever Courtney was planning to do to Fisher.

"Want a ride home?" Courtney asked her. "Dinner? Leftover cupcakes?"

"No, no, and yes. Or rather, no, yes, and yes. Have I ever said no to leftover cupcakes? But I can walk home. I need to work up my appetite for these."

Courtney filled up a box of cupcakes and put it in one of her pink and white bags.

"Let me know if you need anything else. And if you need company tonight, I can be there at the snap of your fingers; you know that, right?"

Nik walked around the counter to give Courtney a hug.

"I know. Thanks."

Of course, once Nik walked home, she'd started to regret not getting a ride from Courtney. Not because the walk tired her out, but because she wished she wasn't alone. As she approached her building she was on high alert for Fisher's silver sports car in the area.

"You're being stupid," she said to herself on her doorstep. "Also, you're talking to yourself in public this time; you should really save that for *inside* the house, Nikole."

She unlocked her front door, and then hesitated on the threshold. Finally, she grabbed a cast-iron pan from her kitchen and, feeling like an idiot the entire time, looked in every hiding place in her apartment. After finding nothing other than a lot more dirty laundry than she thought she'd had, she tried to relax and sat back down at her laptop to check her email.

Fifty-seven more people had emailed her in the two hours that she'd been gone. And not a single one of the fifty-seven was named Carlos Ibarra.

"It was like this, Dr. Ibarra," Luke, his newest patient said. "There was this girl, right?"

Carlos laughed.

"How did I know that that's how this story was going to start? But keep going, all of the best stories start that way."

Carlos listened to the kid's story, took notes, gave him both medical advice—for the sprained ankle that he got from running down the street with the girl (rest, ice, elevation, lots of ibuprofen) and the rash he'd gotten from hiding in the poison-oak-laced bushes behind her house (a prescription cream)—and general life advice (girls who make you go through dangerous situations to prove your worth to them are always exciting at first and then you regret it).

That, of course, made him think about how he'd shoved that cameraman out of the way in order to get Nik safely out of Dodger Stadium. The difference, though, was that was his idea, not hers. But he understood where his patient was coming from—he still felt a rush when he thought

56

about swooping down on Nik and getting her out of the stadium. It was probably just because he didn't do anything dangerous these days other than driving too fast.

He'd had SportsCenter in the background on Sunday morning and was engrossed in the Sunday *L.A. Times* movie section, when he'd heard the announcer say "Can you believe what happened to this poor guy?" He'd looked up at the screen, just in time to see Nik's wide-open mouth and Man Bun drop down onto one knee. He'd been wondering all day how Nik was doing. He wished he'd figured out a way to smoothly get her phone number before he and Angie had left the bar. Maybe sometime he would go back to see if he could accidentally run into her there. She said she and her friends went to that bar a lot, right?

He went back to his office after that appointment, hopefully his last one of the day, unless there was an emergency in the next hour and a half. He typed his notes from his appointments into the online system, making sure to only note the parent-friendly details from the stories that the teens had told him since their parents all had access to their information. With just half an hour to go until his Monday was over, he clicked over to his work email, to see what stupid administrative tasks people had sent him this time.

Nikole Paterson? He clicked on the screen so fast that he accidentally clicked on the email below it first, and had to skim through a message about vaccinations before he realized what was happening and went back.

"I don't know if you saw, but the whole proposal has kind of gone viral." He had, in fact, noticed that the whole proposal had gone viral. She must have heard from everyone she knew, and then some. He had no idea how she'd found his email address, but he was glad she had.

To: Nikole@NikoleDPaterson.com
From: Carlos_Ibarra@ eastsidemedicalcenter.com

Hey! Good to hear from you. I figured you'd want to yell at me about the drinks, but I also figured you and your friends already had too much bourbon to figure out a bill. And yeah, I saw you on SportsCenter. Have you gotten emails and texts from literally everyone you know?

Carlos

He got an email back right before he was about to leave the office.

To: Carlos_Ibarra@
    eastsidemedicalcenter.com
From: Nikole@NikoleDPaterson.com

To answer your question, every single other email in my inbox has the subject line "Was that you?" or "OMG that was you!" and I can't bear to look at any of them. So yes, I've gotten texts and emails (and Facebook messages, and tweets, and LinkedIn messages, for the love of God) from literally everyone I know. I have ignored all of them so far and have been hiding in my apartment almost all day, with a brief excursion to pick up cupcakes from Courtney's shop, but I'm going a little stir-crazy.

Nik

Was that a hint? She didn't seem like a hinting kind of person, but maybe?

To: Nikole@NikoleDPaterson.com
From: Carlos_Ibarra@
      eastsidemedicalcenter.com

If you're in the mood for a friendly face tonight, let me know. About to leave work, want to grab dinner? Text me, I'm at 310-555-4827. I promise I won't say "OMG that was you!"

Carlos

He double-checked his phone all the way to the parking garage, but nothing. Okay, maybe it wasn't a hint. Damn it. It had been a long time since he'd met someone who could laugh at herself the way Nik could, even in the middle of a crisis.

Also, he'd really liked the way she'd looked in that snug baseball T-shirt and those jeans, he wasn't going to lie.

He'd seen way too many accidents in his stint working in the ER to check his phone while he was driving, but he had to fight himself more than once from reaching for it on the way home. But when he pulled up to his apartment and grabbed it out of his pocket, there was nothing other than five group texts about his basketball league.

Just as he walked in the door, his phone chimed.

Going to take you up on that offer for dinner, but this time it's my treat. What time and where? Not a bar, though, I'm still recovering from Saturday.

He was so busy grinning down at his phone that he almost tripped over the Amazon box in his entryway. Worth it.

7:30? Thai? There's a fun place on Sunset, do you know it? Night+Market?

She did know it. He changed into jeans and his favorite T-shirt, killed some time by replying to all of the basketball messages with trash talk, and walked back out the door.

He put his name on the list and hung out by the door and pretended to be absorbed in his phone. She walked in the door at 7:33, not that he was checking. She stood at the door and peered around the restaurant, a guarded look on her face, her sunglasses again tucked into her dark curly hair.

"Hey!" He waved at her. Her face relaxed into a grin when she saw him. She was wearing jeans and a black shirt that looked better on her than any plain black shirt had a right to look.

"Hey yourself. Thank you for rescuing me yet again. If you hadn't suggested dinner, I would have had a half-dozen cupcakes for dinner, hated myself for it, and then had another half dozen for dessert."

He laughed.

"Thai food is definitely a much better idea. Where'd all the cupcakes come from?"

She leaned against the wall next to him.

"I forced myself out of the house today and walked to Courtney's shop. I hung around until closing and she gave me the leftovers."

"That's convenient to have a friend with a

cupcake store." Now that he was looking at her closely, he could see a spot of white frosting standing out against her warm brown cheek and fought his impulse to wipe it off.

"You're telling me. She usually gives any leftovers to the employees at the other shops nearby, as a sort of goodwill/'we're all in this together' kind of thing, but I guess today she thought my need was more important. I certainly wasn't going to argue with her."

They made small talk as they waited for their table, too surrounded by other people to talk about anything important. After longer a wait than he'd hoped, the host finally called his name.

As Carlos walked behind Nik on the way to a table, he admired her shape in her snug jeans. He was pretty sure this woman hated all men at the moment, but he could look, couldn't he?

They both ordered beer before they opened their menus.

"You're going to have to keep me from ordering everything on the menu, I'm starving," he said.

Nik glanced over the menu and grinned.

"Luckily, I heard from you at just the right time before I dove into the box of cupcakes. And I'm glad you wanted to go to this place. I haven't been here in far too long; Fisher didn't like spicy food, so . . ."

He looked up at her with his eyebrows raised.

"Fisher didn't like spicy food, and you went out with him for more than one date? How did that happen?"

She sighed.

"Excellent question, really."

The waitress brought their beers, and she took a sip.

"Never again, though," she said. "I'm swearing off actors. You think you're just casually dating, and then bam, they spring a public proposal on you."

Carlos shook his head.

"Is he a real actor or a wannabe one?"

She laughed.

"You always have to ask that question in L.A., right? A real one, but a terrible one. And that's not even my rage talking; I thought that even while we were dating."

Oof. This woman did not mince her words.

"How did you even meet him?" He shook his head. "You don't have to answer that. You're probably sick of even thinking about this. We can talk about work, or our last vacations, or baseball, or whatever."

She widened her eyes in horror.

"Good God, not baseball, anything but baseball." They both laughed. "As for not talking about this, honestly, I wish I could stop thinking about this. I've probably thought about Fisher more in the past two days than I did in the entire

63

five months that we were dating, that's the wild part. But wait, you probably don't want to hear more about my disastrous love life; you heard plenty on Saturday."

Actually, he'd left right when they'd gotten to the good stuff. And honestly, he was dying to know the details.

"If it helps you to talk about it, I'm happy to listen," he said. Did that sound magnanimous enough? "I talk to teenagers all day; hearing a story about an adult disastrous love life will be refreshing after their stories, I promise."

She pushed her hair out of her face and smiled.

"Okay, but you're going to have to tell me at least one good work story afterward, so I don't feel like such an idiot. You see teenagers; you must have some great ones." She glanced down at the menu. "Wait, let's order first. You already said you were starving."

The waitress stopped at their table, and they ordered far too much food for two people.

"What did you ask?" she said when the waitress walked away. "Oh right, how I met Fisher." She sighed. "Last year, I did a profile of Anna Gardiner for *Vogue*. She only really got big, like, last summer. Right before she got the role that led to the Oscar nomination and *Vogue* cover and everything else, she was in a terrible and short-lived TV show. Fisher was her co-star."

He held up his hand to stop her.

64

"I'm sorry, but you got to meet Anna Gardiner? Most famous people are no big deal, a dime a dozen in L.A., blah blah, but Anna Gardiner? What was she like? Don't tell me she was terrible; I loved that movie."

He was so thankful none of his friends were here to witness him babbling about a movie star—they would make fun of him from here to eternity.

"She was honestly great! Which is the whole reason I met Fisher, actually. Anna and I got along really well, and she ended up inviting me to her birthday party, and that's where I met Fisher. When he asked me out, I was positive that he just wanted to go out with me because he wanted me to write a puff piece about him for something. I sort of never stopped thinking that, actually."

She shook her head and laughed.

"The funny thing is that whenever I went to industry parties with him, when people I knew through my work saw us together, they would look so confused. A few times, when he was on the other side of the room, they even said to me, 'You're here with *that* guy?' I was never sure if that was an insult to me, or to him."

The waitress set their spicy and sweet wings down on the table, and they both grabbed one.

"Anyway, going out with Fisher was very low-stress, until two days ago. I've had such a busy few months of work and Fisher was just a fun guy I hung out with when I had time. I even felt guilty about saying no to his proposal, because I didn't want to hurt his feelings! That was, until . . . well, apparently, I'm not as good at reading people as I thought I was."

He looked closer at her. He was pretty good at reading people, and she looked really stressed about this whole situation.

"Have you heard from him again? Since his bad texts on Saturday?"

She looked up at him.

"How did you know they were bad?"

He gestured to her face.

"That same worried look that's on your face right now was on your face on Saturday night when you told your friends he'd texted you. I figured there was something in there that bothered you, and since you'd just rejected him in front of thousands of people, I assumed it was something pretty nasty." He held up his hand when she started to protest. "I'm not blaming you for rejecting him in front of thousands of people. As a matter of fact, I was pretty impressed that you were honest with him, instead of being nice to him just to make him feel better. But when I saw that look on your face, I figured he wanted to lash out at you."

She nodded.

"He sure did. Which . . . I like revenge as much

66

as the next person, so I get that, but he didn't have to keep going."

He dropped his chicken and sat up straight.

"Is he still texting you?"

She shrugged.

"I'm not sure. The last text I got from him before I blocked him was 'Watch your back.' I'm sure he's just trying to freak me out. I don't really think Fisher is the violent-revenge-for-rejecting-him type." She shook her head. "But I should know better than to say that there's no such thing as one violent-revenge type; anyone can be like that. I didn't tell Courtney and Dana about that text. They would have freaked out, moved in with me, firebombed his house, and reported him to the police, probably in that order. Unfortunately, he succeeded in freaking me out, if that was his motive."

He sympathized with Courtney and Dana. He would want to do the same if anyone texted stuff like that to Angela.

He reached across the table and touched Nik's hand.

"I'm sorry that happened to you. Are you . . . do you live alone?" He shook his head. "Wow, did that sound creepy. What I meant was, are you okay? Are you worried that he'll come to your house if you don't respond to him?"

She started to shake her head and stopped.

"I wasn't at first. I do live alone—I probably

shouldn't tell you that; you're still a stranger, but hey, you have a good sister, you can't be too terrible—and I wasn't worried at all yesterday. But then today, after Fisher's texts, and then all of the tweets and emails from strangers that were way worse than what he said . . . when I walked into my apartment, well. That was another reason I was glad to leave to go to dinner tonight; it was good to get out of there and have some company."

He wanted to ask her what was in those messages from strangers that were way worse than Fisher's texts, but he wasn't sure if she wanted to talk about it. And he wasn't sure if he was ready to hear the response.

Two more platters of food landed on their table. He scooped papaya salad and pork belly onto both of their plates.

"I'm glad I could help, but it sucks that he's made you so anxious about this."

She took a bite of the pork belly and grinned.

"This is delicious, but also it's hot as hell." She squeezed his hand, and he smiled at her. They looked at each other for a long time, their hands still linked across the table. Finally, she broke the eye contact and dropped his hand.

"Okay, please, let's talk about something that isn't me. I deserve your best teen-client story, after that."

He grinned.

"I have a lot of good ones, but my favorite is the kid we nicknamed Santa, because he and his girlfriend tried to hide up the chimney."

She rubbed her hands together.

"Tell me everything."

Chapter Four

• • • • • •

When the waitress brought the check to the table, Nik handed the waitress her credit card.

"This one is on me. I'm still mad at you for paying for our drinks from Saturday. I owed you."

He pursed his mouth and considered.

"Okay, fine, but you get all of the leftovers. Deal?"

He said that like it was a punishment. Which, considering how spicy some of their leftovers were . . . he might be correct about that.

"Deal. I can have them for lunch tomorrow, in between all of the cupcakes."

As they walked to her car, he elbowed her.

"Yes?" she said, in answer to his look.

"I know you're pretty nervous about all of the Fisher stuff. Do you want me to follow you home just to make sure everything is okay? I mean, I'm sure everything is fine, I just thought I'd—"

"Yeah," she said. "That would be great."

Why had she agreed to this so quickly, she wondered on the short drive to her house. She usually hated it when men got all protective about her safety, like she was some delicate flower who didn't know how to protect herself.

But that hadn't been what Carlos had done, and she'd appreciated it. After her panic from this afternoon, it would be nice to have backup for those thirty seconds it took for her to walk through her apartment. Plus, not to be shallow, but the way Carlos's T-shirt clung to his biceps . . . she was pretty sure Carlos could take Fisher down easily.

But wait a second. Was she really going to get some dude she hardly knew to do a walk-through of her apartment just because she got a few nasty text messages? That was ridiculous. She was a grown woman; she'd lived on her own for years; she could take care of herself. She should text him right now and tell him that she was fine and didn't need his help.

Yeah, she'd do that. She reached in her pocket for her phone. When she got home, she'd text her girlfriends and tell them how stupid she'd almost been.

Well, she'd text her girlfriends if she was still around to text them.

She could hear Courtney's voice in her head.

What do you have to lose here? Are you really worried about looking silly in front of a man you barely know? Who cares?

She cared, damn it.

But her friends would kill her if she sent Carlos away and anything happened to her.

Okay, fine. She put her phone back in her pocket.

She parked in the lot behind her apartment building and met Carlos on the front steps.

"Thanks for coming inside with me. I feel like an idiot," she said as she unlocked the door.

"Don't worry about it," he said. "I'm a pretty impressive dude; people feel like idiots around me all the time. I'm used to it."

Despite her rising anxiety, she laughed as they walked up the stairs to her second-floor apartment.

"Did he have a key?" Carlos asked in a low voice.

Nik sighed and stopped on the stairs.

"I never gave him one, but I left my keys around all the time, and it's easy to get keys copied. And there was one time when I forgot my keys at his house for a whole weekend and had to get my set of extra keys back from Dana. I didn't think anything of it at the time, but . . . I'm paranoid now, I guess."

Carlos put his hand on her shoulder, and she relaxed against it.

"Are you ready to go inside? Or do you need a minute?"

She pulled away from him. She never should have done this, but she had no choice now.

"No, no, I'm fine. Let's go in."

He took the key out of her hand and unlocked the door. She could have done that herself, but okay. He pushed it open slowly. Why had she turned off all of the lights before she left her house? Energy-saving nonsense. Now she felt like one of those women in horror movies. One of the ones who got killed in the first fifteen minutes.

Wait, no. Those women never had the sense to get someone else to come with them when they had a bad feeling.

Carlos pushed the door wide open and stepped through it in front of her.

"If the demon gets me, tell my mother I loved her."

Apparently they watched the same kind of movies.

She followed close at his heels as he walked into the living room and flicked on the lights. Everything looked the same as when she'd left it two hours before: her laptop on the desk against her big bay window, her remote on the floor by her coffee table, her T-shirt and—oops—bra on the top of the couch where she'd thrown them off after getting Carlos's text. She saw a smile around his eyes when he turned in that direction, but he didn't let it reach his mouth.

"Is there anywhere to hide in this room?" he asked her under his breath. She shook her head.

She started to walk down the hallway that led to her bedroom, but he put his hand on her shoulder to stop her.

"Let me go first."

He didn't wait for an answer. She stared daggers into his back as she followed him down the hallway. Just because she'd accepted his offer to make sure Fisher wasn't around didn't mean she was okay with him ordering her around in her own apartment. This had been a terrible idea.

When she walked into her bedroom, he'd already flung open the closet doors and was running his hands through the crowded coat side of her closet. He turned around well after she was satisfied that there was no one hiding among them.

"Are all of these coats . . . yours?" he asked her. "You do realize you live in Los Angeles, right?"

"Shut up. It gets cold here sometimes. And I go to New York at least once or twice a year."

He shook his head, with a smile in his eyes.

"Mmm, yeah, that totally means you need twenty coats, absolutely."

She tried not to grin back at him and failed.

He stepped around to the far side of her bed, then went into the hallway and threw open the hall closet. She supposed that Fisher *could* have hidden in there, if he'd been hiding his contortionist talents from her. He glanced at the shelves full of extra bedding, towels, and boxes of sparkling water, and closed the door without a word. He stepped into the bathroom, and she heard the shower curtain swish across the rod.

"All clear in the bathroom, too. Anywhere else?"

She walked down the hall to the kitchen, simultaneously so relieved she was ready to collapse and feeling so stupid she wanted to hide among all the coats in her closet.

"I mean, I suppose if someone was really trying, they could hide in the refrigerator, or under the couch, but I somehow doubt that. I think we're all clear." She opened the refrigerator and pulled out a bottle of wine. "I'm sorry for dragging you along on this wild goose chase. I don't know what got into me. Wine?" She glanced over at him, standing in her living room, and saw him peer under the couch. She smiled and poured two glasses.

"Here." She handed him a glass and sat down on the couch. "Thank you. I'm not usually . . ." She shook her head. "Anyway, thank you. I hope you're not too much of a man's man to drink rosé."

He sat down next to her and picked up the wineglass.

"No such thing." He took a sip of the wine and glanced over at her. "You should get your locks changed."

Okay, that was enough telling her what to do.

"I know I should get my locks changed; I'm not an idiot," she said.

He put his glass down.

"Hey, I'm sorry. Of course you aren't. I didn't mean to suggest that." He looked at her, then looked away. "I'm used to taking care of all of the women in my family, so I have the tendency to go overboard sometimes. I didn't mean to tell you what to do."

She picked up his wineglass and handed it to him.

"It's okay, really. I didn't mean to snap at you." She closed her eyes. "I don't usually give in to fits of paranoia like this, and I hate it. Sorry for taking it out on you."

He smiled at her and patted her thigh. She hated herself for wanting his hand to linger there a lot longer than it did.

"You have nothing to be ashamed of. Every woman needs a big strong man to come and protect her; that's not your fault. It's just because you're naturally weak and helpless, just by virtue of, you know, being a woman and all. You needed a man like me to do the hard work of looking under your bed. I understand that you aren't capable of stuff like that."

She smacked his arm.

"You asshole." She was laughing so hard she had to put her wineglass down. "You had me going for at least five or six seconds there! You were so close to me throwing this wine in your face and literally kicking you out of my apartment."

Carlos laughed and relaxed against the couch cushions. He'd been a little worried that she'd get furious at him for that, but he also thought it might break some of the tension. One of the things that he already liked so much about Nik was how independent she was; he should have known that telling her what to do would piss her off. Angela had gotten mad at him just a few weeks ago for taking her car in to get serviced; she'd said she was fully capable of doing it for herself. He'd told her it wasn't that he didn't think she was capable of it, it's just that he'd felt like it was his job to do it. That hadn't made her less mad.

She waved at his wineglass.

"Drink, drink, I promise I won't knock the glass all over you."

He took another sip. He usually made fun of Angela for drinking rosé. She could definitely never find out that he drank it with Nik and liked it.

"But really, don't feel bad," he said. "It's totally normal to freak out about stuff like this. And my stint in the ER during my residency really opened my eyes to how often this stuff happens to women. I mean, fine, he wasn't here and you felt silly that you had me come up, no big deal. But too many women ignore those feelings or don't want to feel silly, and I've seen some of the aftermaths. Feeling silly is definitely better."

She took another sip of her wine and leaned back. When she'd sat down on the couch, she'd sat down right in the middle, so he'd had no choice but to sit right next to her. They were so close they were almost touching.

"I almost called you on the way here and told you I didn't need you, but I knew my friends would have yelled at me and told me not to be a fool." She paused. "I think I've given other people similar advice, now that I think about it. It's always easier to give people advice than it is to take it yourself."

Should he put his arm around her? He really wanted to, but she'd just had a dramatic breakup a few days ago, and she might smack him and order him out of her house. But she was curled up on the couch next to him like that, all cozy with her wine; this seemed like a prime situation for making a move, right?

"Speaking of giving advice," she said, "you said that you spend a lot of time giving advice to teenagers, and I'm totally curious about your job. What does it mean, to be the assistant director of a teen clinic?"

Okay, it seemed like she just wanted to talk, as they sat here shoulder to shoulder in the dim lighting on her couch while holding glasses of wine. Great.

"Excellent question, and one that I'm still kind of figuring out the answer to. I've only been doing it for about six months, but I love it so far. Basically, all of the health care of the kids that the medical center serves—who are in the twelve to nineteen age group—is routed through our clinic. The goal is to recognize that teens are in a special place, both mentally and physically, and to serve their needs as best as we can."

"I wish my doctor's office had had a teen clinic when I was a kid," she said. "I always remember feeling so grumpy about still going to a pediatrician when I was a teenager, surrounded by babies and toddlers."

She took another sip of wine and picked a piece of lint off of his shoulder. He felt lulled by her touch, the warm night air, by her presence.

And also probably the wine.

She stood up to get the bottle of wine from the fridge and brought it back over to the couch.

"You said you'd only been there for six months—where were you before that?"

She tipped the wine bottle toward his glass and raised her eyebrows at him. He nodded. Was she trying to get him to linger? Had the whole "I'm afraid of my ex" thing just been bullshit to get him to come up to her apartment? Would he care if that was the case? He grinned to himself.

Would he care if a hot girl made up a story about being scared of her ex-boyfriend to get him up to her apartment? Hell no, he would not care.

"I was at St. Elizabeth's Hospital on the Westside. I liked working there a lot, but this job is different from what I'd been doing there, and it's a lot of fun. Plus, it was great to come back to the Eastside and be closer to my family."

But wait. He didn't know this girl that well, but from his few interactions with her, she seemed pretty forthright and honest, almost to a fault. He didn't really think she'd make up a story if she wanted him in her apartment. She would just ask him if he wanted to come upstairs.

Plus, if someone was pretending to be scared, they would have acted much more scared than she did when they walked in. She hadn't been clingy or crying or any of that stuff. She'd just looked tense and angry. And she even hadn't hinted for him to come over; he'd been the one to offer.

"I spend so much time with L.A. people who are from somewhere else; it's always fun to meet a real local," she said. "Do you have a big family?"

He rested his hand on the couch, right by, but not on, her knee.

"Yes and no—it's a big extended family, but Angie's my only sibling. But we grew up right around the corner from my mom's sister, Tia

Eva, and her daughter, my cousin Jessica, who is basically like a sister to me. She's the one I told you about at the bar who I got the 'Is that you?' idea from." He smiled. "That's another reason why this was a good time to move back to the Eastside; Jessie's pregnant now with her first kid, and my whole family is over the moon."

She tucked her hair behind her ears and looked up at him. He liked the way she concentrated on him when he was talking, like she was really listening to what he had to say.

He *also* liked the way the neckline of her shirt kept dipping lower and lower. He had to force himself to not let his eyes linger for too long on her cleavage.

"Are you over the moon about the baby, too?"

Her shirt dipped off one shoulder. He really wanted to reach over and push it off all the way. It took him a minute to remember what she'd asked him. Right, right, Jessie's baby.

"Oh yeah, definitely. You'd think that after being a pediatrician for years now I'd think babies are a dime a dozen, but I can't wait until Jessie has hers. Not that I'm ready in the least to have one of my own, but that's what's going to make Jessie's so fun. Being an uncle is going to be great. All of the fun and none of the responsibility." He laughed. "Plus, this way, my mom will get off my ass about giving her grandbabies because she'll have Jessie's baby to hang out with."

She looked at him sideways.

"Or, she'll be on your ass even more because she'll be so excited about the one baby that she'll want more."

He held his finger up to her lips.

"Shhhhh, don't say that. She knows it's going to be a long time before that happens. I have too many other people to take care of right now. I'm just glad that I'm back on the Eastside. I can be closer when the baby is born, as well as for things like killing spiders—real and imaginary—late at night for Angela."

She took the last sip of her wine and smiled at him.

"She's lucky she has you. I was lucky that I had you around tonight, too." She sat up straight and put her feet on the floor. "Do you have to be at work super early in the morning? It's getting late."

That sure sounded like his cue to go. Damn it. He looked at his watch and barely noticed what it said.

"It's getting pretty close to my bedtime." He put his hand on her arm. "Are you going to be okay tonight?"

Her eyes shot to the door, but she nodded anyway.

"Of course. I'll be fine, don't worry about me."

He'd been on the point of standing up. Instead, he settled back down on the couch.

"Well, when you say it like that, I'm worried about you. Do you want me to . . ." He was going to say, "Do you want me to stay?" but that sounded like he was inviting himself into her bed. And while he'd love to get an invitation there, he didn't want to look like even more of an asshole than he already had tonight. "Do you want me to stay until one of your friends can get here?"

"I feel ridiculous even thinking about doing that, but . . . maybe. Courtney has to be up at the crack of dawn, so I don't want to call her. I can call Dana, though. I don't think she's filming tomorrow. Oh God, that reminds me! Instagram!" She pulled her phone out of her pocket.

He had no idea what the hell that meant in this context.

"Instagram?" he asked.

"Fisher Instagrams his whole life, for 'branding' and his fans or whatever. If he's updated in the last few hours or so, at least I'll know what he's up to."

She typed something into the search bar on her phone while she talked.

"I blocked him on everything, so he can't contact me, but if I'm logged out, I can still see . . . oh my God, Carlos. Look at this! He's in Vegas!"

She turned her phone around so he could see the video of Fisher dancing terribly at some club. He let out a shout of laughter.

"Wow." He scooted closer to her so they could

both watch. My God, she smelled good. He wanted to stay this close to her on the couch for a long time. "Is this guy for real? Play it again."

She played his video four or five more times, and they laughed harder every time.

"This is almost as good as the middle-finger ring picture," she said, still laughing.

He raised his eyebrows at her.

"What middle-finger ring picture?"

"Oh my God. I'm so sorry. I didn't show you. You and Angela left before we looked at his texts. Look at this picture he sent me."

She scrolled through her phone and pulled up a photo of a blurry middle finger with a blue engagement ring on it. He recoiled.

"Oh my God. He seriously texted you this?"

As she'd scrolled to the photo, he'd seen flashes of a few of the texts Fisher had sent her after the proposal. That fucking bastard.

"I know. I know." She was still looking at the photo, and not at him. "You don't have to say anything. I have terrible judgment in men; we all know that now, but this is really incredible, right?"

He stood up. He was glad for her that Fisher was out of town, but now he had no more excuses to stay here.

"It's so incredible that I need to go home now to process that. And also because I have to be up, awake, and ready for patients at eight thirty a.m. tomorrow."

She walked him to the door.

"Sorry for keeping you up, and thanks again."

She reached out to hug him, and he pulled her in tight. Her body nestled up against his felt so good. He wanted to hold on for much longer and forced himself to let go.

"Glad I could be here. Good night. And if you want to stack a chair behind that door after I leave, feel free. No one will know about it but you."

She laughed and reached up to kiss him on the cheek.

"I just might do that, thanks."

Chapter Five

• • • • • •

Nik shut the door behind Carlos and closed her eyes.

Maybe, she thought, if she stood there for a few minutes with her forehead against this door, it would magically take away the far too many feelings going through her head right now.

She gave it about two minutes, but it didn't work. So she flopped back down on the couch and pulled the blanket over her face.

Why hadn't he offered to stay with her that night, Fisher or no Fisher? She would have said "No, you're too busy, I don't want to inconvenience you more than I have," and he would have offered again, and she would have said, "Are you sure?" and he would have said, "Of course," and she would have said, "You really don't have to, but . . ." and he would have said, "I want to!" and then she would have tackled him on the couch. That would have been a much better ending to tonight than her being on her couch alone feeling like an idiot.

Worse, he hadn't even tried to kiss her! She'd given him every damn opportunity—she had practically shoved her boobs in his face—and he'd been all smiling and talking about his cousin and his patients and blah blah blah. Sure, she'd asked him about those things and hadn't asked him, "Do you like my boobs in this shirt, Carlos? I grew them just for you," but he should have gotten that that was what she'd *meant*.

Ugh, and she hadn't even invited him upstairs on some sort of "come look at my etchings" pretext. She'd wanted him for—gag—protection. When she'd unlocked her front door, she'd been so grateful that he was there. She'd felt actually *comforted* by his presence. Even when he'd ordered her around in a way that she would normally hate, she'd still been so relieved that he was there.

How humiliating. She, Nikole Paterson, who prided herself on being self-sufficient and self-reliant and an Independent Woman, et cetera, et cetera, had caved under the slightest amount of pressure and called on a man to come save her. And she'd almost thrown herself at him in the process.

Okay, this was getting way out of hand. Sure, her fingers were dying to run themselves through his thick dark hair, and her hand had lingered a little too long on his bicep tonight, and every time he curved those inviting lips of his into a smile, she wanted to pull him closer. But a rebound with Carlos was a terrible idea, remember? She neither

87

wanted, nor needed, a rebound with anyone! That was why she'd hinted it was time for Carlos to go home. Men were trouble. She'd learned that over and over again. Plus, Carlos was a doctor, and she was done with doctors. They thought they were better than everyone else.

She'd never forget that time when her digital recorder had failed unbeknownst to her during an important interview and she'd burst into angry tears about it to Justin. He'd said, "Come on, Nikole. It's just an interview with an actor; it's no big deal. Unlike in my job, no one's going to die because of a little mistake." She was still mad she'd stayed with him for another year after that.

She shouldn't have let Carlos come over in the first place. Even though he'd seemed nice and, yes, she had wished in a weak moment that he'd ended up in her bed, he still clearly thought that she was a helpless woman who needed him to protect her. He'd joked about that, but was it really a joke?

Letting men see your vulnerabilities was always a mistake. There must be better avenues out there to protect herself against creepy ex-boyfriends than calling for the nearest man to protect her.

"A self-defense class?" Dana asked. "You want us to go to a self-defense class together?"

The three of them were all out at the bar two days later, partly because she hadn't left her apartment since Monday night, partly so she could share her great idea with them.

"It's a good idea!" Nik said. "They're supposed to be very empowering."

Courtney and Dana both stared at her like she had sprouted a second head.

" 'Empowering?' Since when do you use words like 'empowering'?" Courtney asked.

She had a point.

"Sorry, I've been looking at too many self-defense class websites. But doesn't it sound fun to go punch some stuff? It'll be a great workout."

Now Dana looked interested. The poor thing had to constantly exercise. She'd gotten a best friend role in a sitcom the year before, which meant she could never get above a size two, and even that was pushing it.

"That does sound fun, but is this one of those classes where everyone is supposed to share some trauma or something and then you punch it to, like, conquer your fear or whatever?" she asked.

"There are a bunch of different kinds," Nik said. "They teach you how to defend yourself, and—"

"Yes, I got that; it's right there in the name," Dana said.

"Shut up, you know what I mean. It'll help us be more confident walking down the street at night or dealing with creepy guys."

"I drive everywhere, and I've been dealing with creepy guys for over twenty years. What else you got?" Dana drained her drink.

"Hmm, will it also help some of us deal with ex-boyfriends who send vaguely threatening messages?" Courtney asked.

She'd sort of hoped that they wouldn't connect the dots about why she was interested in the class. It was a ridiculous hope, though. Unfortunately, she had intelligent friends.

"You didn't tell me that." Dana sat up straight. "What the hell did he say to you?" She pulled out her phone. "I'm texting my roller derby friends—what's his address?"

Nik grabbed her phone away.

"You don't need to text your roller derby friends. It's not like that."

Dana smacked Courtney on the shoulder. "Why didn't you tell me this was happening? He's freaked her out so much that she wants to take a self-defense class?"

Courtney took Dana's phone from Nik and handed it back to Dana.

"Why am I getting yelled at for this?" She pointed at Nik. "She's the one who should have told you."

Dana squeezed the lime into her gin and tonic before she took a sip.

"Oh, don't worry, I'm mad at both of you. But I know you saw her on Monday. You told me she'd blocked Fisher, but not that his messages had gotten her to the self-defense class state. I'm going to that man's house with a pitchfork."

Even when they drove her crazy, Nik loved her friends so much.

"You don't need to go to his house with a pitchfork." She took a sip of her drink and reconsidered. "At least, wait a few days—he's still in Vegas."

Dana opened the calendar on her phone and made a note.

"Look, this isn't about Fisher," Nik said. Her friends stared at her with identical looks of disbelief. "Okay, fine, it's not *only* about Fisher. It was just . . . when I got home on Monday, after his texts and all of the harassment from random dudes, I was so paranoid. I even . . ."

She'd tried to avoid telling them this, but part of her always knew it would come out in the end.

"So Monday night I had dinner with Carlos, and . . . I was so anxious about all of this that I got him to come check my apartment with me. It made me feel so stupid."

Dana put her arm around her.

"Oh, honey. That sucks, but you have nothing to be ashamed about. It's those assholes who made you so worried who should be ashamed of themselves. I'm glad Carlos was there."

Nik leaned into her friend and nodded.

"He cracked jokes the whole time, thank God.

If he'd been super nice and thoughtful and concerned about me, it would have made me throw up."

"Okay." Courtney put her drink down. "I'm also very glad he was there for you, and I'm even more glad he wasn't all weird about it, but what will make me the gladdest is if you tell us you slept with him afterward."

She shook her head.

"No, guys, seriously, it wasn't like that."

Courtney pursed her lips.

"But why wasn't it like that? He's hot, he's clearly into you, he's the perfect rebound, and good Lord do you need one."

Only the first one of those points was correct.

"No, I told you. I have to swear off men for a while. Every relationship I've had with a man in the past decade has been awful. There was Justin and Fisher, and remember that graphic designer I dated last year, who told me he was in an open marriage on the fourth date? I've had enough."

Courtney nodded, like she'd heard this a million times before. To be fair, she probably had.

"Yes, yes, we know, except we also saw the way you looked at Carlos on Saturday night. Maybe you should swear off men for a while *after* you've had your rebound."

Did they not listen to her, or did they just decide they knew better?

"One: I told you guys, starting anything with him, or any man, is a bad idea. Men always think they can make demands on me, and I'm sick of that. Two: Carlos is clearly not interested in me—he didn't make the slightest move on me on Monday night. And three: if I did want to date someone right now, Carlos is absolutely not that someone."

Dana put her hand on Nik's.

"You've got to get over this doctor thing. This guy is not like Justin. Not all doctors are like Justin."

Nik sighed and took a sip of her drink.

"I know he isn't. Like, I know that intellectually. And I've been over Justin for a long time. I really have been. But it took years after I was over him to get past how shitty he made me feel about my writing. I'm just now at the place where I'm proud of both my work and my career, and I don't want anyone to try to fuck with that."

Dana nodded.

"We know, honey. But you're a very different person than you were when you dated Justin. What would you have done two weeks ago if Fisher had pulled a Justin and told you not to take a great new job?"

"I would have laughed at him," Nik said immediately.

"Exactly!" Courtney said. "To take another example from Justin's greatest hits, what would you have done if that Morton dude you dated had read one of your pieces and had told you to give up writing?"

Nik had to laugh. Her friends remembered everything. Well, almost everything.

"Morris, not Morton. And fine, I would have thrown him out of my apartment. I get your point. I'm in a better place in my life, fine. But still."

"But still what?" Dana threw her arm around her. "Have more faith in yourself, Nik. We do."

Nik refused to let herself cry.

"Oh, shut up. It's only because of the faith you two have in me that got me out of the relationship with Justin in the first place, so there."

She pulled both of her friends into a brief hug. As much as she loved her friends, they were wrong about Carlos, though. Everything they'd said about the guys she'd recently dated had proved it: the reason it was so easy to discount them and their opinions was because she didn't like those guys all that much. Carlos, though, she actually liked. Dating someone you found both smart and interesting seemed much harder. Much riskier.

"To get us back on topic: we *were* talking about how Monday night I asked a man who I barely knew to come to my apartment with me because I was feeling helpless. And if there's one thing I hate, it's feeling helpless."

"You also hate raw peaches," Dana said.

"That fuzz against your teeth!"

"And those five-finger running shoes," Courtney said.

Nik shuddered.

"They make your feet look like hobbit feet!"

"Filled doughnuts," Dana said.

"They ooze!" Nik said. "Especially the ones with red stuff inside—it's like there's blood in there."

"When people have the keyboard sound up on their phone," Dana said.

"Okay, but doesn't everyone hate that?" Nik asked them.

"Beaches," Courtney said.

"So much sand," Nik said. "It gets everywhere. And I mean *everywhere*. I don't know why people love them."

"Rompers."

"Carrot cake."

"Mashed potatoes."

"People who don't use the Oxford comma!"

"Don't forget Chardonnay!"

"Okay, okay, fine, you guys can stop now," Nik said. They would have gone on forever if she hadn't interrupted them. "You're both correct. I hate many things, okay? But feeling helpless is high up there. You happy now?"

It was amazing that two women who were so different in both looks and personality could have the exact same smug smile.

"Yes," they said in unison.

"After all that, now you know you have to go with me to a self-defense class, right?" Nik said.

"Oh." Dana looked at Courtney, and they both looked back at Nik. "We were always going to go with you. We just had to make fun of you first. When's the first class?"

Nik grinned.

"Tomorrow."

Carlos sat down on the corner of his couch with his dinner late on Wednesday night. He hadn't heard from Nik since Tuesday morning—he'd texted her to check in and see how she was doing, and she'd texted back that she was much better and thanked him again. He'd assumed that was a brush-off and he shouldn't text her again, but now he was reconsidering that. Nik's brush-offs didn't seem that subtle, for one thing. He'd seen that at Dodger Stadium. Maybe he'd text her one more time.

Did those Thai leftovers kill you? I hope you ate them yesterday. They get spicier over time.

A few seconds after he pressed send, his phone rang. My God, was it that easy?

He looked at his phone. Angela. Nope, not that easy.

"Hey," she said. "I just got off the phone with Jessie."

His cousin Jessica had just been diagnosed with preeclampsia, and he'd been fielding calls from his mom and aunt about it all day. He'd finally gotten to talk to Jessie right before he left the hospital that evening.

"I talked to her, too," he said to Angela. "Don't freak out. It's still early, but it's a good sign that her doctors sent her home and had her go on bed rest instead of admitting her."

Part of him wished her doctors had admitted her to the hospital—that way she and the baby would be safe and monitored every day in case of any problems. The thing no one told you about being a doctor was how much you would panic when people you loved had anything wrong with them. Doctors knew way too much about the worst-case scenarios.

"You're telling *me* not to freak out? From what Jessie said, you freaked her out! She said her doctors made her feel less stressed about this, and when she left her doctor's appointment, she wasn't too worried, but after she talked to you, she's all anxious again."

His phone buzzed.

Oh wow, really? Thanks for the news bulletin. That would have been a nice thing to tell me on Monday night, not well after I ate them for lunch on Tuesday and had my tongue on fire for 12 full hours. Now I know why you let me have them.

He tried not to laugh. He didn't want to have to explain his laughter to Angela.

"I'm sorry I freaked Jessie out, but she needs to know when she should go back to the hospital. If her blood pressure gets too high, it can be dangerous."

He texted back.

I don't know what you're talking about. I was just being a gentleman.

"She knows all of that; that's what her doctor is for! We all know all of that now. We have Google, too."

He rolled his eyes at his bowl of lentil soup. It was like Angela wasn't even listening to him.

"I didn't know that because of Google. I know because I'm a doctor!"

They all remembered he was a doctor when they needed him, but ignored it whenever they felt like it.

"I know you're a doctor, but stop making her more anxious about everything! She needs your support right now, not you trying to drive her blood pressure up."

Of course Jessie had his support. Jessie was his younger cousin, but only by a year. She had teased him and played with him and laughed at him and encouraged him and been proud of him his whole life. One of the framed pictures he had in his house was of him at three and Jessie at two, both looking dubiously at baby Angela.

Ohhhhhh, is that what being a gentleman is? Letting the woman absorb all of the pain while you take the glory? Now I understand what all of those men who told me they were such gentlemen were saying.

He had to mute his call so he could laugh at that.

"Look," Angela continued. "I know you're stressed right now, coming up on the five-year anniversary of Dad, but—"

He stopped laughing.

"It's not that," he said. He'd been trying to ignore that the anniversary of his father's death was coming up. "I'm just trying to take care of this family, that's all."

Ever since his father's death, Carlos had sort of considered himself head of his family. He'd never say that out loud to his mother or to Tia Eva, but he assumed they thought the same thing. Jessie's dad had never been around, so his dad had always done all of the car maintenance, yard work, and home repairs for all of them. When his dad died, Carlos had taken over all of that. But it was more than just the physical work: he thought of his family as his responsibility. He wasn't going to have anything happen to Jessie on his watch.

"Look, I don't want to fight about this," he said to Angela. "I'm just trying to take care of Jessie the best I know how. I have to work late tomorrow, but I'm going to stop by to see her on Friday."

Don't tell anyone I told you the gentleman code. The other gentlemen out there will murder me.

"Oh great, I have an idea: before you stop by to see Jessie, why don't you go to the doctor? She would love that, and so would I."

He sighed. Not this again.

"Next topic, Angela."

She laughed.

"Fine, but remember what I said. By the way, did you see the video of that proposal pop up everywhere? Wild, right? Poor Nik. I wonder how she's holding up."

My lips are sealed. I mean, until I write the big exposé about this.

"She's hanging in there," he said, without thinking.

Oh shit.

"Oh, *is she?* How do you know that, may I ask?"

Well he definitely could *not* say it was because he and Nik had been texting throughout this conversation. Anytime he even hinted that he enjoyed a woman's company, Angela was convinced they'd live happily ever after. And while he still didn't know what was going to happen between him and Nik, he knew that wasn't in the cards.

"We had dinner on Monday night. She emailed

100

me to say thanks for Saturday—she wanted me to say thanks to you, too, by the way—and we ended up grabbing Thai food."

"Hmmmm. Weird that you didn't mention that she wanted you to say thanks to me. I wonder how that happened?"

Why couldn't they still be talking about Jessie?

"I've kind of had a lot going on this week, Angie. Between being a doctor and taking care of our whole family, it sort of slipped my mind."

"Well, I liked her, and it seems like you liked her, too, so . . ."

Just make sure you don't use my real name in your exposé. Give me one of those hipster baby names, like Carver or Fletcher or Winston.

He never should have let it slip that he'd even thought about Nik after Saturday night. He needed to nip this in the bud right away. Even if something did end up happening with Nik, it wasn't going to be the kind of relationship his sister kept pushing him toward.

"I didn't like her that much. I only had dinner with her because I felt sorry for her. She was dealing with some harassment after the video went public and was freaked out."

Maybe someday he'd be able to date someone seriously, but it was way too soon since his father had died for that. He couldn't put another woman over his mother and sister—not to mention Jessie and Tia Eva. He needed to be able to race to Angie's house when she sprained her ankle or go furniture shopping with his mom on the weekend or change the tires on Tia Eva's car. All of the things his dad used to do. If he was dating someone, he wouldn't be able to do any of that.

"Mmmhmmm," Angie said. "You felt sorry for her, sure. Like I believe that one."

He shook his head.

"Good-bye, Angela. Talk to you later."

How about Atticus? You seem like you could be an Atticus.

He put his feet up on his coffee table and laughed and laughed.

Chapter Six

● ● ● ● ● ●

"I cannot believe you're making us do this," Courtney said as they got out of the car. "You know I avoid all situations where the correct attire is athleisure."

Nik zipped up her hoodie and ignored her.

"Oh hush," Dana said to Courtney. "I like that outfit on you. I've been trying to tell you for months how much more comfortable you'd be in leggings or yoga pants at work all day."

Courtney shook her head as they walked toward the gym. Nik had almost avoided this class in principle because it was called "Punch Like a Girl," but it was the only class on the Eastside that started in the next few weeks. And it somehow felt urgent for her to do this *now*. It wasn't that she really thought Fisher—or any of the other creepy guys who sent her messages— would actually do anything to her. It was more that she'd realized that she would have no idea what to do if any of them did.

She couldn't wait to tell Carlos that she was taking the class. She was pretty sure he'd get a kick out of it. That was, if she ever saw him again. They'd texted for hours last night, and on and off again today, but that didn't mean anything.

"I don't care how comfortable leggings are; I like my dresses for work, thank you very much," Courtney said. "I spent years dressing in ugly plus-size suits for corporate America. It's a relief to wear A-line dresses in ridiculous patterns. Plus, I run a cupcake shop that I named after myself; dressing like a cupcake is very hashtag on brand."

"I cannot believe you said 'hashtag' out loud like that." Dana pulled her hair up into a ponytail. "You've clearly been doing too much store-related social media lately. We might need to have an intervention."

Courtney pulled her phone out of the pocket in her leggings.

"Are you kidding me? I just hit twenty-five thousand Instagram followers! I'm doing something right." She smiled at a picture of a cupcake before she tucked her phone back in her pocket. "Yes, I know I'm obsessed; you don't have to tell me twice."

Nik pulled out her own phone. Who knows, that source may have emailed her back!

I swear to God, a patient today told me she babysits for a kid named Kaftan.

She hid her smile.

The gym was a big, kind of anonymous-looking

104

building with only a metallic gold sign over the door that said NATALIE'S GYM.

"Where did you find this place?" Dana whispered to Nik. "I've never seen a sparkly gold sign at a gym before."

"Shhh," Courtney said. "I feel more at home at this place already if there are sparkles involved."

Nik ignored them and went up to the blond woman in a pink tank top sitting at the front desk.

"Hi, I signed up online for three of us for the class." She refused to say the name.

"Punch Like a Girl? Fantastic!" The incredibly thin, perky, ponytailed woman beamed at her. "What are your names?"

"Nikole Paterson, Dana Carter, Courtney Park," Nik said, pointing at herself and each of her friends in turn.

"Nice to meet all three of you!" the woman said. "It's a sliding scale, so just let me know what you're comfortable paying. Usually you can pay for one class at a time, but for this class, we like you to pay for the whole six weeks in advance, so we can count you in for the whole run of the class."

Nik handed over her credit card. She'd never heard of a sliding scale gym in L.A. before, especially not a cute one like this. That would have been useful when she was just starting out, but luckily, she could afford to pay the list price now.

"Great!" The woman stood. "You're all paid up and checked in, the locker rooms are through there, and we'll be in Studio A for the class—starts in ten minutes!"

"Great!" Nik said back, and was immediately ashamed that she'd adopted the other woman's exclamation points. This was just like how whenever she went to the South, she started drawling and saying "y'all" after the first five minutes.

None of them needed the locker room, so they shuffled into Studio A. It was a big, brightly lit exercise studio, with shiny wood floors, mirrors covering one wall, and a water fountain in the corner. A big sign by the door told them—in more metallic gold letters—to turn off their phones and put any personal items in the cubbies by the door.

"Are we in kindergarten?" Dana said, gesturing toward the sign. "I don't know about this place, Nik."

Courtney quickly shed her jacket and tucked it and her purse into a cubby.

"I obey any sign that sparkles at me—you know that," she said to Dana. "Have an open mind! You're too used to your high-pressure SoulFit or CrossMethod or whatever the hell it is you do when you work out."

Dana raised her eyebrows at Nik.

"Some sparkly signs and this woman is all in.

I've never seen her change her mind so quickly about anything."

Thank God her friends were with her. There were many things in life she would cheerfully do alone—go to a movie, out to dinner, on an international trip—but she never would have had the guts to come to a class like this alone.

She took out her phone to turn it off, and what the hell, send one more text.

Now you're just making things up, but I swear I just heard someone at the gym call someone else Sunshine.

At seven on the dot, the blond woman from the reception desk bounced into the center of the room.

"Welcome, everyone!" All of the murmurs quieted down, and everyone turned to her. "I'm Natalie, and I'm so glad to see all of your beautiful faces here today!"

Oh God. This was the kind of person who said "all of your beautiful faces." What had she gotten them into? She saw Courtney and Dana exchanging glances.

"So, as you all know, this is a six-week course to teach women how to fight." She smiled at the half circle of women gathered around her, and they all smiled back. More or less. "Some of you probably signed up for this class thinking about how they do self-defense classes for women in the movies. You know, a man all dressed up in lots of padding, and everyone gets to beat him up and knock him down; we all laugh, right?" They all nodded, more sure of themselves this time. That was exactly what Nik had wanted. To be able to punch a man and walk away from the class confident knowing she could.

"Well, that's not what we do here." Natalie's voice had changed. It was still pink and sparkly, but somehow had steel behind it, too. "We don't want this to be some fake empowering nonsense that lets you leave here after you knock down a man covered in padding, who was unable to move and who'd given you, like, ten minutes of warning that he was going to try to attack you. What the hell good does that do you?"

Hmmmmm. This was getting interesting.

"If we did that, you'd leave after six classes, still completely unable to face whatever it was that drove you to sign up for this class. That's not what I'm about. In my classes, we're going to face those fears head-on. And we're going to teach you how to punch like a girl. Because you know what?"

Beyoncé's "Run the World (Girls)" suddenly blasted from the invisible speakers in the room, and the whole class jumped, then laughed, then sang along.

"That's right. We run the world, girls. Don't ever let anyone forget that." Natalie beamed at them. Nik suddenly noticed the size of her biceps.

She had definitely misjudged this woman by her blond hair and cheerful voice, that was for sure.

"I know, I know, you're all looking around for the punching bags and boxing gloves. That's next week. Today we're going to start with loosening up and learning some form." She smiled at them, a smile that felt like a hug. How did she do that?

"Okay, everyone!" Natalie bounded to the front of the class and faced them. "Now, we're going to learn proper form. We have to get your hands, your arms, your shoulders, your back, and your legs all in order." She demonstrated a punch, her ponytail swinging. "That's what you are all going to look like before the end of next week's class. Now, let's talk about how you stand. That's the most important part."

Nik imitated Natalie's stance. She already felt stronger. She bet if Carlos saw her now, he wouldn't think she was some sort of weakling.

Well, okay, she still didn't know how to throw a punch, but she would very soon, which was the important part.

"We get to use punching bags next week, you guys!" Courtney said as the three of them walked out of the gym an hour later. They were dripping with sweat and had huge grins on their faces. "I can't wait."

Nik looked over at Dana.

"What did you think, D? I know this one became a convert as soon as she saw the sparkles, but you were more skeptical. You going to keep going with us?"

Dana jumped into the front seat of Nik's car.

"Absolutely. Now that I think about it, I've always wanted to know how to punch someone in the jaw."

"Same here," Nik said.

Carlos woke up extra early on Friday morning and went for a run. The hell with apples; it was a run a day that kept the doctor away.

He was so tired of Angela bugging him about going to the doctor, and lately Jessie had been doing it, too. They'd started bringing this doctor thing up over a year ago when he made the mistake of letting it slip that he hadn't been to the doctor in years. He knew it was because they were just paranoid about something happening to him like it had happened to his dad, but he was fine—he kept telling them that. He knew his own family history all too well; he didn't need to go into detail with someone else about it. And he already knew everything he needed to do for his health, and he didn't need some other doctor bugging him to cut carbs and exercise more, blah blah blah.

He'd planned to take a few hours off on Friday afternoon, so when he left work early, he drove down to Los Feliz to the bookstore he liked there, Skylight Books. He'd promised Jessie that he would pick up some books for her to read while she was on bed rest. He was pretty sure that Jessie was more stressed about having preeclampsia than she'd let on to him. Books would help her relax, no matter what she was reading.

"Looking for anything in particular?" a voice next to him said. Oh thank God, someone on the staff to give him advice.

"I am, and I need some help." He turned around to find Nik standing next to him, that worried look on her face from Monday night replaced by a grin.

"Hey! What are you doing here?" he asked. He pulled her into a hug. He'd been on the point of asking her to get a drink last night, but she'd gone radio silent on him for a few hours, and when he heard from her again, it would have been way too late.

"I'm here all the time," she said. "Today there's no particular mission other than seeing if I can find a book I'm in the mood for. I have stacks of brand-new books at home, all of which I was excited to read when I bought them, but now . . . none of them seem quite right to me."

He nodded.

"Yeah, I know how that is. All of the books that you have are sad books when you're in a happy book mood, or vice versa. Or dense when you want a page-turner."

She smiled up at him. Her skin almost glowed

in the warm light, her hair bounced as her head turned, and her huge smile made him feel warm inside. He couldn't help but to smile back at her.

"Exactly! All of the books I have right now are either very smart nonfiction books about very important issues that I would rather jump in front of a moving train than read right now or novels where all of their *New York Times* reviews said the writing was 'beautiful,' and I don't have the patience for beautiful writing right now. What are you looking for?"

They walked a few steps together, away from the woman who seemed to be bothered by their above-a-whisper-level conversation.

"I'm shopping for my cousin who's on bed rest, and she's obsessed with true crime. Books like that stress me out, but she can't get enough of them. But since I can't read them without having nightmares, I have no idea what I should get her. Plus, she's a librarian, so I'm always terrified to buy her books."

Her eyes lit up.

"It's your lucky day because you're looking at Southern California's true crime book expert. I'd call them my guilty pleasure if I believed in guilty pleasures. I can give you as many recommendations as you have bookstore dollars to spend."

Well then. It was his lucky day for more than one reason.

She picked up a book from the shelf they were standing in front of and paused.

"Wait, is this the same pregnant cousin you were telling me about the other night? What happened?"

He'd forgotten that he'd told her about Jessie. He was impressed that she'd remembered.

"Yeah, Jessie. She has preeclampsia. We found out this week." He tried not to let on how anxious he was. "She'll be okay, we think—it's not the most serious kind, but it's going to be a long twelve weeks for her."

She squeezed his arm.

"Oh God, that must be so stressful." She turned back to the shelves, her hand still on his arm. He resisted the urge to flex. "Okay, this just means we've got to get her some excellent books that will make her happy to stay on the couch. Do you know what she already has?"

They walked out of the bookstore forty-five minutes later, a bag of books in each of his hands.

"Can I buy you some coffee to thank you for your help?" he asked her.

"Absolutely not, I owed you this favor," she said. "But I can buy you coffee to thank you for your help on Monday night."

He laughed.

"Okay, how about I buy you coffee and you buy me coffee then?"

She steered him down the street.

"Deal."

They ended up at a coffee shop with outdoor seating a few blocks away and sat down at a shady table with their iced espresso drinks.

"Preeclampsia can be scary, right?" she asked. "How is your cousin doing?"

Thank God *someone* understood that.

"It can be really scary, yeah. I think Jessie's doing okay, but I'm not sure if she's taking this seriously enough. She's only twenty-eight weeks, so we're all just hoping the baby stays put for at least another two months."

He'd been terrified when he got the first text from Jessie. Thank God it wasn't as bad as he'd initially thought, but that terror hadn't completely dissipated.

She touched his clenched fist. He forced his fingers to relax enough to clasp her hand without breaking it.

"What's making your face do that?" she asked him.

He scrunched up his face at her, and she laughed.

"My face do what? What is my face doing?"

She touched his cheek with her free hand.

"You have a dimple in this cheek right here. All afternoon and evening on Saturday, I saw it winking at me. The same thing happened when we were in the bookstore just now. But as soon as we sat down, the dimple disappeared. And lines appeared up here." She drew a line across his forehead with her finger. He closed his eyes at her touch. She dropped her hand, and he opened his eyes.

"Remind me not to go to Vegas with you," he said. "You'll let everyone know all of my tells!"

"Oh no." She shook her head. "I'm an excellent Vegas buddy. I'll tell YOU everyone else's tells."

He laughed and sighed. His face was probably doing that thing again, but he couldn't help it.

"This early in her pregnancy, for her to get this diagnosis—there's a lot that could go wrong. I don't want the rest of my family as anxious about this as I am, so I'm trying to be calm about this when I talk to them. I'm just worried."

"Where's her spouse in all of this, or is she single?"

He shook his head.

"No, she's married, her husband's great. But Jessie and Angela and I grew up together, she doesn't have any siblings, so I'm sort of her big brother, as well as Angie's." It had always been his job to take care of Jessie and Angie. And since his dad died, he'd made an effort to always be there for them, even when he'd lived all the way over on the Westside. Jessie was still his responsibility, Jon or no Jon.

"Anyway, I was supposed to go out of town this weekend, but I'm going to have to cancel. My best friend Drew got engaged last week and he and his fiancée are having an engagement party in Berkeley. I was supposed to fly up tomorrow morning, but I can't leave Jessie now. I still have to cancel my flight and call Drew and tell him I'm not coming."

He sat up straight and tried to shake all of this off. Why had he just let all of these stupid emotions out to this woman who barely knew him?

"Sorry for spilling all of that. I'm sure you didn't come get coffee with me in order to hear all about my family drama."

She shook her head and squeezed his hand.

"Well, you didn't go get dinner with me in order to become my private security guard, so I'd say it's about even." Her face lit up. "Ooh, here's a thing that I bet a pregnant woman on bed rest will love: cupcakes. Courtney's shop is just a few blocks away. Want to walk over there?"

Chapter Seven

• • • • • •

Nik shook her head when she saw the pink and white polka-dot Cupcake Park sign. What was she doing bringing Carlos here? She would never hear the end of it from Courtney. But he'd looked so sad about his cousin. Cupcakes were the first thing she could think of that might cheer him up.

"Hey!" Nik said to Courtney, who stood behind the counter with a smirk on her face. "I brought you a customer."

Courtney waved as she carefully placed an assortment of cupcakes into a box for the woman standing at the register.

"Hey, Carlos, good to see you again. Welcome to Cupcake Park. Nik can give you the rundown of all of the flavors while you wait. She knows them almost as well as I do."

Nik gave him a wry smile as they went up to the counter.

"As much as I hate to say this, she is correct. I curse the day one of my best friends opened a cupcake shop so close to my apartment. And unfortunately, it looks like business is booming, so she'll be here for a while, tempting me with her delicious sugary treats. I think she did this to get revenge on me for something."

Courtney and her customer both laughed.

"I can't tell if you're the worst possible advertisement for my store or the best. I guess time will tell."

The customer picked up her bag containing two big boxes of cupcakes.

"Get the strawberry ones," she said. "Those are my favorite. Those and the coconut-lime ones. Ooh, and the matcha ones!"

Nik shook her head after the customer left the store.

"All of those are very good, but she's wrong. He should get the confetti ones and the lemon ones."

Carlos smiled at Courtney.

"Those flavors all sound great, but I need to start with some red velvet. These are for my cousin, and those are her favorites."

Courtney smirked at Nik, and Nik put her head in her hands.

"What did I say?" He turned from one to the other.

"When I was opening this place, I insisted that I needed to have red velvet cupcakes. Nik argued *strongly* against them. She said my whole shop was going to be about unusual and interesting flavors, and that red velvet cupcakes weren't good enough for me."

"They taste like nothing!" Nik said. "They're just a vehicle for cream cheese frosting, but you can put cream cheese frosting on other cupcakes!"

"I guess I can see who won this argument," he said, and gestured to the case full of red velvet cupcakes.

"A good cupcake shop has got to have some crowd pleasers," Courtney said.

Courtney was always so happy that she'd been right about red velvet, damn her.

"You're shopping for your cousin?" Courtney asked Carlos. "Any special occasion, or a just because cupcakes are great?"

He smiled at her, but he had that sad look in his eyes again.

"Sort of. She's pregnant and newly on bed rest, so I wanted to bring her some cheer."

"Oh no, your poor cousin. Okay, some cheer, coming right up. How many do you want?"

Carlos put his bags of books on a chair.

"A dozen. At least. If I know my family—and I do—everyone is going to be coming by her house in the next few days, and they'll all eat one, minimum."

"Okay, got it." Courtney pulled out a big pink box. "Here, I'll put together an assortment of Cupcake Park's greatest hits, and Nik can take you into the back to show you my kitchen, aka my pride and joy. One question: how do you feel about spicy food?"

He looked at Nik and they both laughed.

"I feel great about it. Why? Do you have a spicy cupcake?"

Courtney grinned her slightly evil grin.

"Nik, you tell him all about my spicy cupcake while I put together this box of treats, okay? And yes, yes, I'll give him some of the confetti cupcakes."

Nik led Carlos through the door marked employees only and tried to ignore Courtney's knowing look. It was like she thought the whole reason Nik had brought Carlos here was for Courtney to start up the rebound refrain again.

To be fair . . . she'd been thinking a lot about that moment on the couch the other night. Maybe too much about it. If Courtney *did* start up the rebound refrain again, she might be somewhat more receptive. Maybe.

"How long has this place been here?" Carlos put his hand on her lower back to steer her around some cardboard boxes stacked on the floor.

"Just over a year." Would he slide his hand up her back to put his arm around her shoulders? Come on, give her this one thing. YES. YES, HE WOULD. She leaned toward him and tried not to let her smile show her triumph.

"Did she have another bakery somewhere else?"

Nik shook her head. How could he expect her to have an actual conversation with his arm around her like that, and his warm body right next to her?

"No, she used to be an investment banker, isn't that wild? But she'd saved up a ton of money and had always loved baking. About a year and a half ago, she saw this place for lease and took the plunge."

"Wow," he said as they walked through the kitchen. "That's inspiring."

She nodded and looked up at him.

"Agreed." She wanted to touch his hair so badly. It was slightly too long and a little messy from the wind. If she could just brush it back with her fingers . . .

She felt a buzz from his pocket, and they both jumped and pulled away from each other. He shook his head and reached for his phone.

"That was Jessie, wondering when I'm coming over. I should probably . . ."

She nodded.

"Yeah, let's go get your cupcakes from Courtney."

They emerged back into the store. Courtney's smirk was in full bloom. Nik glared at her, but it didn't make the slightest impact.

Carlos pulled his wallet out of his pocket and handed her his credit card. "Thanks so much for the cupcakes. I'm sure Jessie will love them."

"My pleasure." She ran his card and handed him the receipt. "Thanks for coming by, and I hope this isn't the last time. And make sure you warn everyone about the spicy chocolate cupcakes; they're the ones with the chili pepper on top."

He laughed and waved good-bye as they left the store.

"Thanks for bringing me here," he said to Nik as they walked to his car.

They stopped in front of his car, parked just a few doors down from Cupcake Park.

"Keep me posted," she said. "About how she liked the cupcakes, and how she's doing."

He opened the trunk and put the books and the cupcakes inside.

"I will," he said. "And about how she likes those fucked-up books, too."

She laughed.

"Please do."

He opened his arms for a hug.

"Thanks for all of your help today. With the books, and everything else. Now I definitely owe you a drink. Next week?"

She let the hug linger and kissed him on the cheek when she eventually pulled away.

"Absolutely. Text me and let me know what works for you."

She pulled out her phone as soon as he drove away, certain about what she would find.

Sure enough:

If you don't get your ass back to my store,

I'm going to murder you with my bare hands.

Nik grinned and walked back to Cupcake Park.

Why did Jessie have to text him right then? He'd been about two seconds from kissing Nik, and unlike Monday night, he'd been pretty sure she would have kissed him back. And then the damn text from his cousin had to get in the way.

He was already mad at Jessie for how nonchalantly she was treating her preeclampsia, and she had to go and do this to him, too? Now she was in for it. That was, if he could concentrate on anything other than how good Nik smelled, and how soft her skin was, and how he'd wanted to pull off her clothes right there in the bakery kitchen.

Jon opened the front door almost as soon as he knocked. Carlos walked in, carrying the bookstore bags in one hand and the cupcake bag in another.

"Hey, man, how're you holding up?" Carlos asked him. Carlos had been very suspicious when Jessie had introduced him to the skinny, white, bearded English professor she was dating, but now he liked Jon a lot.

"Okay, except for your cousin over here trying to kill me." Jon smiled at Jessie with so much love and worry in his eyes that Carlos had to look away.

Jessica was reclining on the couch like a

123

pregnant Cleopatra. Her long dark-brown hair and big brown eyes added to the resemblance.

"Carlos!" Jessie smiled up at him. "I was wondering when my good-for-nothing cousin was going to stop by."

He set the bags down on the coffee table and leaned in for a hug.

"What's your blood pressure right now?"

Jessica pulled away.

"Come on, Carlos. This is your cousin, not your patient. Take a deep breath."

He knew she was his cousin. He wouldn't be half as worried if she were his patient.

"Don't give me that 'take a deep breath' nonsense. Come on, what's your blood pressure?"

Jessie reached for her bottle of water and took a swig.

"Now that we're on the topic, what's your blood pressure, Carlos? When's the last time *you* went to the doctor?"

"Oh my God, Jessie, don't do that right now. This is serious!" Jon shot a look at him, and he realized that snapping at his pregnant, sick cousin probably wasn't the right move.

"Yes, yes, I know it's serious. Can we get to that?" She pointed at the bag on the coffee table. "What'd you bring me? Wait, I mean . . ." She arranged her face into a perfect fake look of surprise. "For me? You didn't have to bring me a present, Carlos! No really, you didn't! Okay, fine, if you *insist*." She grinned at him. Despite his irritation with her, he couldn't keep from grinning back. "How'd I do? Did I look just like Taylor Swift?"

"Fantastic, you were perfect. No one would have known the truth." He gave up on the medical questions for the moment and handed her the carefully wrapped stack of books. "Here, dig in."

She squealed and tore into the wrapping paper. He had to remember to thank Nik for getting the bookstore to wrap the presents. He would have just handed Jessie the bag.

"Oooh, I've been wanting to read this book! I didn't know it was in paperback, awesome." She tore through the books, and when she looked back up at Carlos, he was surprised to see her eyes full of tears.

"You asshole. These are all so perfect. Thank you."

She reached her arms up, and he hugged her again, longer this time.

"I know how you feel about being bored, so I thought some reading material was in order. I'll be around all weekend, so if you get tired of reading, I can come entertain you."

She narrowed her eyes at him.

"What do you mean you'll be around all weekend? Angie told me you were leaving tomorrow to go up to Berkeley for Drew's engagement party."

He had forgotten he'd told Angie about that. Damn it, why did she have to tell Jessie everything?

He shook his head.

"Oh no, that's not this weekend. She must have heard me wrong. That's in a few weeks."

Would she buy that?

"I always know when you're lying; you know that, right? I refuse to let you miss out on your best friend's engagement party. I'll be *fine*. I have Jon here, and Angie is fifteen minutes away, and my mom and your mom and God knows how many doctors. You can't hover over me like this for the rest of my pregnancy."

There was no way he could go; she knew that.

"Jessie. Come on. I can't leave now; you know that."

She set her mouth in that stubborn way she'd been doing ever since she was a toddler.

"No, I don't know that. As a matter of fact, here's what I do know: if you try to come over this weekend, I'm not even going to let you in my house. So you might as well go to Berkeley because you're not going to see me if you're here."

He turned to Jon, hoping he would talk some sense into her.

"You know she'll do it," Jon said.

Unfortunately, he did know.

"Fine." He shook his finger at her. "But I swear

to God, Jessie, you had better text me if anything happens. Promise me."

She rolled her eyes at him.

"I promise. Are we done with that?"

He nodded.

"Now!" She pointed to the cupcake bag, just out of reach. "What's in the pink bag?" He sighed and pushed it toward her. Leave it to Jessie to keep her mind on her presents.

"Oooh, it's heavy. Hmmm, what place did my hipster cousin discover?"

"I'm not a hipster!" he yelled. This is what he got for his pains.

"Carlos. You hang out in Silver Lake. Come on."

"I have a perfectly normal haircut! I don't have a beard or Warby Parker glasses! I *never* wear a hat."

She laughed harder and looked at Jon.

"I love doing this to him. He gets so mad every time!" She pulled the cupcake box out of the bag and opened it. "Oooooh. Red velvet cupcakes! And . . . is that Funfetti? Gourmet Funfetti cupcakes?" She took a cupcake from the box and took a bite. "Oh my God. If this is what hipsters eat, I've changed my mind about them; I want you to be the hipsterest hipster in all of Los Angeles if you're going to bring me baked goods like this. Jon, you've got to try one."

He grinned at the look on her face and at the

frosting on her nose. He was so glad he'd been able to make her happy, even though he was still furious at her. The cupcake store had clearly been a good idea. Another thing to thank Nik for.

"So I heard you picked up a girl by using my story. You're welcome."

Angela *really* told Jessie everything.

"I did not 'pick up a girl.' I just helped someone out of a difficult situation, that's all."

Jessie took another bite of her cupcake.

"Mmmmhmm. Just one question: have you seen this girl since you helped her out of that one difficult situation?"

Thirty minutes ago, and I was this close to pushing her up against a wall to kiss the hell out of her until you texted me and interrupted us, he didn't say.

He picked up one of the spicy cupcakes to play for time. After one bite, he had no idea why Courtney had warned him about the chili powder.

"As I'm sure you already know from my chatty little sister, I met up with her for dinner a few days later, but it was no big deal."

When should he text Nik about going out for drinks? He'd said "next week" so he should probably wait until then to ask. But he could text her tonight about what a hit the books and the cupcakes were.

Jessie pursed her lips at him.

128

"You always say things are no big deal, but I don't believe you anymore."

How had their conversation become all about him? Time to turn this back to Jessie.

"Do you know what IS a big deal? Preeclampsia, that's what's a big deal."

Jessie and Jon both went into peals of laughter. He glared at them.

Wait. There was the chili powder. Oh wow, it kind of snuck up on you, didn't it? He mentally apologized to Courtney for doubting her.

"Oh, Carlos, thank you for that. I haven't laughed so hard in at least a week."

He made a face at her.

"Hah hah hah, I'm glad that you found that amusing, but seriously, Jessie . . ."

She held up a hand to stop him.

"Seriously, Carlos. I love you, but you are not my doctor. You're not even an OB. I know what I'm supposed to be looking out for here. Please relax so that I can relax. Go on your trip. Celebrate with your friends. Drink lots of champagne, since I can't. And chill out."

He didn't think he was going to be able to relax until she'd safely delivered the baby, but he figured telling her that at this point was probably not a good idea.

"Fine. Can I make you some dinner, then?"

As soon as he got home from Jessie's, he called Drew.

"Hey, man, how's it going?" Drew asked when he answered the phone. "Ready for the party?"

"Very. I always told you that you crazy kids would make it."

"Yeah, yeah, yeah," Drew said. "You told me so, I know. I'm never going to be able to ignore your advice again in my life, am I? Anytime I try, it's going to be 'Hey, Drew, remember that time you almost let Alexa—you know, the love of your life—get away from you?' and I'm going to have to give in. What a nightmare."

Carlos laughed.

"Yes indeed, your life seems like a total nightmare. I feel so bad for you."

"You should," Drew said. "You absolutely should. I had to make pancakes this morning. Me! Making pancakes! I spent hours on the couch afterward to recover."

"What a tough life."

"It's terrible and I love it. Speaking of, what's going on with you? Any women I should know about?"

He flashed back to that moment with Nik in the bakery.

"If you're trying to get me to settle down like you, dude, it's not happening. You know that's not me. But are you at home? Do you have a second?"

Drew's voice got serious.

"What's up? Something wrong?"

130

Carlos walked into his kitchen to see if he had any beer in his fridge.

"You remember my cousin Jessie, right?"

Oh thank God, there were two bottles in the back.

"Yeah, of course. Is something wrong with the baby?"

Drew knew him too well.

"Jessie has preeclampsia."

"Oh." Drew paused. "How far along is she? When did they find out?"

"Twenty-eight weeks, and just a few days ago. Her doctor isn't that worried, and she's on bed rest, but . . ."

They went over the details of Jessie's case, like they'd done together about other patients hundreds of times, back when they worked together and would bounce questions and ideas off each other. Turning Jessie into a patient, and not his cousin, gave him some of the distance he needed.

"Okay. I feel a little better. Thanks." He wished Drew still lived in L.A.

"No problem, man. Let me know if there's anything I can do. We'll miss you this weekend, but I totally understand that you can't leave Jessie now."

Carlos opened his second beer.

"Oh no, you're stuck with me. Jessie refuses to let me stay in L.A. this weekend. She said if I don't go up there and go to the party, she won't allow me in her house. Thank God I already told you I'd cook stuff for your party. I'm going to need to keep busy the whole time."

Drew laughed.

"That sounds like your family. We can go to the store after I pick you up from the airport tomorrow morning."

He already had some snacks in mind to make for the party. Fancy pigs in a blanket would keep him occupied for a while, for starters.

"Perfect. Hey, on a different topic: did you see the thing about that failed proposal at Dodger Stadium last weekend?"

Drew groaned.

"Did I ever. Thank God that happened after I proposed to Alexa; otherwise I would have totally lost my nerve."

"Yeahhhh, so, funny story. I was sitting right behind them when that happened."

"What? Are you kidding me?" Carlos heard some commotion in the background, and then Drew clearly talking to Alexa. "That proposal I told you about! Carlos was there. He was sitting right behind them." Drew came back on the phone. "Alexa is dying over here and says you have to tell me all the details."

"Put him on speaker!" Alexa shouted in the background.

Carlos laughed and told the story, with all of

the details he could remember. After spending all day talking about scary topics, it was fun to tell them about how he'd met Nik.

"Wait, so after you threw this unsuspecting, traumatized woman into your car—and then drove her through L.A. in that terror mobile, you and Angela went out drinking with her?" Alexa asked.

"I can't believe you would say something like that about my car! Is this what happens when people get a ring on their finger and stop being polite?"

"The entire world knows you're terrifying to be in a car with," Drew said. "Finish the story."

"Some friend you are. But, yes, that's pretty much exactly what happened. Except we weren't just with her, we were with her and her two best friends. It was me and four very angry women. I was just grateful I got out of there alive."

The three of them cracked up, and Carlos wished again that they all lived in the same city.

He would tell Drew the rest of the Nik story sometime when Alexa wasn't also there. Nothing against Alexa, but this was a guy kind of conversation. Maybe soon, he'd have more than an almost kiss to tell him about.

"Okay, guys, I'd better run."

"Talk to you soon," Drew said. "Keep me posted on Jessie, okay?"

Carlos nodded, even though he knew Drew couldn't see him.

"Will do, buddy. Thanks."

"Anytime."

Chapter Eight

• • • • • •

When Carlos left work on Wednesday, all he wanted was a very strong drink. His day had been full of minor disasters: a patient's dad had yelled first at the patient, then at Carlos; he'd called a patient by the wrong name, and then had called her by a different wrong name when he tried to apologize; a nurse had dropped a tray of urine samples on his shoes. Thank God he'd had an extra pair of shoes in his office.

Well, there was one other thing than just a strong drink that would put him in a better mood . . .

"Oh hell, why not?" he said to himself and scrolled to Nik's name in his phone.

Hey, you in the mood for that drink?

They'd been texting on and off since they'd seen each other last, but until now neither of them had mentioned getting together again. He kept almost bringing it up, but each time it was either so early in the day that it would look too premeditated or so late in the evening that it would look like a booty call. Now seemed like just the right time, but with his luck today, she'd be out with another guy already.

He drove toward the grocery store while waiting to see if she'd answer. He could stop for gas at the station next door. And if she said no, or even worse, didn't answer, at least he could splurge on some good bourbon.

Just as he pulled into the grocery store parking lot, his phone buzzed.

I am absolutely in the mood for that drink, but I can't tonight. Courtney's in the midst of a cupcake crisis; we have to deliver a zillion cupcakes up into the hills, her help bailed on her and her car broke down so we have to do it all in mine.

Apparently, Courtney was having a day like he was.

Oh, the hell with it. He had no other plans tonight but to sit on the couch and yell at his TV screen.

Do you need help? I'm not far away, and my car is 100% functional.

He got her text back within seconds.

Are you sure? That would be a lifesaver, but seriously, if you're busy, it's no problem.

Did he really want to spend his evening driving cupcakes around? No, of course not. Did he have an ulterior motive for volunteering to help? Obviously.

On my way.

When he got to Cupcake Park, Nik was standing in front waiting for him.

"You're our hero. Drive around the back into the alley, that's where we can load up. Just FYI, Courtney is freaking out, so don't be surprised when you see her."

He waved and drove on into a narrow alley around the corner. He pulled up when he saw a rack full of cupcake boxes and parked behind Nik's car.

"Carlos!" Courtney came running to the car, with many colors of frosting all over her pink and white apron. "You're a hero and a saint, and I'll find a way to thank you but I can't do that right now because we're in a time crunch. Help us load up."

Carlos jumped out of the car.

"Aye aye, captain."

They very carefully loaded what felt like hundreds of boxes of cupcakes into the two cars, while Courtney ran back and forth bringing more boxes out.

"Only on the floor!" Courtney shouted. "No boxes on seats! They'll fall off at the slightest hit of the brakes and disaster will strike."

He couldn't look at Nik, otherwise he knew he would laugh out loud.

"See what I meant about her freaking out?" Nik said as soon as Courtney went back inside.

He nodded.

"You weren't kidding about a cupcake crisis."

They unceremoniously tossed all of the crap

that had been in both his and Nik's trunks into the back room at Cupcake Park to maximize the space for the cupcakes. When they were all loaded up to Courtney's specifications, she programmed the address of the place they were going into Nik's phone, and took Nik's car key out of her hand.

"I'll take your car and meet you two there." She pointed her finger at Carlos. "No crazy driving, do you hear me?"

He turned to Nik.

"Why would she say that to me? I'm an excellent driver."

Nik laughed at him and got in the passenger seat.

"You'd better drive like you're transporting a tiny baby. If a single one of those cupcakes arrives with even slightly smashed frosting, Courtney will murder you."

He pulled out of the alley and zoomed toward the freeway.

"I'm offended that you would even feel the need to tell me that. I've been driving on L.A. freeways since I was practically a toddler. Those cupcakes will arrive in perfect condition, mark my words." He revved the motor at a stoplight, and Courtney, in the car next to his, looked over at him in horror.

"You just woke up the baby in the back seat, and it's pissed," Nik said.

He sped through the light when it turned green and laughed on his way to the freeway entrance.

"I was in a terrible mood, but that look on Courtney's face just cheered me right up. She might kill me, but it'll be worth it."

"Oh, she will definitely kill you, but she'll kill you after you get her cupcakes to the event." Nik relaxed into his passenger seat. "Speaking of babies, how's your cousin?"

He ran his hand through his hair and sighed.

"She's hanging in there, thanks for asking. Oh, she told me she tore through that Jamestown book and loved it. I'm not sure if that's because she was anxious or bored, but either way it helped, so thanks for the recommendation."

"My pleasure." He glanced back in her direction just to see her smile. "It's always good to find people who seem nice and normal and share my love for this genre. It makes me feel less evil to be so into such terrible stories. Wait. Your cousin is nice and normal, isn't she?"

To be honest, he'd always kind of thought that Jessie's love of true crime showed the evil side to her, but he probably shouldn't say that out loud.

"I guess that depends what you're comparing 'nice and normal' against," he said.

Nik laughed.

"Well, you and your sister both seem . . ." She looked sideways at him. "Nah, I take that back.

Your sister seems nice and normal, maybe. You, I don't know."

He shook his head.

"See, this is what happens when you go out of your way to help people—they spend the whole time insulting you."

Nik patted him on the thigh. He wished she would leave her hand there, but no luck.

"But seriously," she asked, "did you have to go far out of your way to come help? Where do you live, anyway?"

He pretended he was checking to change lanes just to look over at her. He would have driven from clear across the city just to see the way she looked in that tank top.

"Atwater Village, not too far from here. But I was even closer, because I was at the Vons in Silver Lake when I got your text."

"Oh wow, Atwater Village is such a great neighborhood," she said. "How long have you lived there?"

Her hair was back in one big ponytail. His fingers ached to pull it out and run them through it.

"Let's see, it's the end of May? Almost six months. I bought it in January, which is a terrible time to move, especially with a brand-new job. But it was all kind of a fluke. I lucked into it. The seller had just gotten a new job on the East Coast and had to sell fast, so I got a good deal."

"Congratulations, that's fantastic," she said.

"I still can't believe I'm a homeowner." Sometimes when he looked at his house keys, it still blew him away that the place was all his. "It's tiny, but it works for me."

He pulled onto the freeway exit.

"Oh look, there's Courtney in my car," Nik said, gesturing to the car in front of them at the light.

"Have you been friends for a long time?" Carlos asked.

Nik nodded.

"We went to Stanford together. We lived next door to each other junior year. One night she got locked out and knocked on my door, and we've basically been friends ever since."

He and Courtney both turned to head up into the winding roads into the hills. He hoped that none of the cupcake boxes moved while they went around curves. As much as he'd teased both Nik and Courtney on the way here, he really did want the cupcakes to arrive looking perfect.

"Is that how you met Dana, too?"

She nodded.

"Yeah, but not in the dorms. I met Dana through a theater group on campus. One night, the director hit on Dana in a pretty gross way, and Courtney came with me to rescue Dana." She shook her head and laughed. "Long story short, that guy woke up the next morning with spray paint all over his beloved car. I'm not going to say how it happened, because no one ever found out. I'll just say that Courtney is a really good person to have on your side."

He'd be sure to keep that in mind. He loved his car too much not to.

"Did you move to L.A. together?"

She shook her head.

"No, Courtney moved here right after graduation and has been here ever since. I moved to New York after graduation, but I couldn't stay away from California too long."

He had always fantasized a little about moving to New York, but both the weather and the distance from his family had always held him back.

"Do you think you're going to stay here?" he asked.

One of her curls had escaped from her ponytail. She tucked it back in.

"Oh yeah. I've been in L.A. for six years, and it's home now. I can't imagine living anywhere else."

He nodded.

"Granted, I've lived in L.A. most of my life, but I agree. Also, how much farther?"

Nik looked at her phone for the directions.

"Only half a mile."

He grinned at her.

"How much do you think Courtney is freaking out now?"

Nik leaned back against her seat and considered.

"Well, she'll definitely be calmer now that we've got your help, but she's always hyped up before she does an event. She'll be in drill sergeant mode when we get out of the car; I'm going to prepare you for that now."

Just then, the GPS told them that their location was up ahead on the right. Courtney was already there. She jumped out of the car right when they pulled up and came straight over to his car, already talking.

"Listen to me very carefully. Do not take a single box out of this car without my supervision. Open the trunk and all of the doors, but don't touch anything yet. I'll go inside to see where we should unload, I'll be right back."

She pulled her apron off to reveal an identical clean apron underneath, flipped her head upside down and redid her ponytail, and walked up to the house. Carlos got out of the car and obediently opened his back two doors and the trunk. He and Nik leaned against the car, almost, but not quite, touching.

He looked down at her. That rogue curl had escaped her ponytail again. He couldn't resist tucking it back in. She smiled her thanks at him.

"Hey." She put her hand on his arm. "Thank you so much for helping us. We could have done this ourselves; it just would have been much more stressful for both of us, especially Courtney."

He slung his arm around her shoulders.

"Does this mean that I get free Cupcake Park cupcakes for life? Because I think that would be an appropriate token of gratitude."

Nik relaxed against him.

"I don't know about for life, but I'm pretty sure you're going to get quite a few free cupcakes out of this. Just make sure to say—"

Courtney came racing out of the door, flanked by two waiters.

"We have reinforcements! Okay, everyone. I'm going to hand the boxes out of the cars to each of you, and we'll all walk inside carrying a box and put them on the designated table in the kitchen. Nik and Carlos, follow Andre and Kevin here once you have your cupcakes. We'll do this until we get them all unloaded."

As the five of them went back and forth from the cars to the kitchen, Nik shook her head at herself. Most people who had the hots for the sexy doctor nearby would ask him to get a drink, or would text him increasingly suggestive jokes until he got the hint, or would "injure" themselves and call him in a panic, preferably while wearing a casually elegant sundress and a sexy bra. No, she'd asked him to come help her and her panicked friend drive dozens of cupcakes up into the hills and then carry them as gently as they would bombs about to detonate. And she was wearing an old tank top and torn jeans. And not the artfully torn kind.

Courtney owed her big for this one.

"Okay." Courtney glanced at the clock after the four of them had stacked all twenty boxes on the table. "I need to set up my trays and arrange the cupcakes, but I don't need help for that; I have plenty of time. Thanks to you two. You can go."

Nik turned to Carlos and hugged him.

"Thank you so much. Go and have your relaxing evening." She turned back to Courtney. "Where should I wait for you?"

Courtney looked at her like she was an idiot.

"You don't have to wait; you can go, too."

Nik returned her look.

"You don't have a car, remember? I have to drive you home."

Courtney pointed at Carlos.

"He can drive you home. I'll bring you back your car tomorrow. If you're waiting around for me, it'll stress me out."

Nik looked at Courtney. She saw the glimmer in Courtney's eyes. Ohhhhh. Courtney was trying to throw the two of them together. Nik looked away.

"I can drive you home, no problem," Carlos said.

Courtney looked victorious. No one ever called her subtle.

"Are you sure? I'm not really on your way, am I?" Nik asked him. Why was she asking him that; what the hell was wrong with her? Just get in the damn sports car with the hot man, Nikole.

He shrugged.

"No, but you're not that far out of my way."

Courtney winked at her and turned to open the cupcake boxes.

"Thanks for your help, Carlos. Your next dozen cupcakes are on me."

"Are you sure she doesn't need us to stay and help?" Carlos asked as Nik got back into the passenger seat of his car.

Nik shook her head and put her seat belt on. Okay, this was it, right? She didn't remember how to do this kind of thing. She hadn't been at all interested in the past few guys she'd dated until well after they'd asked her out . . . and sometimes, not even then. Should she ask him if he wanted to get that drink after all, on her? Should she just invite him up to her apartment when they got to her place and pounce on him? Or should she just wait to see if he made a move?

"Oh, she definitely doesn't need us. Courtney is the ultimate micromanager when it comes to her cupcakes. She only let us carry the boxes tonight out of sheer necessity."

Carlos nodded and turned the car on.

"Well, she's done a great job so far doing it all herself," he said. "I get the impulse."

She could put her hand on his leg or something? Why was she so bad at this? She was usually *great* at flirting with men. Had she lost her mojo?

"I do, too, but I wish she had more reliable help. Thank goodness I live close by and could race down to the store today."

Carlos touched her hand.

"You're a good friend. She's lucky to have you."

Nik felt her cheeks get warm.

"Oh, well—"

His phone rang, and he pulled it out of his pocket.

"Oh shit. I'm going to have to take this. Sorry about that." He pulled over under a clump of trees and turned the car off.

"Hey," he answered the phone. "Is something wrong? What's your blood pressure?"

Really? His cousin, right now? She tried not to let out a frustrated sigh. She was pretty sure this meant the universe was against this whole rebound idea.

She sat there silently, trying not to listen. Which was impossible because he was two feet away from her. She pulled out her phone to text Dana so she wasn't too obviously eavesdropping.

Sitting here, next to Carlos, I think I've forgotten what to do with men, all I can talk about are cupcakes and I keep laughing too loud, help—erase erase erase erase. Just because he was facing out his window didn't mean he wouldn't turn around at any moment and be able to see everything she was typing.

"Don't give me this 'I just wanted to talk to my cousin' bullshit—you know I'm going to worry whenever you call me from here on out. And I already told you that engagement party was fun, and that I think two of Alexa's friends secretly have the hots for each other. Did you forget that phone call? Oh! I get it! You're bored stiff. You're used to talking to people at work all day and now you're stuck at home. I get it, bed rest would bore me to tears, too. We have to find more ways to entertain you. What about those books I got you?"

Carlos turned to her and smiled, and she smiled back. He reached up and tucked that annoying curl that kept falling out of her ponytail behind her ear. God, she loved it when he touched her like that.

He moved his hand down from her head to her shoulder. His fingers moved gently, up and down her bare shoulder. She sighed.

Suddenly he let out a bark of laughter. It made her want to laugh along with it.

"You've read how many?" He looked down at Nik with a huge smile on his face. "Which was your favorite?"

Oh good, she could stop pretending she wasn't listening.

148

"You loved them all?" He held eye contact with Nik, and his smile got even bigger. She could feel a matching smile spread across her own face. "I'll be sure to tell my friend who recommended them how you felt about them.

"I guess I'd better buy you some more. In the meantime, I've heard there's this thing called Netflix. You should look into it."

He kept smiling at Nik. It took all she could to resist leaning against him. His eyes crinkled with the laughter she could tell he was holding in.

"As a matter of fact, people *do* tell me that I'm funny. I'll bring more books on Saturday, okay?"

He hung up the phone and tucked it back into his pocket. He pushed his hand through his hair and smiled at her.

"As you heard, Jessie loved the books."

She bit her bottom lip. Good Lord, this man was more attractive by the second.

"I'm glad." She leaned toward him and willed him to start playing with her hair again.

A car shot past them on its way up the hill, and they moved away from each other.

"We should get you home."

He turned the key and gunned the motor to get them back onto the roadway. The engine sputtered and stopped.

"Uh-oh." Carlos turned the key again, and nothing happened. "Shit."

"Did you run out of gas?" she asked him.

"What? No, that's impossible. I never run out of gas. I went to the gas station tonight, right after I went to the grocery store . . ." He trailed off, then looked at her in horror. "I didn't go to the grocery store. I didn't go to the gas station! I was on my way to the grocery store when I got your text. Shit. I did run out of gas."

She patted him on the shoulder.

"It's okay; it's no big deal. We can call Triple A. You do have Triple A, right?"

He nodded, but made no move toward his phone or wallet.

"I never run out of gas! I can't believe I let this happen to my car. I never even get down below a quarter tank, but this week has been so busy and I let it go way longer than usual."

Nik narrowed her eyes at his steering wheel.

"Didn't you notice your gas light go on?"

He refused to make eye contact.

"The thing is . . . I always keep my gas tank at least a quarter full, so the gas light in this car has never gone on before. So . . . yes, it went on, but I was preoccupied, and I'd never seen it before so I didn't . . ." She held her laughter in so well, even when he finally turned to look at her, but something in her eyes must have betrayed her. He frowned at her. "The gas light in this car is in a weird place, okay? Are you laughing at me?"

She shook her head and rubbed her hand up and down his arm.

"No, I'm not laughing at you. I'm desperately trying not to laugh at you, here."

She knew how touchy men were about their cars. He would probably get mad at her for that, but she couldn't help making fun of him.

But he grinned at her.

"Okay, fine, I will admit that this is a little funny." He put his arm around her shoulders and lowered his voice. "You have to promise to never tell anyone about this, though. I have a reputation to uphold."

She nodded and turned so her lips were almost touching his ear.

"Cross my heart; it's our secret. Just one question: do you think you maybe want to call Triple A to get us out of here?"

He pulled his wallet and phone both out of his pocket.

"Right, of course."

He made a face at her when he got off the phone.

"They're on their way, but it'll be a while. Apparently, 'out of gas in a safe spot in the hills' is low priority."

Nik took off her seatbelt and leaned toward him.

"We might as well get comfortable while we wait for them." She looked around the car. "How long have you had this car, anyway?"

He closed his eyes for a moment before answering her.

"Almost five years."

His car had confused her, ever since she'd gotten to know him a little bit. He didn't seem like the kind of guy to be obsessed with his bright red sports car, but from his reaction when the car had run out of gas, that seemed like exactly what he was. Granted, people in L.A. tended to care about their cars more than anywhere else she'd ever been, so maybe it was just that.

"Why did you buy it?" she asked. "A celebration of a new job or something?"

He shook his head, but didn't say anything. He ran his fingers down the steering wheel. The silence went on so long that she didn't think he was going to answer her at all. She opened her mouth to ask him another question when he finally spoke.

"My dad died. Almost five years ago, my dad died."

Oh God. Leave it to her to ask the asshole question.

"Oh Carlos, I'm so sorry. You don't have to . . ."

He shook his head and kept talking.

"My parents didn't have lots of money—they always managed to give us all of the important stuff, but they were both school teachers for thirty years; they were never flush. But it turned out that he had a ton of life insurance. Some in my mom's name, of course. But some in mine, and some in my sister's. After he died and I got this enormous—to me, at least—check . . ." He paused for a second before continuing. "Well, I didn't know what to do with it. I deposited it in my savings account, and just let it sit there for a while. I was going to use it to pay off some of my med school loans. I probably *should* have used it to pay off some of my med school loans. But then one day, I took a different way home from work. I saw the sun gleaming off of a bright red sports car with a big price tag on the windshield. I turned straight into the lot and bought that car an hour later. My dad always liked flashy things. Sometimes I feel like that was a stupid way to use his legacy, but . . . I think he'd like this car a lot."

She pulled him into a hug. His head dropped down on her shoulder, and they sat there together for a few minutes, breathing with each other.

"Thanks for telling me," she said.

"Thanks for listening," he said.

His hands moved up and down her back, and then gently through her hair.

She turned her head and kissed his jaw. His cheek.

He pulled back to look at her. She looked back at him: his kind big dark-brown eyes; his thick almost-black hair that she was dying to touch; his warm skin, with stubble already visible along his jawline; that hint of a dimple in his cheek; his lips, a dusky pink, not quite smiling, but looking like they would smile at any minute.

He lifted his hand from her shoulder and stroked her cheek, and she smiled.

He slid his hand around to the back of her neck and pulled her toward him. And finally, *finally,* he kissed her. Soft, at first. Not tentative, but slow. Gentle. Tender. She hadn't realized just how much she'd wanted him to kiss her until just this moment. She kissed him back the same way, happy to let him take the lead, as long as he stayed here in this car and kept kissing her.

Her hands went up into his hair, that hair she'd been wanting to touch for so long, and she sighed with some combination of relief and lust.

That sigh seemed to signal something to him. He pulled her tighter against him, and his hand ran down the side of her body. His lips, his tongue, got stronger, and she met his urgency with her own. He pulled away, and she almost moaned in frustration, but then he trailed his mouth down her neck, kissing and biting and kissing again, until her hands gripped his hair and she gasped.

He raised his head.

"You liked that?" he asked, as he nuzzled her ear.

"God, yes," she said.

"That's what I was hoping," he said. She turned her head and kissed him again.

"I've been wanting to do this ever since I met you," he said.

"Oh my God, me, too," she said. She didn't realize how true that was until she said it out loud.

They looked at each other and laughed. He brushed her hair back from her face and smiled at her. That same smile that had made her trust him at Dodger Stadium. She pulled his face to hers and kissed him again and again.

She started to pull away to say something witty, but he ran his tongue around her lips, so she had no choice but to open them and meet his tongue with her own. His hands kept moving, this time up and down her torso. He lingered beneath her breasts and then started making long, slow, circles around them that got progressively smaller and smaller.

"I like that, too," she said, breathing hard.

"Good. I hoped you did. Because I really like doing it," he said as he reached her hard nipples. He leaned forward to keep kissing her as he touched them. Why had she held off kissing this man for so long?

"Are we . . ." He touched her in a way that made her gasp and lose her train of thought for a second. "Are we going to get in trouble if someone finds us like this? We are up in the hills, after all. I don't know if a lot of people who look like us live up here."

He pulled back, but his hands lingered on her breasts.

"You're right. I definitely don't want some rich dude who lives up here to call the cops on us. I haven't made out in a car since . . . my God, since I was in high school, I think." His hands slid down to her thighs. "The problem is, and the thing that I'd forgotten is . . . making out in cars is really hot."

She glanced down and saw the clear evidence of how turned on he was.

"Mmmm, it is, isn't it?" She put her hand on his knee. "Do you know that this is the first time I've ever made out like this in a car?" He watched her fingers trail up and down his thighs, never getting quite where she knew he wanted them to be.

"Never? How is that possible?" he asked, not raising his eyes.

"I have no idea, but I was clearly missing out." Her fingers did little loops on the insides of his thighs, and he let out a breath.

"Uh-huh. Is your first time everything you wanted it to be?" He raised his eyes to hers.

"Everything and more." She leaned forward to kiss him and to move her hand higher.

HONNNNNNNNK.

They sprang apart and looked up at the mechanic's truck parked in front of them. Carlos's cheeks got red and he bent down to reach for his wallet.

"You the one who called about running out of gas?" The guy was at the window, a leer on his face that Nik wanted to smack off of it. Maybe after a few more self-defense classes she could.

"That's me." Carlos got out of the car and handed him his driver's license and AAA card.

Nik looked out the car window without seeing a thing. Holy shit, this really seemed to be happening. Was she sure she wanted to do this? She'd *felt* sure while Carlos was kissing her. But she still felt hesitant. Something about Carlos seemed different than the guys she usually went out with. She didn't know if it was different good or different bad. The uncertainty made her nervous.

After far too much chatting, the mechanic poured a gallon of gas into Carlos's tank and gave him a screen to sign. He winked at her before he got back in his van. She rolled her eyes.

"Oh my God." Carlos got back in the car and shook his head. "I haven't gotten caught in a car making out with a girl since I was seventeen. And then it wasn't even my car! I'm twice that age now; at least the car is a lot better." He wrapped his arms around her. "And the girl is, too."

Okay, hearing that was almost worth getting checked out by the mechanic. She lifted her face to him, and he kissed her hard.

Chapter Nine

● ● ● ● ● ●

Carlos stopped at the gas station at the bottom of the hill.

"I should fill up here, even though it's like twenty cents more expensive than it is near my house." He leaned over to kiss her. Now that he'd started kissing her, he couldn't stop. She kissed him back so hard it was a struggle for him to pull away and get out of the car.

Had he made it weird when he brought up his dad to Nik? Did she think his reason for getting the car was stupid? Some people had, which is why he never told people the real reason anymore. He just let them think he was one of those L.A. dudes who liked sports cars. He didn't know why he'd told her.

When he got back in the car, they grinned at each other and both leaned in for another kiss. He felt like a horny teenager. He loved it.

Finally he turned the key and pulled out of the gas station. Within seconds, they were both singing along to Beyoncé as they shot down the freeway. She smiled at him as she sang along, and he sent silent thanks to Courtney's flaky employee, her broken down car, and the entire concept of running out of gas for getting him here.

A few songs later, and they'd pulled up in front of her apartment. She ran her hand from his knee up his thigh and smiled at him.

"Are you going to come inside?"

He tried not to grin as big as he wanted to, but he was pretty sure he failed. His terrible day had officially turned around. He couldn't wait to pounce on her as soon as they walked into her apartment.

As she unlocked the door to her building, he thought of something.

"Did you get your locks changed?"

Fuck. Why did he ask her that? She'd snapped at him once for bringing that up. What was wrong with him?

She held up a brand-new key.

"Last week. I felt stupid for doing it, but then I remembered what you said about how feeling silly is better than the alternative."

Oh thank God, she wasn't mad at him.

As they walked up the stairs to her apartment, she smiled wryly.

"I also convinced Courtney and Dana to take a self-defense class with me. Well, it's really more of a boxing class, actually."

Well, he hadn't expected that.

"Wow, that's great. How was it?"

She stopped at her front door to unlock it with the new key.

"It was surprisingly fun. There's only been one so far, but I'm happy I'm taking it."

"That's awesome. I'm impressed."

He was also glad that she'd trusted him enough to tell him she was doing it. And flattered that she'd gotten her locks changed at least in part because of something he'd said.

When they walked into her apartment, he was ready to throw her down on the couch, but she walked into the kitchen before he could reach for her.

"Do you want some wine?" she asked him.

Hmmm. He couldn't be wrong about why he was in her apartment, could he? He had been here before, and nothing had happened then.

No, this was different. She'd seemed like she'd wanted to pull his clothes off in the car. Maybe she was just nervous now that they were back at her apartment? He wasn't sure what was going on, but he'd better take her lead on this.

"Sure." He sat down on the couch. "More of that rosé, maybe?"

She laughed and opened the refrigerator.

"I *think* you're making fun of me and my rosé, but I don't even care, because I love it. As a matter of fact, yes, I do have another bottle of rosé open now—though this time it's a different one—and I'm going to pour us both glasses of it, take that."

She came over to the couch with glasses of wine for each of them. Okay, she sat down right next to him; she was clearly not keeping her distance. He put his arm around her and pulled her close.

"I have to confess I have been known to make fun of my sister for her love of this wine, and it kills me that I actually liked the one you gave me last time because now I might have to eat my words to Angie." He took a sip. "Actually no, there's no way I'd do that. But this is terrible—I definitely like this wine."

He let his fingers drift into her hair, and she relaxed against him.

"Oh no, you've discovered a kind of *wine* that you like, and it happens to be *pink* wine. What will you ever do with yourself?" She swatted his thigh. And then left her hand there. "You can't possibly let a *woman* know that she was right about wine; that's impossible."

He shook his head. He finally pulled that ponytail holder out of her hair and let her curls spring free.

"No, that's not it. I'm happy to let women know they're right about many things. My boss was right about the diagnosis of the kid I saw today. You were right about the books I bought for Jessie. Jessie was right when she told me I'd get into med school. It's just that I can't ever admit to my *little sister* that she was right about something I've been teasing her about for years. Come on now."

"Mmmm." She looked up at him. "I'm an only child; it's possible that I don't get all of the big brother–little sister relationship nuances, so I'll that one go." She rested her head on his shoulder. "Oh! What did Jessie say her favorite of the books was?"

He was trying to concentrate on what she was saying, but between her fingers gently massaging his knee and feeling her sigh as he stroked her hair, his mind was in many places.

"Um, what did she say? Oh! She said her favorite was the Jeffrey Dahmer book. I don't understand either of you. If I read those books, I would have nightmares for weeks."

She set her glass, still half full, on the coffee table.

"People have said that to me. Maybe I just don't have very vivid dreams." She brought her hand up and drew it through his hair. She plucked his glass out of his hand and put it on the coffee table next to her own. "Or maybe I just dream about other things."

He smiled. The preamble was apparently over. He turned to face her and pressed her down onto the couch until she was underneath him.

"Yeah? What is it that you dream about?"

162

She grabbed the bottom of his button-down shirt and pulled it over his head.

"This." She pulled him against her and kissed him.

Mother of God. He thought he liked kissing her when they were making out in the front seat of his car, but that was clearly only an appetizer. There, she'd seemed enthused, but still tentative. Now, she was both passionate and forceful, as if to make it clear she was all in. Her hands moved under his T-shirt and up and down his back, pressing him harder against her. He moved his attention to her neck, kissing her smooth brown skin.

"Do you dream about that, too?" he asked her.

"My God, yes," she said.

He blew gently over her skin and kissed the cool spot. He did it again lower, and then again lower. He loved the way her fingers tensed on his back. He drew his hand up and plucked her nipple. She arched her back and moaned. He kept kissing her neck and playing with her nipples until he thought both of them were going to explode.

"We both have way too many clothes on." He pulled her tank top off, to reveal her black lace bra underneath. "Mmmm, this is a very pretty bra. But right now, it's in my way." He reached around and unsnapped her bra and tossed it over the couch. He sat back to admire her.

"That's better."

She shook her head.

"You said we both had too many clothes on, but I didn't see you take any off."

The woman had a point.

He stood up, tugged his pants off, pulled his T-shirt over his head, and stood in front of her in his boxer briefs.

"Is *that* better?"

She smiled and nodded, her eyes roaming all over his body, but coming back to focus somewhere right around his waistband.

"Much better."

She didn't bother to get up, but pulled her jeans off and threw them on the floor next to his clothes. He took a long look at her curvy body. Holy shit. He climbed back on top of her.

Oh thank Athena, Aphrodite, and all the other gods for the many crises tonight that had resulted in Carlos in her bed. Okay, it was her couch, but this wasn't the time for details. She was very glad she'd gotten over her weird—and stupid, in retrospect, now that she'd seen him without clothes on—anxiety about this guy. The way that he looked at her body . . . well, that kind of look was exactly what she needed after this past week and a half. He looked at her like her body was a joy to behold, like he couldn't wait to touch her, kiss her, like he was lucky to be here with her without any clothes on. Damn right he was.

She was feeling pretty fucking lucky herself right now. This man definitely knew how to touch a woman, that's for sure.

"We need to get these off of you," he said, caressing her sensible black cotton underwear. She'd had no idea she was going to be having sex later when she'd left the house that day, okay? At least they were bikini cut. She lifted her hips to give him better access.

He shook his head.

"No, not that way." He got up off the couch, pushed her coffee table back out of his way, and turned her around until she was sitting forward. "Okay, now." He hooked his fingers in her underwear and pulled them to the floor. Then he pushed her legs apart and knelt at her feet.

"Mmmm." He stared straight in front of him with a hungry look on his face. "That's even better." He reached back and pulled her toward him. Well, maybe he tried to pull, but she was so eager for what she knew was coming that she fairly launched herself at him.

Good *Lord*. She lay back on her couch pillows, gasping for air. She thought she liked it when he kissed her mouth, that was nothing to what those lips and that tongue—dear God, that tongue— could do to other parts of her body. It felt so good she wanted it to go on forever. She thought there was no way for it to get any better. And then he

165

added his fingers to his lips and his tongue, and she came so hard she saw black spots floating in front of her eyes.

"Holy shit," she said as soon as she could talk. And then she did something she'd never done after an orgasm before: she started giggling uncontrollably.

"What's so funny?" He sat back up on the couch, and she leaned against him until they were laying down again, her tucked into the curve of his arm.

"Nothing," she choked out. "This was just not at all how I expected my day to go. I didn't even . . ." she tried to catch her breath. "I didn't even have my good underwear on!"

He glanced at the clothes littered across the floor, then back at her.

"Who cares about what kind of underwear you had on when you have that body underneath it?" He ran his hand down her torso, the side of her hip, her thigh. Something inside of her melted.

"You jackass."

"What?" He froze. "What did I say?"

She shook her head.

"You can't say shit like that when my condoms are all so far away in my bedroom. Because now I want you to fuck me right this second."

He jumped into a runner's stance.

"Where are they? I can run fast. Especially when I'm motivated."

"Top drawer of the nightstand. Go."

She relaxed back on the couch and laughed as he raced to her bedroom. She could feel the shit-eating grin on her face. Ahhhhh, that butt in motion was fantastic.

He was back in less than thirty seconds, true to his boasting. He dropped his boxer briefs to the floor and ripped open the condom packet. Thank God enough lights were on in her living room so she could see he really was as big as she'd thought he was. Sometimes touch could be deceiving, especially with layers of clothes in between, but boy was this not one of those times.

He was back on the couch and on top of her as soon as he'd rolled the condom on. She wrapped one leg around him to bring him in closer, and he groaned in her ear and moved faster. So she did it with the other leg and he bit down on her shoulder.

He took her hands and moved them to the arm of the couch behind her.

"Hold on."

She obeyed him and was glad she did. She held on for dear life and met him thrust for thrust as he pounded into her, faster and faster, until he finally roared and collapsed against her.

He lifted himself up a little while later and kissed her cheek.

"I'm never going to make fun of rosé again if that's the result." He stood up and went over to the kitchen to throw out the condom. "Pink wine, man. Who would have thought?"

She laughed and curled up in the corner of the couch.

"There's more in the fridge." She pulled the blanket that hung on the back of the couch over herself.

He opened the fridge and took out the bottle.

"Look, lady. Some of us need a little bit of a break before we have more *rosé,* okay? Let a man breathe for a minute."

Oh, she would let him breathe as long as he wanted if he did it with that grin on his face and that swagger in his walk.

"I'm just glad I introduced you to the glory that is rosé, that's all. You take your time. I don't want to rush you."

He topped up both of their glasses and carefully pushed the coffee table back to its normal spot before getting under the blanket with her.

"You know what would look great on that table?" he asked her, nodding at her coffee table.

"What?" She stared at the table, trying to figure out what he meant. It was just a chestnut wood coffee table, nothing fancy, but the perfect height for propping her feet up to watch TV. What did he think would look good on it, coasters or coffee table books or something?

"A large pizza. With everything. That much rosé makes me hungry."

She shook her head.

"Not everything. No blue cheese or olives. Everything other than that."

He reached down to the floor for his pants and pulled his phone out of the pocket.

"I can live with that. Large pizza with almost everything coming up."

He called some pizza place she'd never heard of and ordered a monstrosity of a pizza. As soon as he listed the toppings on the phone, her stomach rumbled. Apparently, that much . . . *rosé* . . . made her hungry, too. Well, that, and she hadn't eaten since lunchtime.

"I've never ordered from this place before, but this sausage is great," she said as she picked up her second piece. Carlos was already on his third.

"Look," he said, when his mouth was no longer full. "You don't know me that well yet, but one thing you should know is I'm very good at ordering food. I know you didn't trust that this pizza was going to be good. I could see it in your eyes when I ordered. I'm not even going to make you admit that you were wrong, because that's the kind of guy I am. But that should be the last time you ever doubt me on food matters."

She reached for her wineglass to wash down the delicious grease.

"Noted. Does that mean you're a good cook, too?"

He shrugged, but that cocky grin was still on his face.

"I mean, yes, I'm a fantastic cook, but I try not to brag about it." His grin widened and she laughed. "I don't do enough cooking these days, though, what with work and everything else."

"How did you learn to cook?" she asked.

He took another bite of pizza.

"Originally, from my mom. She taught both me and my sister all of her specialties, and then I taught myself how to cook other stuff. First, when I was a poor student, and then when I realized that cooking was meditative for me, a way to relax and take a break and be alone with my thoughts."

He shook his head and was silent for a moment.

"In med school I used to make huge pots of chili for my roommates, and we would all eat it for a week. My buddy Drew and I met when we were in this fellowship together. It was so stressful and exhausting. We both happened to have the same day off one week, so I invited him over to eat enchiladas and watch the game. We were so tired that we both fell asleep on the couch after we ate and woke up just as the game was ending." He laughed. "We've been friends ever since."

She laughed, too. She and her friends had bonded over revenge; he and his friend had bonded over food and a nap. That sounded about right.

Speaking of sleep . . .

"Hey, what time is it?" she asked him.

He checked his phone, on the coffee table along with the now almost empty pizza box and wine.

"Ten thirty." He put his wineglass down. "I hadn't realized it was so late. I'd better be going."

"Oh." She put hers down, too. "Oh, okay. You probably have to get up early, I guess."

He stopped halfway through standing up and sat back down.

"Didn't you . . ." He paused for a few seconds, shrugged, and continued. "Just to be clear—do you want me to go? Because if you do, it's no problem, but if not, I'm happy to stay."

"No!" She shook her head and put her hand on his knee. "I mean, no, you don't have to go. Sorry, that must have sounded like a hint, that's not what I meant. I was just thinking it was about time we left the couch. We haven't even made it into my bedroom yet, and we finished the bottle of rosé, so . . ."

He took her hands and pulled her up off of the couch with him.

"Lead the way."

Chapter Ten

• • • • • •

Nik woke up the next morning significantly later than she usually did. As a writer who worked from home, she generally had to keep herself on a pretty strict schedule or she would get nothing done. She almost always forced herself to keep to that schedule, even though everyone she knew—including Fisher—had made fun of her about how rigid she was about it.

But when you woke up in the wee hours of the morning because a big, warm, strong man was kissing you awake, and then you spent the next hour doing delicious things with him in your bed before he had to leave to get to work on time, it was only natural that you'd fall back asleep and not wake up until . . . holy shit, it was nine thirty.

She stretched luxuriously in her big empty bed and smiled at her rumpled sheets. She felt like the queen of the world. She liked this feeling.

She stumbled into the kitchen, naked and pleasantly sore. She'd forgotten to set up her coffee maker the night before—she had been a little distracted, okay?—so she tossed out yesterday's coffee filter and turned her coffee grinder on. She hummed as she scooped coffee into the machine, measured out the water, and got her favorite coffee cup down from the cabinet. While the coffee brewed, she went back to her bedroom for her robe. Not that she minded being naked, but she'd left the windows open overnight, and the morning air was chilly.

Would she see Carlos again? He didn't seem the type to sleep with her and then disappear, but you never knew with men. She hoped she'd see him again, though. The sex was fantastic, and he made her laugh. That was a pretty rare combination in her experience.

She sat down on her couch with her coffee and dug into her bag for her phone to check her email. She took one sip and laughed at herself. Check her email, what was she thinking? If she knew her friends, and she did, she would have many text messages to respond to first.

Sure enough, Courtney had texted her and Dana early this morning.

Nik, I have your car, let me know if I can come pick you up this afternoon and get it back to you. Also DID YOU BANG CARLOS I AM BETTING THE ANSWER IS YES BUT I NEED TO KNOW IMMEDIATELY.

Then Dana:

Wait, what? I thought she was still being all wishy washy about it? What happened? I need details, how did I miss this?

173

Courtney filled Dana in, Dana responded with many exclamation points, the two of them had a nice long chat about her long before she was awake.

Good morning, friends. I'm around anytime today for a car exchange. Also, yes.

She couldn't resist teasing them a little.

She hummed as she checked her email. Okay good, she'd gotten the go-ahead from the studio to do a profile of the up-and-coming black female director, her piece on that school teacher in Fresno who had taken in ten of his students as foster kids was going to run in the *Times* Sunday magazine in a few weeks, and the editor she hated working with was resigning and moving to New York for a magazine she also hated. What an excellent morning.

Yes? YES??? We get a hell of a lot more than fucking yes.

She laughed out loud at Courtney's text.

Nik will give us the details as soon as she wants to give us the details.

Dana was always the nice one.

However. She had better want to give us the details within the next two minutes, or I'm never going to let her borrow my shoes again.

Not that nice. She'd better respond.

I don't know why Courtney even asked the question, she orchestrated the whole thing! Don't worry, you'll get all the details tonight after class. Long story short: it was excellent, you both were right, he left a few hours ago, and I'm exhausted and very smug. I probably won't get any work done this morning but I don't care. I have no idea if I'll ever see him again but it was still worth it. Happy?

She went to the kitchen for a refill on the coffee and heard numerous texts come in as she poured it.

From Dana: We have to go through an hour and a half class with you doing your "I Just Had Sex" face before we hear the details? I'm going to kill you.

From Courtney: Yessssssssssss. I think this is worth skipping class for, don't you??? Wasn't one class enough?

From Dana: No, we have to go, we already paid for the whole six weeks.

From Courtney: I hate you so much. Can't we get the dish before class, then?

From Dana: I'm filming all afternoon and I won't allow you to hear about this before I do.

From Courtney: Ugh fine fine, that's a legit excuse, but still, I'm dying over here. And N: I would bet you're going to see him again.

And, right as she read that one, another text jumped onto her screen:

I hope you got back to sleep this morning after I left. You going out of town for Memorial Day weekend, or are you free Friday night?

She took another sip of coffee with a big grin on her face and texted her girlfriends.

Apparently you'd win that bet. See you both tonight. She set her mug down on the coffee table, stood up, and danced in her living room for a full minute before texting Carlos back.

Friday night works for me!

Wait, no. Right before she pressed send, she deleted the exclamation point. She was all for being straightforward and not playing games with guys, but he didn't need to know a text from him literally made her dance.

She also didn't need to tell her friends how right they were that a rebound had been exactly what she needed. They would be sure to tell her that themselves.

When Nik walked into class that night, Courtney and Dana were both already there. And both glaring at her.

"I texted that I got out of work early and we could meet up before class. Why didn't you answer?" Dana whispered.

Oops. She'd put her phone in lockdown mode this afternoon to get work done and had forgotten to take it off. She had gotten a ton of work done, so that was a positive. A negative was that her friends were going to kill her.

"Sorry, I was working, and my phone was off," she said. Their expressions did not change. She couldn't help but laugh, which just made them glare all the more. "Okay, I will tell you one small detail to get you even more excited for the full story: we didn't even make it out of his car before we started kissing."

Dana high-fived her.

"I'm still mad at you, but also, I'm thrilled at how unlike you that is."

Dana was wearing a very cute hot pink sports bra, and that brand of workout leggings that looked amazing on tall, willowy people like her, but terrible on anyone else. Nik looked down at her own old Stanford T-shirt and comfortable yoga pants and sighed. She'd been paranoid for years after moving to L.A. that Dana would decide to ditch her and Courtney for other actress/ model types. There was something about being in this city, where looks were so important, that made you doubt everything you'd been confident about, including your friends. Dana had never wavered, though. Now Nik was ashamed that she'd ever doubted her.

"Hi, class!" Natalie said. They all immediately switched their attention to the front of the room. Today her hair was up in an impossibly high topknot.

"I'm super excited about our class today! Today you all get to use . . . punching bags!"

The whole class applauded, even though the punching bags had been already hanging up throughout the room when they walked in, so it was kind of self-evident they were going to use punching bags today.

Carlos had seemed so surprised and pleased when she'd told him about this class. He was always cracking jokes, so she'd steeled herself for him to make fun of it, but he seemed almost proud of her.

"Remember, punching bags are pretty big and heavy, so you're really going to feel it when you punch them. But before we get to the bags, let's go over the form lessons we learned last week. Did you all practice like I told you to?"

There was faint applause from the class. Nik had definitely intended to practice. She'd gone home all hyped up and ready for it, and she'd thrown a few punches at imaginary people in her apartment that night. But then, she got sore. And busy. And after a few days of not practicing, the idea of practicing sounded intimidating, and it sounded much easier to not practice, so that's what she did.

Dana was clapping with energy, though. Overachiever. She'd probably practiced every day.

"Not as many as I hoped, but that's okay. Practicing by yourself can get a little scary, right? Don't worry, we'll get you guys over that hump today." "Stronger" by Britney Spears blared out through the speakers. This woman was magic with the music. "Now, watch me." She stood in the stance she'd taught them the week before and did a fierce one-two punch at the air. "Remember, that's a jab. Now you guys do it. Make sure you're a good distance away from each other, and I'll walk around the room and check in on you."

Nik imitated her and punched the air. OW. All of those hours of athletic sex made turning that way pretty painful. She wouldn't give up a second of it, though. She grinned, stretched, and punched the air again.

"Good job, Nik!" Natalie was suddenly behind her. "Remember, elbows in and keep those feet planted, okay? You've got some real power behind that punch—keep it up!"

Why did she usually hate people who spoke like cheerleaders, but somehow when Natalie did it, it actually did inspire her to keep it up? Maybe because it actually seemed sincere coming from her.

"Excellent, Dana. I can tell how much you've been practicing. Keep that thumb secure. Great work!"

Nik turned around to make fun of Dana for being the teacher's pet, but Dana was beaming so hard she didn't have the heart to do it.

"Other side!" Natalie shouted to the class. They all turned and kept going as she finished her loop around the room.

"Okay, everyone! Great job. Now you all get boxing gloves. And look, I know that in a real situation you're not going to be able to pull out your boxing gloves before you can defend yourself or a loved one. But we have to protect ourselves as we learn how to do this, don't we? You learn how to punch these punching bags hard with these gloves on, and you'll be able to break a man's jaw with your bare fist. I guarantee it."

Ahh yes, that's the other reason she didn't mind Natalie's sugar-sweet attitude. Because every so often, she could see the cyanide hidden in there.

Natalie walked them through wrapping their hands with tape and putting on gloves. Nik held her fists up in the air. She nodded at them with a triumphant smile. Her whole body felt stronger, just with these on.

There were two rows of punching bags hanging in the room, one on each side. She, Dana, and Courtney were all in a line.

"Okay, great! Everyone is ready. Now, remember everything I told you, remember your form, and start punching!"

Nik stood back, paid attention to her form, and sent her fist flying into the punching bag.

Holy shit. Natalie wasn't kidding. That thing was like a brick wall. But it was pretty satisfying to see it swing from her jab. She threw another punch.

After a few minutes, Natalie was at her side.

"Nik! You're doing so, so great today—just look at you."

She grunted, tried to make her form perfect, and punched again.

"Oh, that was a good one. Excellent job. One question: why did you sign up for this class?"

Nik looked at the punching bag instead of at Natalie.

"Eh, I thought it would be fun to come with my girlfriends, you know."

Natalie patted her on the shoulder and smiled.

"Of course! Okay. Now tell me the real reason."

Nik turned to look at her, and Natalie was smiling back, as bright as could be. Nik sighed.

"My ex-boyfriend was a real asshole." She realized that could describe more than one person. "Actually, too many of my ex-boyfriends are assholes."

"You aren't alone there!" Natalie stood behind the punching bag and held it still. "Okay, now picture their faces on this punching bag. And then punch the hell out of it."

Nik took a step backward, stared at the bag, and let her fist fly. It felt great.

"Fantastic!" Natalie said.

Nik grinned.

"That was fantastic, wasn't it?"

By the time they made it to the bar after class, all three of them were high on pure adrenaline.

"Did you see me punch that bag?" Courtney

asked the other two. "By the time we're done with this class, I'm going to have it flying across the room. I promise you."

"I'm going to be so fucking sore tomorrow, and I don't even care." Nik made a fist and flexed her just visible muscles. "My biceps hurt right this second, and I'm not even mad about it. That was awesome."

Dana said nothing; she just beamed at the damp table.

Pete dropped their drinks off at the table, and they all thanked him.

"Now do I get to say 'I told you so' about this class? Aren't you guys glad you did it with me?" Nik asked them.

"I am *very* glad we did it with you," Dana said.

Courtney shook her head.

"Sure, fine, the class is better than we thought, but Dana and I have a much bigger 'I told you so' coming up."

She'd walked right into that one, hadn't she?

"What did we sayyyyy?" Courtney said to Dana, her hand raised high in the air. Dana high-fived her, with a small, but just as smug, smile on her face. "We told you that you needed a rebound, didn't we? I can't believe we've waited this long. Tell us everything."

Nik couldn't keep the smile off her face as she told them the story—or most of it, at least.

"Thank God we convinced you to get over that

whole bias against doctors thing," Dana said.

"Oh, I still don't like doctors, but in the end I couldn't help myself," she said.

The three of them all laughed.

"Wait." Nik had a terrible thought. "What if Carlos doesn't realize that this is just a rebound? What if he's a serious relationship kind of guy? I don't want to accidentally get into another Fisher situation."

"Oh, come on." Courtney laughed. "This is Los Angeles. There is no such thing as a 'serious relationship kind of guy' in this city. You don't know this because you aren't looking for one, but I promise you, men like that don't exist here."

Nik shook her head and drained her drink.

"That can't be true. Remember all of those cozy little couples holding hands at brunch last time we went? Also, one of the supposedly mythical serious relationship Los Angeles men *just* proposed to me, remember?"

Courtney rolled her eyes.

"Fisher doesn't count. Everything about that proposal was fucked up. And all of the couples we saw having brunch were there after their third successful date, but they'll move on to someone else within three weeks to three months, maximum. Serious couples don't go to brunch; they stay home and cook for each other. Everyone knows that."

Courtney liked making bold pronouncements

about what "everyone knew," most of which just made Nik laugh. But this time . . . Nik's mind flashed back to some cozy brunches she'd made for Justin. She gratefully took her new drink from Pete.

"Okay, but what about all of the married people? You're not going to claim that there are no married people in all of Los Angeles, are you?"

Courtney sat up straight and winced.

"I think I'm already sore from that damn class. Yes, of course there are married people in L.A. People arrive in L.A. in serious relationships or already married, that's the only way it happens. No one meets a spouse in L.A., except for celebrities, and those relationships are all fake, anyway."

Dana, who had been rolling her eyes throughout all of Courtney's decrees, nodded.

"Our cynical friend over here is wrong about everything except that last thing. Celebrity relationships are all fake."

Nik narrowed her eyes at Dana.

"Wait, you can't mean *all* celebrity relationships. Even I know in my heart that John and Chrissy—"

"Back to Carlos," Courtney said. "I knew he was worthy. You told me how much he liked the spicy cupcake. And I believe we all remember that Fisher did not."

All three of them nodded.

"Excellent point." Nik waved at Pete and pointed at their drinks to request another round. "I feel like, in the future, all you need to say is 'Fisher liked that' to steer me away from someone, or 'Fisher didn't like that' to steer me toward them."

Pete put their drinks down on the table to a flurry of thank-yous.

"However." Nik took a sip of her gin and tonic and smiled. "I do have to thank Fisher for one thing: if he hadn't proposed to me at Dodger Stadium, I never would have met Carlos. And after last night, well, that would have been a real shame."

The three of them clinked glasses.

Carlos walked into his apartment on Thursday night with an enormous grin on his face. He should be exhausted, after getting barely any sleep at Nik's place last night, then racing home just to shower and change and head to an extra-long work day, but he didn't remember when he'd felt less tired. He was ready to go back to Nik's tonight to keep going. If only.

He was very glad he'd texted her this morning about Friday night. He'd almost waited, in the interest of being chill about everything, but then he remembered how much he'd hesitated to ask her out for drinks in the first place, and how ridiculous that felt now.

He walked into his kitchen to see what he could scrounge up for dinner. When his phone rang, he was certain for about a second it was Nik calling him. He glanced at the screen and shook his head at himself.

"Hey, Angie."

"I heard you talked to Jessie last night."

"I did." He'd almost forgotten about that. It had happened right before he realized he had run out of gas. "She sounded good, but bored. She said I have to get her more books. I'm going to try to do that tomorrow or Saturday."

When he'd suggested Friday night to Nik, he'd had no real plan in mind other than to see her again. But then she'd texted him back asking him what he was in the mood to do, and he felt like the answer she was looking for was not "sex on your couch, then pizza, then more sex was pretty great last night— we could do that again?" The guys she tended to go out with were probably "fancy pizza place in Silver Lake where you had to stand in a long line" kinds of guys, and nothing against guys like that, but that wasn't him.

"Jessie told me you yelled at her. You have to stop doing that! It's going to make her blood pressure worse, I already told you that. And I looked up preeclampsia, and—"

"Angela. Are you really trying to tell me something about medicine you found on the Internet right now? Seriously?"

But also, he had to come up with an idea for something to do with Nik—before they got to the good part—that made it clear this thing wasn't on a path to a proposal. He liked her a lot, and the sex had been great, but he was not on the hunt for a girlfriend, let alone a wife. All he wanted from Nik was to have someone to blow off steam with every once in a while, whether that was more great sex or more great sex plus a few drinks or more great sex plus some joking around, et cetera.

"I'm just saying, if you want Jessie to relax, you're going about it the wrong way. The books were great and so were the cupcakes. Keep doing things like that. Stop hounding her about her blood pressure."

Why did his family always say things like this to him? He wasn't "hounding" Jessie; he was just trying to make sure she was taking care of herself. He wished he had some of Nik's rosé right now. Hell, he wished he had Nik with him right now.

"Fine. I just wanted to make sure that she's taking this seriously. I don't want anything to happen to Jessie or the baby."

He walked over to his pantry, his favorite room in this house. He hadn't had time to cook for a few weeks, and he'd missed it. All of the chopping and stirring and puttering around relaxed him after a long day. He put a big pot of water on to boil.

"I know," she said. "She knows that, too. Just try to be more gentle about it with her, okay?"

"Okay, okay, I promise. Satisfied?" he said to his sister. Nothing else would get her off the phone.

He hoped Nik understood that he wasn't looking for a girlfriend. He thought so. Because after everything that had happened with Fisher, both at the Dodgers game and afterward, he was pretty sure Nik was in no mood to get back into a relationship. But was there a way to make that clear to her without acting like he assumed she'd fallen in love with him or something?

Oooh. Here was an idea. He put his phone on speaker so he could text and keep talking to Angela.

What's your feeling on Mexican food? Any interest in checking out my favorite taqueria?

There. A date at a taqueria should say "fun, but not serious" right on the label.

"Hey, speaking of medical stuff." Angie's voice got really casual. Too casual. "Have you thought any more about making that doctor's appointment? Just you know, with Jessie having these issues, and our family history and all, it's good to . . ."

"Angela." He grated cheese harder than necessary into a big bowl. "Stop. Don't worry about me, I'm fine."

"I know that's what you say, but what does it hurt to get a few checks?"

He was so tired of this conversation. He didn't want to go to the doctor, and he didn't need to go to the doctor.

"Angela. I'm fine. I eat healthy, I run, I get enough sleep, I'm making myself a salad for dinner right now. Relax. Channel your worry about Jessie in a more productive way than bugging me, like knitting or chopping wood or something calming."

He reached into the back of his pantry and found his pepper grinder. He ground a bunch of pepper on top of his mountain of grated cheese.

He checked his phone, just to make sure he hadn't missed Nik's text. Not that he assumed that people would always text him back immediately, but this morning when he'd asked Nik if she wanted to hang out on Friday night, she'd texted back pretty quickly.

"Knitting? Chopping wood? Have you never met me before? I tried to knit a scarf once and ended up almost cutting off the circulation in my fingers. And do you think I live in a cottage in the woods and have an ax? I live in Los Angeles, remember? The way we do stress relief here is yoga classes, acupuncture, and weed."

"Okay, great." He added salt and a handful of dried spaghetti to the now boiling water. "Go to yoga, go to acupuncture. As your older brother, I cannot advise you to do that last one, but if you do it, maybe you'll stop bugging me, and we'll all be happier and more relaxed!"

Maybe Nik was offended that he was only suggesting a taqueria. Maybe she wanted him to be one of those "standing in a long line for fancy pizza" kinds of dudes. Maybe she was standing in one of those lines with another guy right now.

"Yes, well, I'll see what I can do."

He pulled his tongs out of a drawer and stirred the pasta with them.

"Hey, have you talked to our friend from Dodger Stadium lately?" she asked. "I told you I liked her, didn't I?"

Maybe she'd said yes this morning just to pacify him but he'd never hear from her again, and his text would be just out there in the universe, unanswered, forever.

"Nope. Anything else you need to nag me about tonight?"

"Shut up and go eat your salad. Talk to you tomorrow."

Ten minutes later, he sat down at his kitchen table with a big bowl of cacio e pepe. Okay, yes, it wasn't a salad, but man couldn't live on lettuce alone, could he? Plus, he'd worked off a lot of calories with Nik the night before.

His phone buzzed.

Come on, I've lived in California way too long not to love Mexican food, what an insulting question. If I get over the insult, which I'm not sure I will, checking out your favorite taqueria sounds great.

He laughed at his phone and put down his fork.

A thousand apologies. But who knows, you may not like everything at this place. Some of it might be too spicy or too weird for you.

He took his first bite.

Want to bet?

He grinned.

Chapter Eleven

• • • • • •

Nik woke up on Friday at her usual eight a.m. and immediately thought about her date with Carlos that night. Okay, it wasn't a *date* date. It was just a glorified hook up, with food first—she was pretty sure they both knew that. But still. Whatever it was, she was excited about it.

She forced herself to work all morning, but by noon, her mind was wandering to where they'd go tonight, how he would look, and oh shit, what she should wear. The last time he'd seen her it was after she'd raced out of her house when Courtney had called her in a panic, and she had not at all been prepared to see anyone, let alone him. She needed to show that she could look good if she tried.

Something casual, chill, and cool. Something she would look incredibly sexy in, but still looked like a normal outfit to wear to a taqueria on the Friday night of a holiday weekend. All of that should be no problem at all for her, the person who had worn her holey Stanford T-shirt and threadbare yoga pants almost every day this week.

She dug into the back of her closet, the place she put stuff that she bought whenever she got a big rejection and let her online shopping fingers roam free.

Oooh, that leather jacket. She'd bought it last month when the *New Yorker* had rejected a piece she was sure they'd love. It had arrived in the middle of one of L.A.'s spring heat waves, so she hadn't even tried it on and had stuck the box in her closet.

She opened it and winced at the number on the receipt. What had she been thinking? Was it too late to return this?

Then she put it on. Holy shit, this thing made even her old yoga pants look hot. She adjusted the zippers and grinned at herself in the mirror. If she wore that, plus her one sexy pair of jeans that gave her an ass like one of those rap guys' girlfriends, she could wear any shirt and she would look great.

She sat back down at her desk and looked at her to-do list, full of crap she had no desire to do. After fifteen minutes of trying to make phone calls and just getting voice mail boxes—some of them full—she gave up. It was Friday afternoon; everyone on the East Coast had already cut out of work by now, and everyone on the West Coast was pretending they had. She might as well join them.

After an hour and a half of yoga, an hour of

yoga recovery flat on her back on her couch, a shower, and an hour of trying on shoes and makeup to go with her outfit, she was ready for Carlos, only two minutes after he was supposed to pick her up. Luckily, he was five minutes late.

"Hey! I'm outside. Sorry I'm late," he said when he called. "Should I come up, or . . ."

"No, I'll come down," she said. She felt ridiculously high school. She rolled her eyes at herself. This wasn't a date, remember?

Carlos was standing at the door when Nik walked outside. She'd kind of expected him to be waiting for her in the car. That made her feel even more high school, but in a good way.

"Hi," she said to him.

He grinned at her.

"Holy shit, you look great."

She tried to keep her smile from stretching across her entire face but may have failed.

"Thanks! So do you." She reached up to hug him and he leaned down to kiss her. She hadn't quite expected them to be at the kiss hello stage yet, but she liked kissing him so much she'd take any excuse to kiss him.

"Hungry?" he asked, when they finally pulled away.

She wiped her lip gloss off his mouth with her thumb and walked with him to his car.

"Starving. I only had a salad for lunch in preparation for this meal." In retrospect, she should

194

have at least had a snack after yoga. Oh well, at least she knew there would be plenty of food where they were going.

He opened the passenger door for her.

"That is one of the biggest compliments anyone has ever given me," he said.

She smiled at him as he started the car.

"You said you were the food expert. I'm trusting you here."

"You were right to trust me, and I'm very grateful, especially after I insulted you so gravely by questioning your allegiance to Mexican food."

She shook her head sadly.

"I'm still not over that. You're going to have to give me a little time."

He squeezed her thigh before moving his hand back to the gearshift.

"Take all the time you need."

He accelerated as he got onto the freeway.

"You know, I never learned how to drive a stick." She traced the outline of his fingers with her fingertips. "But boy, do I like watching other people do it."

He glanced down at her hand, then looked back up at the road.

"My dad made both me and my sister learn to drive stick before we could learn an automatic. He said if you learned an automatic first, you got too lazy to really learn how to drive, but if you learned how to drive on a stick, you'd be a better driver for life." He frowned at her, but still with a smile in his eyes. "I still can't believe you had the gall to say I drive too fast. Me, of all people."

She lifted her hand from his and pointed at the speedometer.

"You're currently going fifteen miles over the speed limit, Mr. Safety First."

He shrugged.

"I can't help it if everyone else on the road is so timid, can I?"

She laughed and shook her head and settled back into her seat.

"I hope you have passenger-side airbags and good insurance."

Fifteen minutes later, after a drive through some of the less gentrified parts of the Eastside, they pulled up in the parking lot at his new favorite taqueria.

"Here we go," he said. "Taqueria de los Campos. Before we go in, really, is there anything you won't eat? I mean, other than blue cheese and olives."

"Oh, there are plenty of things I won't eat other than blue cheese and olives, but I don't think those things are going to be at a taqueria."

He narrowed his eyes at her.

"What do you mean? Have you never been to a real taqueria? There are lots of things there that plenty of people don't eat." He paused. "Wait. Do you go to . . . Chipotle?"

She laughed and opened the car door.

"Okay, yes, I have been to Chipotle in my time, but I've also been to a lot of real taquerias. I've lived in California most of my life, I told you!"

He got out of the car and came around to her.

"Hmm, okay. Where in California?"

He still sounded very suspicious.

"I grew up in Sacramento. My parents still live there and are very confused about why I live in L.A. now without what they see as a stable job, instead of moving back home. They're very supportive of my career, even though they don't understand it."

Carlos grinned at her.

"I've seen how that goes with some of my cousins who have jobs their parents have never heard of. Sacramento is respectable, but I'm still reserving judgment on your taqueria cred. What are the other things you don't eat?"

They walked the short way up to the entrance, and he opened the door for her.

"Jell-O in all forms, custard in all forms, but especially when it's inside of a doughnut, chicken breast, carrot cake, raw peaches—cooked ones are fine—and shredded coconut. There, are any of those things going to be inside of a taco?"

He sighed in relief.

"Chicken breast could potentially be inside of a taco, but don't worry, I would never order it

197

here. And I promise, this place does not have any Jell-O or carrot cake tacos."

When they got up to the front of the line, Carlos ordered in Spanish without consulting her. She regretted her inability to speak the language. Sure, she spoke a little Spanish, just from living in California, and the bits that she'd learned from listening hard when she did interviews of Spanish-speaking sources with the assistance of interpreters. She'd taken French in high school and college, a decision she'd lamented for years once she realized how useful even semi-fluency in Spanish would have been to her life.

"What do you want to drink?" he asked her.

"Pineapple agua fresca, por favor," she said to him, in her not terrible but also not good accent, which Carlos and the counter guy both laughed at.

He paid, and they slid into an empty booth with their drinks and their order number on a stick.

"Did you grow up speaking Spanish?" she asked him.

He shook his head.

"No. My parents emigrated when they were both young—my mom was three; my dad was eight. They both grew up only speaking Spanish at home and English at school, and they got teased a lot for their accents and not speaking English well enough. They didn't speak Spanish to me or Angela when we were kids because they didn't want the same things to happen to us. I wish . . ." He sighed, and she resisted the impulse to grab his hand. "That's a long way of saying that no, I didn't, and I wish I had. Especially growing up in L.A., everyone would look at me and hear my name and speak to me in Spanish, and I couldn't respond. I didn't really learn until college. I took it in high school, but I always felt self-conscious about it there, I guess."

She took a sip of her agua fresca. She'd had other friends who grew up with Spanish-speaking parents who had the same thing happen, and they'd both hated and understood the choice that their parents had made.

"Sixty-three?" A man picked up their number and put two huge trays of food in their place.

"Oh my God."

There were so many tacos in front of her. Thank God she was hungry. She counted at least six different kinds, but there were at least two of each kind. And there were chips, and guacamole, and a big dish of refried beans and rice. It was a good thing her jeans were stretchy.

He laughed at the look on her face.

"I can't decide if you're excited or horrified."

She shook her head and kept her eyes on the food.

"I can't, either."

He picked up the squirt bottles of salsa at the

corner of the booth. She reached for another, but he took it out of her hand.

"Wait. Only certain salsas go with certain tacos." She started to object, to say that she could select her own salsa, thank you very much, but she reconsidered.

"Okay, food guru, tell me what to do here."

He touched her hand and flashed a smile at her. She'd last seen that smile on Wednesday night, right before he pulled off her underwear. She was not in the habit of asking men to tell her what to do, but apparently, they liked it.

She wasn't planning to *get* in that habit, but it was always good to know these things.

"Well, when you put it that way . . ." He lined up the plates of tacos in front of her and added the salsa of his choosing to each one. "Now. Rank them. I'll tell you what everything is afterward."

She rubbed her hands together and took off her leather jacket. This date was already more fun than her usual "drinks at a hipster bar, dinner at the upscale pizza place next door afterward" L.A.-style dates.

She took bites of each taco in succession, and then second bites of all six.

"Okay." She looked down at all of her tacos, and then across the table at his; while she'd been tasting each one carefully, he'd decimated his.

"First, I have to say, ranking these from number six to number one doesn't give number six enough credit. I would eat this taco every day if I could, let's be clear." He motioned for her to get on with it. She picked up a plate and set it at the far end of the table against the window. "Six."

"Carne asada, but I'm sure you already knew that." She nodded and tried not to smile like her favorite teacher had just complimented her in front of the whole class. She put another plate next to the first one.

"That's tripas. Are you sure that wasn't too weird for you?"

Tripe. Huh. Okay, that was a little weird. She hadn't really expected tripe to be one of the things she'd eat tonight. Or that she'd rank it over steak.

"If it had been too weird, would I have kept eating it?" She hoped he didn't notice that she didn't quite answer the question.

She hesitated for a few seconds with the next selection, then moved a third plate over.

"Carnitas!" He pulled the basket of chips toward him and squirted salsa on one of his empty plates. "Only fourth place for carnitas, wow."

She couldn't tell if that was a good wow or bad wow.

"I loved the carnitas! I've always thought carnitas was my favorite before, and it hurt me to put it in fourth place, but . . ."

He dipped a chip into his salsa with a huge grin on his face.

"This is fun. Keep going."

None of the guys she'd dated in the past five years would have even imagined ordering this much food for two people. Not even for four people. Thank God she wasn't here with any of them.

She moved a fourth plate into line.

"Cabeza in third place!" Carlos said.

And she'd never dated anyone who would have ordered her a cow head taco. A delicious cow head taco, to be clear.

He rolled his sleeves up to his elbows, and she couldn't hold back a sigh at the sight of his forearms. Did men have any idea how sexy it was when they did that?

She moved the next plate in line.

"Lengua." He dug into the bowl of guacamole with a chip. "Well, you should have ranked that one the first, but you can't get everything right."

Why was she not surprised that his favorite was the tongue?

"As much as I love that one . . ."

"Mmmm, you sure do. I know that now." He smirked at her, and she tried hard not to laugh.

"As I was saying, as much as I love that one . . ." She pushed the last plate into line. "This is my favorite."

He held out his hand, and she slapped it.

"Respect. Al pastor is an excellent taco favorite to have, especially here."

She finished the al pastor taco and raised an eyebrow at him.

"So did I pass?"

He stopped, a guacamole-laden chip halfway to his mouth.

"What do you mean pass?"

She rolled her eyes at him.

"This test. I know it was a test, don't even try to pretend it wasn't."

At first he shrugged and didn't meet her eyes. Then he gave her a puppy dog smile.

"Okay, yes, you definitely passed, but I didn't really intend it to be a test. It was just that . . ."

Nik spooned some rice and beans onto a plate. She was already so full that putting more food on her plate seemed ridiculous, but she couldn't not try the rice and beans, could she? When she had a little bit of both on her plate, she sat up straight and looked Carlos in the eye.

"It was just that what? I'm going to make you finish that sentence now."

Carlos sighed and put his fork down.

"It was just that you kind of seemed like a girl who stayed in the safe parts of L.A. and who moved in bougie kinds of circles, and who . . . who . . . I wasn't sure how you would react to a place like this and food like that."

She didn't break eye contact. He'd thought that maybe she'd get distracted by the food on her

203

plate, but she'd clearly listened to every word he'd said.

"And who . . . dates the whitest of white guys? Is that what you were going to say?"

Well, yeah, but he'd caught himself at the last second.

"I was, but I thought the better of it!" Shit, she was going to get mad at him for this, wasn't she? She had every right to.

She laughed and reached for another chip.

"Don't judge me by Fisher, come on now. I'm not going to claim that he's the only white guy that I've dated, but he's definitely one of the worst."

He'd take her word for it. She seemed more relaxed about the Fisher thing than she had the last time they'd talked about it. Maybe it was her self-defense class making the difference.

"How's your self-defense class going? Are you kicking some ass?"

She put up her fists.

"I sure as hell am," she said, before putting her fists down. "I didn't really expect to enjoy the class; I think I expected it to be some empowerment bullshit, but I feel like I'm learning a lot, and it's actually really fun. The instructor is the owner of the gym, and she's pretty fantastic."

He'd kind of expected her class to be some empowerment bullshit, too. His dad had made Angela take a self-defense class when she went off to college, and Angie had complained about it the whole time. She'd said it was just talking about your feelings and beating up a dude covered in padding, but that she hadn't really learned how to defend herself. He'd had to take her into the backyard and show her how to throw a punch to feel comfortable with her leaving.

"Oh man, I'd love to hear more about that. That's the kind of place I'd love to silently pass their brochure to some of my patients. And their moms, though I bet it's outside their price range."

She shook her head.

"Probably not—that's one of the interesting things about it. She has a sliding scale for membership and all of the classes. Pretty great."

"Wow." As he well knew, it was hard for low- or even moderate-income people in L.A. to access a lot of the stuff that hipster L.A. took for granted. "Are you planning to write about it? I read that Anna Gardiner thing you told me you wrote for *Vogue*; it was great."

"You read it?" If he had known she would look so flattered when he told her that, he would have told her days ago. "Thanks, I'm glad you liked it. I actually hadn't even thought about writing about Natalie's Gym, but that's an idea." She shrugged. "We'll see."

"What other kinds of writing do you do? Is it all freelance, or are you on staff somewhere?"

"All freelance. After college, I got a job at

the *New York Times*, which was overwhelming and amazing. I learned a ton about writing and researching there, especially about investigative reporting, just from listening to some of the reporters there and asking them a lot of questions." She made a face. "And asking for feedback on my own work, which was horrible at the time but ultimately very valuable."

He grinned at the look on her face.

"They were very blunt, huh?"

She dropped her head into her hands.

"You have no idea. God, I still get humiliated sometimes when I think about the draft of a story I gave one guy. Oh, it was so bad, and he told me, in lots of detail, why it was so bad. But you know, that one terrible conversation was probably worth at least an entire class of journalism school." She took a sip of her water. "Then I came back here to be an editor for the *L.A. Times* entertainment section. It was such a different job, but I learned a ton about the ins and outs of the industry here in L.A."

Hers was a very different part of L.A. than the one he'd grown up in. The part with the movie stars and the rich people that he'd always known existed, but it seemed so foreign compared to his life that it could have very well been across the country.

"This was a long way to answer your question about what kind of writing I do. I left the *L.A.*

Times about a year and a half ago. There was a big buyout, but I was ready to go. I was getting tired of only doing celebrity stuff, as entertaining as it can be. Now I do a good combination of writing: some celebrity profiles, especially women of color. But also some investigative journalism, and other short fun pieces when I have time for them. It's been a little scary, but also fun to craft my career in this way."

He nodded. He'd known some of that from when he'd Googled her to find that Anna Gardiner story, but not all of it.

"What kind of investigative journalism? Who pays for stuff like that these days, other than like, the *New Yorker*?"

She grinned.

"I had a piece in the *New Yorker* last week, actually. My second piece there."

He'd walked right into that one, hadn't he?

"Holy shit, that's awesome! What was the story about?"

"Thanks. This one was a celebrity piece; it was a profile of a screenwriter who has two movies coming out this summer. I was really glad to get to write about her." Her grin lost a little of its sparkle. "I was really excited to see it in print, but I just realized I didn't even open the magazine. It came the same day as the Dodgers game, see."

He suddenly hated that Fisher guy. What a way to ruin the joy of her accomplishment.

He looked at their table: plates of half-eaten tacos lined up neatly, the beans and rice basically untouched on both of their plates, their drinks all empty.

"Do you want to get dessert?" he asked.

She laughed, and the sad look disappeared from her face.

"Oh my God, no, are you kidding me? I'm way too full to even think about dessert. I can't remember the last time I said that."

They waved good-bye to the staff as they walked out and got in his car. A few blocks down the road, she cleared her throat.

"I might be accused of being bougie by asking this, but I'm going to do it anyway: do you ever worry about your car, parking it in neighborhoods like this?"

He nodded.

"Nah, that's just common sense. At first I barely drove it anywhere but to work and home. I was so paranoid about break-ins, or accidents, or other cars parking too close to me. I *never* did valet, which in L.A., as you know, made everything more difficult."

He flicked his blinker on to turn onto the freeway, and thought about those first months after. A lot of it he barely even remembered. He only knew certain things had happened because friends had mentioned them later. Sometimes he'd searched through his emails for something unrelated and come across emails he'd sent friends, thanking them for their card or the food they'd sent or for coming to the funeral, and he had no memory not only of sending the emails but of receiving their card or food or seeing them at the funeral. It had been such a terrible time; he was glad that there was a fog over his memory of a lot of it. The car probably wasn't the only reason he'd barely gone anywhere but to work and his mom's house for months.

"What made you change?" she asked.

He shrugged and started to give her a bullshit answer. But the only answer he could think of was the truth.

"My friends, really. Especially my friend Drew. Some of it . . . a lot of it, probably, wasn't about the car at all, but was about my dad." He'd tried not to let anyone figure out what a hard time he was having with his dad's death. He especially didn't want his family to know. He knew he had to be there for his mom and for Angie, to be the rock they needed.

"One day at work, we were talking about a new case that had come in the day before. It was a middle-aged man who died suddenly of a heart attack, the same as my dad. When they described what happened and started asking questions for us to answer, I had to leave the room. I didn't think anyone noticed me leave. But that night, Drew asked if I wanted to get a beer when we both got off. We didn't talk about it, at all, but . . . it helped. And then the following week, he convinced me to join a basketball rec league. I knew he was doing it to force me out of the house for something other than work, but I did it anyway. And it helped."

He didn't look at her, but he could feel her watching him, listening to every word he said. She didn't touch him, but the softness in her voice felt like a caress.

"A sudden heart attack. That's terrible. I'm so sorry."

He nodded, very glad that they were in a car in the dark and she couldn't see the tears in his eyes.

"Thanks. Anyway, the car. I think I mostly realized I couldn't live in fear anymore. I mean, sure it could get broken into outside the taqueria, or I could have an accident any day to or from work. Plus, I bought the car in honor of my dad—how did it honor him for me to be afraid to go anywhere in it? Good God, I can't imagine how ashamed he would have been if I didn't want to go to a taqueria because I was scared of what might happen to my car, you know?"

Why the hell was he talking to her about his dad? He never talked about him, not even to Angela or his mom. He'd decided to stop talking—or even thinking, for the most part—about his dad almost six months after he'd died.

It had been too hard for him to deal with otherwise.

Fucking journalists, they knew just the questions to get you going.

"I'm glad you had good friends." She put her hand on his, and he thought she was going to say something else warm and sympathetic, which might be more than he could take right now. "I'm also glad you discovered that taqueria, because oh my God was that food good."

He laughed, relieved she'd changed the subject.

"So am I. I love that place. I try not to go there too often. I always eat too much when I'm there."

They talked about tacos the rest of the way to her apartment.

"I know this is insanely bougie of me, but so be it," she said as she opened her apartment door. "Do you want some sparkling water? It always makes me feel better after I eat an enormous meal. I have like four different flavors, minimum."

She kicked her shoes off by the door, so he followed suit.

"Hmmm, that depends. What flavors?"

She threw off her leather jacket, walked into the kitchen and opened the fridge, while he sat on the couch.

"Grapefruit, lemon, berry, and mango."

He sighed dramatically.

"Lime is my favorite, but I guess I can settle for grapefruit."

She grabbed the water out of the fridge and brought it over to the couch.

He drank some water, put his glass down on the coffee table, and put his arm around her.

"Sparkling water is good at settling your stomach after a big meal, but do you want to know something else that works for that?"

She rose her eyebrows.

"Hmmm, what?"

He ran his hand up and down her bare arm.

"Some good, healthy physical activity."

She took another sip of her water and set it down.

"Oh wow. I'm so glad you told me that. I'd always read the opposite, that you shouldn't eat before any strenuous activity."

He shook his head vigorously.

"Oh no, no, that's outdated advice. I'm a doctor, see, so I know all of the new and up-to-date research on this." He reached up and tugged on one of her curls, released it, tugged on another one.

"Mmmm. I'm so grateful that I have you, a fancy doctor, to tell little old me about this." She pulled him against her.

"I'm so glad you appreciate me." He kissed her neck and then trailed kisses down to the hollow between her breasts.

"I definitely do." His thumbs were on her nipples, hard peaks beneath the thin fabric of her shirt. She closed her eyes.

"The more strenuous, the better for your digestion, really." He pushed her back against the couch and lifted her shirt.

"Wow, that's so good to know. What . . ." She sucked in her breath and paused before she could continue. "What should we do? We could go for a nice walk."

He pulled her shirt off and tossed it to the side. Her breasts were full and luscious inside her sheer black bra. He couldn't stop looking at her. And touching her.

"A walk is a good idea. From what I remember from last time, the walk to your bedroom is really long. It took us a long time to get there. That seems like the perfect length for a walk to me."

She smiled up at him.

"Whatever you say, doctor."

He stood and took her hands to pull her up off the couch.

Chapter Twelve

• • • • • •

"You should be honored. My friends were very nice to you tonight," Nik said.

Carlos and Nik were walking to his car the following Friday night. He'd texted her before leaving the hospital to see if she wanted to go out, and she'd texted him back that she was out with her friends, and he should come join them. He'd really wanted to see her, so he went. But that had made him nervous that this was more than a casual hookup thing to her.

Maybe he should talk to her about it, even though he hated bringing up stuff like that. But they'd been seeing kind of a lot of each other, and he didn't want her to get the wrong idea. After the taqueria last Friday night, he'd hung out at her house well into Saturday afternoon. And then they'd met up for burgers on Tuesday night and gone back to her place for some healthy adult exercise. And they'd been texting a lot this week. Were they spending too much time together?

Granted, she didn't act like the women he'd gone out with in the past who had wanted to be his girlfriend: she hadn't insisted on week-end plans far in advance or pushed him to invite her over to his house or told him he was the kind of guy who would be a great father. But making him spend an hour with her and her friends when she knew all he wanted was to be taking her clothes off was getting close.

"That was them being *nice?*" he asked. He was sort of kidding, but . . . only sort of.

She laughed.

"They only quizzed you for like five minutes."

It had felt like far longer.

Sure, he'd met her friends right after the baseball game, but that was before they'd started sleeping together. Did this whole "come meet me and my friends" thing mean she was getting the wrong idea about what he wanted here?

If he had to end things with her, he was going to be so mad. He hadn't had sex this good, with someone he actually enjoyed spending time with in . . . shit, since he could remember.

"Courtney gave you more than one compliment. That's basically a declaration of lifelong devotion coming from her."

When he'd told her how much he'd liked her spicy cupcake, she had told him that said something good about his character.

"Well, I'm glad, I guess, but please don't kill me if I say I'm glad they both had to get up early tomorrow morning so I could get you alone."

She looked at him out of the corner of her eye and smiled.

"That sounds promising. What did you have in mind?"

He grinned as they approached his car.

"Well, you know me. Before I do anything strenuous, I need a good dinner. What are you in the mood for?"

"Do you want to go out? Or get takeout?"

He put his arm around her.

"I can do either, but the idea of takeout on your couch sounds pretty great right now. It's been a long week."

She put her arms around his waist, and he pulled her close.

"How's your cousin doing? Everything okay there?"

He nodded.

"Thanks for asking. She's hanging in there, but I'm always on edge about it. Every time I get a call from anyone in my family, I jump. I would say that I can't wait for this to be over, except that the best outcome is for it to be like this for another nine or ten weeks, which seems unbearable right now."

He sighed and opened the passenger door for her.

"Thanks for listening to me ramble about my family, I appreciate it. I can't really talk to them about it, because then they all flip out."

She leaned over to kiss him when he got in the car. The kiss lasted for a long time.

"Ramble all you want," she said. "You just held up very well under cross-examination from my two best friends, so I owe you a night of lots of listening, something fun on the TV, and . . ."

He cocked his head to the side.

"And?"

"And whatever else you ask for," she said.

He grinned. He would worry about the other stuff later.

Nik woke up early the next morning, with Carlos sound asleep against her. Good God, this guy was fun. He had certainly taken her "whatever else you ask for" to heart, with very good results.

She turned back toward him and he nuzzled against her neck.

"Mmm, so you are awake," she said.

"I'm not awake. I'm having the most fantastic dream."

He had such a scratchy voice first thing in the morning. Just hearing it gave her goose bumps.

"What kind of dream?"

He ran his hand from her knee up her leg to her hip and rested his whole palm against her butt.

"I'm in bed with this incredibly sexy woman, for starters."

God, she liked it when he touched her.

"Mmm, tell me about her."

His hands kept moving up and down her body. They stopped to linger at her breasts, and she closed her eyes and sighed.

"Oh, she's something else. She's smart, she's funny, she surprises me at every turn, and her body . . . I just can't get enough of it."

That was definitely an excellent thing to hear from a man who woke up in your bed.

"She sounds incredible. Tell me more about the dream."

He pushed her onto her back and knelt above her.

"In my dream, we had amazing sex last night . . . multiple times, actually. God, what a great dream this has already been. And now . . ." He leaned down to kiss her mouth. "And now, if I'm lucky, we might get to do it again. Oh wow, I hope I don't wake up."

She played with his hair and relaxed at his touch.

"I hope you don't, either."

Now his mouth was on her breasts, and she sighed.

"Mmmmm. This is a great way to not wake up; I've got to say."

"Mmmmm?" He lifted his head. "Oh, you like that? I think there's an even better way to not wake up. Let me see if you agree."

He threw the covers to the foot of the bed and pushed her legs apart. She looked down at his head between her legs and grinned.

"Oh, I think I like this dream of yours a whole lot. Do you think you'll—OH MY GOD."

Those were the last discernable words she said for a long time.

When they both finally caught their breath, he kissed her cheek.

"Okay, you're going to think I'm crazy saying this after all of that food we ate last night, but . . . I'm starving."

She laughed into his chest.

"Well, you did have lots of good, healthy physical activity. It makes sense that that would make you hungry."

He rolled on top of her and tickled her.

"Oh, you're making fun of me now? Just for that, I'm going to make you breakfast." He sat up. "That is, if you have anything I can cook?"

She nodded.

"I went to the store the other day. There should be stuff in there. I'll make the coffee."

He pulled on boxers and went to investigate her kitchen. She grabbed a robe out of her closet and went to the bathroom before joining him. By the time she got there, he had a pile of food on her counter.

"Are you going to make *all* of that?" She opened the coffee maker and pulled out yesterday's filter and tossed it in the garbage.

"I'm deciding what to cook. A true artist takes time at his work."

She turned on her coffee grinder and scooped grounds into the fresh filter.

"Okay, Picasso. I make coffee strong; that okay with you?"

He laughed while he pulled bowls out of her cabinet.

"That's fine, but if I had said no, what were you going to do? I already know you wouldn't have made weaker coffee for me."

She poured water in the machine and turned it on.

"No, I would have just made sure you didn't use all the milk in whatever you're cooking in case you needed a lot of it for your cup."

He opened another cabinet.

"Good point, because I was thinking about making pancakes since I see you have syrup here. Any objections? Also, where's your flour?"

She reached for two mugs from the cabinet above the coffee maker and took the opportunity while his back was to her to admire his ass in his gray boxer briefs.

"No objections at all to pancakes, as long as you make bacon, too. And the dry goods are all under there."

He added a lot of sugar to his coffee, but she tried not to judge him for that. Some of her best friends added a lot of sugar to their coffee.

Once he was all set with ingredients and pans, she sat at the kitchen counter with her mug of coffee and watched him cook. Just as he flipped the first pancake with a flourish, she heard Courtney's voice in her head: *serious couples don't go to brunch; they stay home and cook for each other.*

Oh shit. Was this a sign that he wanted to be serious? She'd assumed it was clear that that wasn't what she was looking for right now, given the whole "dramatic breakup that he and thousands of other people witnessed just three weeks ago" thing, but maybe her state of mind wasn't clear to him?

Did she need to have an actual conversation about this with him? She hated having conversations like that.

But then . . . she'd avoided having an actual define-the-relationship talk with Fisher, and that didn't work out all that well.

Come to think about it, Carlos did seem like a serious relationship kind of guy. He was kind and considerate; he was close to his family; he'd just bought a *house,* for the love of God. Men don't buy houses if they don't want to get married soon after that. Damn it.

Carlos set a plate of golden brown pancakes and crisp bacon in front of her with a smile. She tried to smile back at him.

"Wow. What service."

He half bowed.

"I try. Syrup?"

She took a bite just as he sat down next to her. Oh, this was terrible. Not the pancakes—the pancakes were fantastic, that was the terrible part. If she never had these pancakes again because she'd accidentally found the one man in Los Angeles who wanted a serious relationship, she was going to be so mad.

"So, uh. The only problem is that . . ." She took a sip of coffee and tried the beginning of that sentence again. "I just wanted to . . . right now, I'm not sure if I'm . . ."

He looked at her like she had three heads.

"Nik. What are you trying to say?"

She shook her head out of frustration with herself.

"I'm sorry, I'm not making any sense. It's just that after the whole Fisher thing, and with work being so busy right now, I'm not in a good place for any sort of relationship. But like, this whole thing . . ." She gestured toward him, the kitchen, the couch, the bedroom. "This whole thing is great. And I like spending time with you a lot. I feel like we're becoming good friends. Just with"—she waved her hand in the direction of the bedroom—"that stuff going on, too. So I just wanted to see where you were with everything."

No one would believe she made her entire living by putting words together. Did any of the words she'd just said make sense in that order? She had no idea.

"OH." His shoulders relaxed, and he grinned at her. "Well, thank God for that, because I think this whole thing," he mimicked her gesture with his fork, "is great, too. And to be honest with you, between work and everything going on with my family, I don't have the energy for anything even approaching a relationship. So if you're cool with keeping *this* casual, so am I."

She let out a deep sigh and picked up a piece of bacon with her fingers.

"Excellent." She bit into the bacon, and the salty sweetness of the bacon and syrup combined exploded in her mouth. What a great morning.

He stood up, walked around the counter to get the rest of the bacon, and tossed a strip onto her plate.

"I promise we can hang out and eat pancakes and drink rosé and I won't propose to you on a JumboTron."

She clinked her coffee mug against his. Oh thank God. They wanted the exact same thing. This was perfect.

"That sounds pretty ideal."

Chapter Thirteen

• • • • • •

Carlos was just driving out of the grocery store parking lot a week and a half later when Drew called. It had been a brutal day at work, so he'd decided to cook something elaborate for dinner to help himself relax.

"Hey, man, what's up?"

"Hey!" Drew's voice boomed through the speakers in his car. "How's the assistant director doing on this fine Wednesday?"

Drew had been the whole reason he'd even applied for the job in the first place. He hadn't actually seen the opening, but Drew—all the way up in Berkeley now—had and had emailed it to him immediately. Carlos had jumped at the opportunity to move back to the Eastside, but he hadn't been sure if they were looking for someone with his background for the job. When he got it, Drew maintained that he'd known he would all along.

"I'm still alive; that's the best thing I can say after today at work."

"Ahh, one of those days, huh?"

Carlos sighed.

"One of the worst kinds of days. You know the kind."

"Well, maybe this will make it better: you around this weekend to hang out with your best friend and his fiancée?"

Carlos downshifted as the light changed.

"Oh, you mean Jake and Melissa? Yeah, I'm probably going to see them this weekend, why do you ask?"

"I ask because you can go fuck yourself, that's why I ask," Drew said, and both of them cracked up.

"Okay, but seriously, you and Alexa are coming to town? You need a place to stay? You know I live on the Eastside now, right? I don't know if you know how to get to this side of town."

"You are such an asshole. Yes, I know you live on the Eastside now. But we don't need a place to stay. Alexa's got to go down there with her boss for a conference, so I'm tagging along."

"Awesome. Everything was so crazy at the engagement party I barely got to talk to you." He hadn't seen Drew since Christmas-time and Alexa since before that. "I'll get to congratulate you two in person."

"And we'll get to see the new house, I hope?" Drew asked.

"Of course, but I haven't put in the basketball hoop yet."

"And meet whatshername?"

He never should have told Drew he was sleeping with Nik; he knew he'd get the wrong idea. But Drew had texted him the day after they'd first slept together and had asked if he'd seen her again, and it was impossible to not say he'd seen a hell of a lot of her the night before.

"Her name is Nik. I can check to see if she's free, but I told you, this thing with her is very casual."

It was a *frequent* casual thing—they'd only started sleeping together three weeks ago, and they'd already seen each other six times. But after Nik had been the one to bring up that she didn't want a relationship, he wasn't worried about how often they saw each other anymore.

How had he gotten so lucky? It was so rare for him to find women who didn't want a relationship, especially women who were interesting and funny. Not to mention hot. Thank God Nik had dropped into his life.

"Yeah, yeah, you told me. But, you know, check to see if she's free Saturday night. We'll even come to your precious Eastside."

He thought Drew and Alexa would both like her a lot, though. Alexa had always laughed at his jokes, so she'd like Nik's sense of humor.

"All it takes to get you to the Eastside is for you to move to the other end of the state."

"Yeah, yeah, yeah. I'll text you our flight info and details, okay?"

Carlos pulled into his driveway and grabbed the groceries from the back seat.

"Sounds good."

"Hey, how's Jessie?"

Carlos had just checked in with her before leaving work. He knew she was getting sick of him checking in on her every day, but that didn't mean he was going to stop doing it.

"Going stir-crazy, but otherwise hanging in there."

"Okay, I gotta go. Go make your risotto or enchiladas or whatever."

Carlos laughed as he set his groceries down in the kitchen and took the risotto rice out of the bag. It was good to have friends who knew you better than you knew yourself.

He turned on the basketball game to keep him company while he cooked. One of the only things he'd made the time and effort for after moving into this house was to put his TV on a pivot, so he could watch it in the kitchen while he cooked, and then turn it so he could watch it from the couch while he ate. The ideal set up, really.

He chopped an onion, sliced the fresh mushrooms and soaked the dried ones, and peeled the asparagus. The rote movements gave him the feeling of zen that this kind of cooking always did for him. He couldn't think about the stuff that had happened at work that day or worry about what would happen tomorrow when he was busy carefully dicing an onion so that all of the pieces were the exact same size. Just as he turned the heat on underneath his big sauté pan, he heard his phone buzz and grabbed it out of his pocket. Nik.

I just finished a huge story and I'm starving, want to get dinner?

He texted her back without stopping to think.

I'm in the middle of making dinner. Want to come over? How do you feel about mushrooms?

Holy shit, what was he thinking? He never invited women over to his place; it was kind of a thing of his. After a few way too fast relationships in his mid-twenties, he'd learned to keep the women he was dating away from his space. If women came to your place, they always wanted to change things to how they liked them, probably in preparation to move in all too soon.

I feel great about mushrooms. What's your address? I'll leave here in about fifteen minutes. Does that work?

Okay, but wait. This was Nik. She'd made it very clear to him that this was a rebound for her, just quite not in those words. And unlike a few of the conversations he'd instigated with women about keeping a relationship casual where they'd *said* that was fine with them but had made it clear shortly afterward that that was absolutely not fine with them, he knew that Nik hadn't been bullshitting him.

4242 Sequoia Street. See you soon.

Plus, Nik was fun to cook for. She'd gone crazy over those pancakes he'd made her. And it seemed like they'd both had busy days. Some stress release with her in his big bed sounded like an excellent way to end this day.

As Nik walked up the front steps of Carlos's little gray cottage, she suddenly felt shy about basically inviting herself over to his house. Had he really wanted her to come over, or did he just ask because she'd texted him out of the blue and he didn't know what else to do? She wished she'd called him instead, even though the two of them never talked on the phone—it was always easier to tell from a voice how someone really felt than from a text message. Well, it was too late now. He opened the bright red front door before she reached it.

"Hey." Okay, he looked normal. "Come on in."

The house was as masculine and put together as Carlos always was. The living room had a big fat leather couch, a huge TV on one wall, and a fireplace against the other. She dropped her stuff by the door and followed him into the big open kitchen that looked like something out of the Williams Sonoma catalog.

He moved back to the pan on the stove and started stirring. He was wearing a soft blue cotton T-shirt, the gray pants that he'd clearly worn to work, and patterned socks that made her hold back a smile.

"This kitchen is incredible. You told me you were a good cook, but I didn't know you were, like, copper-pots-hanging-from-the-ceiling good."

He glanced up at the pots and shrugged. Was that a blush she saw? He wouldn't meet her eyes.

"The copper pots were definitely an extravagance. To be fair, the first one was a house-warming gift from Angie. But when I bought a house with a beautiful rack to hang pots, what was I supposed to do?"

She thought about her collection of high heels that she almost never wore but kept buying because of the built-in shoe shelves in her walk-in closet that displayed them so beautifully. She nodded.

"Obviously you had to buy pots to fill it; I get it."

He handed her a glass of wine.

She took a sip of the wine as she looked around the kitchen and big open living room. She liked it. Even without anything but the TV on the wall, it felt like a home.

"I didn't even ask what you wanted to drink. Sorry, I didn't have any rosé," he winked at her, "but that should go well with dinner."

Wait. This seemed way too cozy, didn't it? His nice little house, his big warm kitchen, Carlos at the stove, stirring together things that smelled delicious . . . maybe Courtney had a point after all.

No. They'd talked about this, remember? Carlos had looked *very* relieved when she'd said she wasn't in the place for a relationship. This wasn't that, this was just one friend making dinner for another friend. She and her friends did this all the time. This time, she and her friend would just happen to have sex afterward, that's all.

"I wouldn't dare to question you on wine. You told me to always trust you with food and drink recommendations, and I took that to heart."

She took another sip of wine and tried to let herself relax. She'd spent days wrestling with a big story that she still didn't know if she was good enough to write. While she'd had moments of thinking she'd nailed it, the rest of the time she worried it was a complete failure.

"Everything okay?" he asked.

She nodded.

"Yeah. I've just been holed up in my apartment for the past three days finishing that story, and now that it's done, I feel like I'm coming out of a coma." She took her sweater off and tossed it on a stool. "It's great to relax here with some wine and have you cooking a delicious-smelling dinner for me." He looked back down at the food with a smile. Was he blushing? Maybe.

"Thanks for inviting me to share your dinner, by the way. What are we having?"

He looked back up at her.

"Risotto. I hope you like it."

Wow, he wasn't kidding about being able to cook.

"I don't know anyone who knows how to make risotto. I'm pretty sure I've only had it in a restaurant."

He laughed as his big wooden spoon made rhythmic circles in the pan.

"Oh, I love making it." He poured some liquid from the smaller pot on the stove into the big one and stirred some more. "It's funny; I don't even really like eating it that much. I mean, I like it, but I would never choose to order it in a restaurant. But I love to make it."

She took another sip of her wine and looked around at his kitchen. He had four bowls lined up next to him, two with mushrooms in them, one with bacon, one with cheese. And then there were the two pots on the stove. But most amazingly, other than a cutting board with a knife sitting on top of it, there were no dirty dishes anywhere. The rest of the kitchen looked spotless.

"It seems like a lot of work for a Wednesday night," she said.

He nodded.

"It is—that's why I love it. When I've had a really long or difficult day, it relaxes me to cook. It gives me a break in the day to concentrate on something else. And risotto is especially great,

232

because after you do a whole bunch of chopping, then you just have to stand there, preferably with a glass of wine, and slowly stir the rice until it's just right. Every so often, you add some liquid, and you stir some more. You can't rush it; you can't turn up the heat or add the liquid all at once to make it go faster. It's ready when it's ready. And so you just stand there and keep stirring, and everything settles down by the time the food is ready."

She'd never heard anyone be so eloquent about risotto before.

"Wow. I feel more relaxed just hearing you talk about making it."

He looked up and met her eyes, and she could feel his smile all the way down to her toes.

"What a nice compliment from the person who wrote that heartbreaking story about foster children in the *Times* Sunday magazine."

Now it was her turn to blush and look away. She didn't expect him to have read that story. She couldn't remember the last guy she'd dated who had read any of her work. Well, Justin had, but only ever to tell her how bad it was.

"Oh, you read that? I didn't . . ." She looked up at him and smiled back. "Thank you. I was proud of that story."

He poured more liquid in the risotto and kept stirring.

"Good. You should be. It was excellent. It's

such a hard topic—I know from dealing with it with my patients who are foster kids—and you handled it so thoughtfully."

She sipped her wine so he wouldn't be able to see the sudden tears in her eyes. She cleared her throat.

"Thanks for saying that. It means a lot. I was feeling pretty down about my work today, so it was really good timing to hear that."

He reached out and touched her shoulder.

"I can't believe that someone as good as you ever feels down about your writing, but I'm happy I could help you realize how amazing you are."

She laughed. If he only knew.

"I think all writers feel down about their work sometimes . . . or most of the time. At least, I hope they do and I'm not the weird one here." She swallowed and looked down into her glass. "But also, I had an ex who was pretty insulting about my writing, and despite everything I've accomplished since then, sometimes it's still hard to get him out of my head."

Good Lord, a few sips of wine on a hard day and she started spilling everything.

Carlos touched her hair, then her cheek.

"Well, he was obviously an asshole who doesn't know anything about good writing or good people, and I'm glad for more than one reason that he's an ex."

She smiled at him.

"Me too." God, was she ever glad. "It feels stupid to still dwell on something a jerk said years ago, but for some reason I remember some of the negative stuff people have said about my writing like it's imprinted on the inside of my eyelids, and it's much harder to remember—or believe—the compliments."

He poured more wine into her glass.

"Well, now that you've told me that, I'll just have to repeat my compliments a few times, maybe in different words so they'll stick. Hey, Nik, I really loved that piece you wrote, especially how you managed to make it hopeful while acknowledging the pain."

Oh shit, now he really was going to make her cry.

"I wasn't fishing for a compliment there, but thank you."

Why was she so emotional tonight?

It was probably just because she was about to get her period and was feeling sensitive about everything. Plus, even though she couldn't remember the last time a guy she dated had given her a compliment on her writing, her friends did all the time.

See? She and Carlos *were* friends. They had actually been friends first, pretty much from the moment he'd pushed that cameraman out of the way at the stadium. They'd gotten to know each other pretty well before they started sleeping together and had had some pretty deep conversations about their lives long before they'd even thought about getting naked.

How refreshing, to actually be friends with a guy you were sleeping with.

"Um, can I help with anything?" she asked.

He shook his head and poured more liquid into the pan.

"Nope. But it's going to be about twenty more minutes until dinner is ready; do you want a snack?"

Oh thank God. After his wonderful speech about how you couldn't rush risotto, she'd felt like she couldn't mention that she could eat a horse right now. Maybe two.

"Sure," she said. "What do you have?"

He handed her his wooden spoon.

"Here, stir this."

She stood barefoot on the warm tile floor of the kitchen and tried to mimic the way she'd seen him stir the risotto. She heard him behind her open a door, then she heard plastic crinkle. After a minute or so, he came up behind her and took the spoon from her. She leaned back against his body and felt his warmth surround her.

"Here. I only gave us enough to stave off hunger, but not enough to spoil our dinners." He set a bowl down on the counter next to the stove. When she looked in the bowl, she started laughing.

"Are those Flamin' Hot Cheetos?"

He grinned.

"They are indeed. The best snack food ever invented, and I will hear no argument."

"No argument here. I love that a pediatrician had Flamin' Hot Cheetos tucked in the back of his pantry. Makes me feel a lot less guilty about my secret snack drawer."

They demolished the Cheetos in about three minutes flat and spent the rest of the risotto cooking time talking about their favorite snack foods.

"Okay, I think we're ready." He took bowls down from the cabinet and nodded over to the living room. "Sorry, I don't have a dinner table yet. I got rid of my old one when I moved because it didn't work in this space, but I haven't had time to get a new one yet. I just mostly eat at the coffee table."

"Oh no." She set her wineglass down and shook her head sadly. "I wish you'd told me that before I came over. I can't eat a meal at a coffee table! Don't you know who I am?"

He grated cheese on top of a bowl of risotto and handed it to her.

"Oh, I'm sorry, your royal highness, please forgive me?"

She took the bowl and picked up her wineglass.

"I'll make an exception in this case, but I don't

237

want you to think this is going to be a common occurrence."

He waved toward the living room.

"Go sit down, and I'll bring everything else over."

She padded into the living room and sank down into the couch.

"What is *in* this couch?" she asked him, when he came back into the living room, his bowl in one hand and forks for both of them in the other. "Angel wings? Unicorn feathers? Actual clouds from heaven?"

He set the food down onto the coffee table and handed her a fork before he went back into the kitchen.

"That couch is super comfortable, right? I got it at a furniture store's going-out-of-business sale—I always think those sales are fake because, I swear, some of those furniture companies go out of business like twice a year—but I don't even care if this one was fake because I love this couch and will defend it against all enemies."

He came back to the couch with his wineglass, the wine bottle, and a pile of napkins.

She topped off both of their wineglasses.

"Does . . . does your couch have a lot of enemies? Forgive me, I don't have a leather couch made of pillows sewn by a goddess, so I don't know these things."

He picked up his glass, his face serious.

"Oh yes. It's one of the hardest things about owning a couch like this. People try to storm your home all the time to destroy it because they think anything this magical must be a sin. They warn you about this at the furniture store before you buy it. They had to put a guard on it in the showroom. It was crazy." He looked at her with a straight face until her laughter finally made him crack a smile.

She stuck her fork into the risotto and took a bite.

"Oh my God."

He looked up, his fork halfway to his mouth.

"What? 'Oh my God' what?"

She was too busy eating to answer at first.

"Oh my God, this risotto, that's what 'Oh my God!' I had no idea it was going to be this good!"

His most smug smile spread over his face, but she didn't even care.

"Tell me more. What's so 'Oh my God' about it? I want details, please."

She waved her finger in his face and retreated to the far corner of the couch.

"Stop talking to me. I need to concentrate when I eat this."

When she was almost done with her bowl, one of the things he'd said about why he liked making risotto came back into her head.

"So what happened at work today that made you need to make risotto?" she asked.

He sighed and put his own fork down.

"It was just a really shitty day, with some of my least favorite parts of this job."

She took a sip of her wine and looked at him. He seemed like he wanted to talk, but she wanted to tread lightly. She still didn't know him that well.

"Least favorite as a doctor, or least favorite as a person? Not to say that doctors aren't people, but . . . you know what I mean."

He took her bowl without asking and went over to the kitchen to get them both seconds.

"Yeah, I know what you mean," he said when he came back. "No wonder you're such a good writer. You ask good questions. Least favorite as a person. Or rather, least favorite as a person who is also a doctor, and therefore has to be professional when I really just wanted to punch that man in the face. Calling CPS isn't nearly as satisfying."

Child Protective Services.

"Abuse?" she asked.

He nodded.

"Yeah. Stepdad. The girl was getting the cast off of her broken arm; I wasn't there when she came in for the arm, so I don't know what happened then, but a few things she said when I was taking it off worried me, so I managed to get him out of the room and got the details out of her." He stared down at his knees and sighed.

"It's not new to me. I've seen it before, but it's a stomach punch every time."

She moved closer to him and took his hand. He held on tight but didn't say anything. She didn't ask any more questions; she figured now was the time to just be silent and let him talk or not talk as much as he wanted.

After a few minutes, he looked up at her and shrugged.

"On top of everything else, it makes me think of my dad. Which sucks, because between Father's Day this coming weekend and the anniversary of his death next Friday, I try to avoid thinking about my dad as much as possible in June."

She squeezed his hand. She hadn't realized that the anniversary of his father's death was right around Father's Day.

"Why does this make you think of your dad? Because he was so much better than that guy?"

He laughed and let go of her hand, but only so he could put his arm around her.

"Well that, too. But also because I remember when something similar happened to one of his students. This was when Angela and I were younger; I think I was around twelve and she was ten, something like that. And he sat us down at the kitchen table and told us that his student had come to him, and how if anyone tried to do anything like that to us, we could come to him, and if any of our friends were dealing with something like that, we could always come to him. My mom tried to stop him at one point, told us we were too young to hear all of that, but he said 'Susana, they need to know this, it's important!' " She ran her fingers through his hair, and he leaned his head on her shoulder. "He was right. It was important."

After a few minutes, he sat up and looked down at their almost empty dishes.

"Hey, do you want some ice cream? I went a little wild at the grocery store tonight. I have three flavors."

Wine, risotto, and three kinds of ice cream. It's like the man knew she was coming over.

"Bring them all out."

He stood and picked up her dishes.

"Will do. I'm sorry if this was too heavy. We can talk about something else."

She shook her head.

"I wouldn't have asked if I didn't want to talk about it. It's not too heavy."

He came back a few minutes later and set a bowl with three scoops of ice cream in it in front of her.

"What do we have here?" she asked.

"Dark chocolate brownie, vanilla, rum raisin," he said.

She took the spoon he handed her.

"I like all of those things." They sat together,

eating ice cream and not talking for the next few minutes.

"Does Angela remember that? About your dad?" she asked him.

He shook his head.

"I have no idea. Angie and I don't really talk about my dad. Sometimes she brings him up, but it's too . . . I don't really want to talk to her about him. Partly it's because she's always bugging me to go to the doctor, probably because she's scared something will happen to me, too, but I'm too busy to deal with all of that right now. But also, it makes me too sad, I guess, which is stupid. It'll be five years next Friday. I shouldn't be sad about this anymore, but I guess I am."

There were so many things that she wanted to say to him, but who the hell was she to tell him how to deal with his grief over his dad's death? She'd never experienced that before. But one thing she knew for sure.

"It's not stupid," she said. "He was your dad. Of course you're still sad."

He wrapped his arms around her.

"Yeah. He was my dad," he said. "And he was a pretty great dad."

She took a deep breath.

"I bet Angela is still sad, too. It might make you feel better to talk to her about it. She's the only one who knows how it feels to have lost your dad."

He nodded slowly.

"That's true. She is."

She rubbed her hand against his stubbly cheek. Would he get mad at her for this?

"I know you're busy and I'm sure you're fine, but maybe think about going to the doctor? Just to make Angela feel better?"

He stiffened up.

"I'll think about it."

She maybe shouldn't have said anything.

"I'm sorry, it's probably not my business."

He shook his head.

"No, it's okay. One of the things I like about you is that you always say what you mean."

Huh. That was a thing that most people *didn't* like about her. She leaned up and kissed him on the cheek. He turned and kissed her on the lips.

"Thanks for listening. I'm sorry if I—"

She held her finger up to his lips to stop him.

"No apologies. We all need a shoulder to lean on sometimes. I wouldn't have offered mine if I didn't want to."

Carlos knew Nik well enough at this point to know that she didn't do anything she didn't want to. But he was used to being the one offering his shoulder for people to lean on. He wasn't sure how he felt about it being the other way around.

He couldn't believe he'd talked to her about his dad. He didn't talk to anyone about his dad. It had been kind of nice, actually, especially since Nik hadn't pounced on the topic and asked him a million questions. She'd just mostly listened.

"Oh, hey, Angie is at Jessie's house tonight for dinner. I should check to see if there have been any updates."

She took a spoonful of rum raisin ice cream.

"No problem. How's Jessie doing?"

"Bored, but okay. We just need to keep her there."

He pulled his phone out of his pocket to see four texts from Angie. His heart rate sped up, but when he clicked on them, they were four different selfies of her and Jessie together. At least, he thought the fourth one was of the two of them.

"What the hell is this picture?" He showed Nik the last one, with two faces covered in some white material with holes cut out for eyes and lips.

She shook her head at him, a disappointed look on her face.

"For someone with a sister and a cousin who's like a sister, you should know what a sheet mask is. The best kind of girlfriend activity. You pop them on, relax for ten to twenty minutes, usually take a few selfies, and take them off. You should try them; I bet it would help after a long day at work."

He laughed and put his arm around her.

"That's what a big-screen TV and basketball were invented for."

She handed him the remote from the coffee table and leaned her head on his chest.

"Speaking of, I'm impressed at your restraint. I know the playoffs are on."

So he turned on the game, and they spent the next hour curled up on the couch watching the second half of a pretty exciting game between two teams he couldn't care less about. His ideal post-work wind down kind of game—he got all the fun of the lead changes and the great shots, but none of the up and down emotions of a true fan of either of those teams.

"Ahhh, that was excellent," he said when the buzzer blew. Nik didn't respond. He pushed her hair back from her face. She was fast asleep, her head still on his chest. He bent down and kissed her forehead.

"Hey," he said in a low voice. "Time for bed."

Her eyes fluttered open, and she looked confused for a few seconds before she realized where she was. She sat up straight.

"I fell asleep, didn't I? I'm sorry."

He stood up and held out a hand to her.

"You missed an amazing game. I bet that breaks your heart. Let's go to bed."

He led her into his bedroom and she looked around.

"This is nice," she said. "Very peaceful."

He was just glad his clothes were no longer all over the floor and were in the hamper in the closet.

"Thanks. It is peaceful, but maybe too peaceful? I had no time to paint before I moved in here, and I keep thinking of painting this room, because it feels kind of depressing with all of the gray. Maybe some weekend I'll try to tackle it, once I figure out what I want instead."

She put her arms around him.

"As long as it isn't Dodger blue, any color works for me."

He leaned down to kiss her.

"I'll keep that in mind, though you know, I *am* a Dodger fan."

She ran her fingers through his hair and kissed his stubbly cheek.

"I know, don't remind me. I keep trying to forget that," she said as she unbuckled his belt.

"And here I was, about to say that if you were too tired for sex tonight, it was okay." He unbuttoned her jeans and pushed them to the floor. She kicked them to the side.

"Why did you think I took a little nap? I had to rest up."

She wrapped one leg around his waist, and he put his hands under her butt and lifted her. She laughed and wrapped her other leg around him.

"Well then, we need to make good use of that nap of yours, don't we?" He dropped her down on his bed. He liked the way she looked there, unsmiling, with her eyes roaming over his body. "You look good in my bed. I can't believe it's taken me this long to get you in it."

She stretched her arms above her body in a way that accentuated her breasts, almost, but not quite visible in her thin tank top.

"I can't believe it, either," she said. "I think it was because you didn't want to share this incredible bed with me. First your couch, then your bed—you are incredible at selecting furniture. I could stay here forever."

He pulled his clothes off before crawling above her onto the bed.

"Well then, you're in luck, because I'm going to keep you here for a damn long time. We have . . ." He glanced at the clock as he pulled her tank top over her head. "Eleven hours until I have to get up in the morning. Eleven and a half, if I push it. You're going to be very familiar with this bed."

She propped herself up so she could unhook her bra and tossed it to the side. Thank God she did—he was agile, but unhooking a woman's bra from behind her back while he was kneeling over her in bed might have been too much for even him.

And now those breasts of hers were bare for him. He cupped them with his hands, enjoying their fullness, their hard nipples in the middle of his palms. She stared up at him, her eyes heavy lidded, a smile hovering around the corners of her mouth.

"Do with me what you will, Dr. Ibarra. Your bed, your rules."

Holy shit, did that get him hot. He took a deep breath, and her smile got bigger.

"Oh, you like that, do you?" She glanced down. "Mmm, I can tell you like that."

He bent down to kiss her.

"If I had known it would be this fun to get you in my bed, I would have managed it weeks ago." He looked her naked body over and grinned. "Okay. Here's what we're going to do first . . ."

Chapter Fourteen

• • • • • •

When Nik woke up the next morning, she was alone in Carlos's big pillowlike bed. She wondered briefly where he was, decided it was either in the bathroom or on a phone call, and abandoned thought to luxuriate in his fluffy blankets against her bare skin.

That was until she heard him coming back into the room. She stayed right where she was, ready for him to get back under the covers with her.

Instead, he leaned down and kissed her cheek, the only part of her body that wasn't covered by his blankets. She pulled down the covers and smiled up at him.

"Good morning," she said.

"Good morning," he said. "How do you feel about coffee?"

She smiled and turned over to face him. He had on gray sweatpants and nothing else.

"I feel great about coffee, but you know that. I always feel great about coffee."

He smiled back at her. Her hair probably looked insane right now. She usually tried to at least put it in a ponytail after they'd gone to bed, but last night . . . well, there hadn't been time.

"Excellent." He put a mug of coffee on the bedside table next to her. "Here you go."

She looked over at the mug, and then back up at him.

"Really? You made me coffee?" He nodded at her like the answer was obvious, which she guessed it was. She still couldn't believe it.

She sat up in glee. He'd actually made her coffee? He brought it to her in bed? No one had brought her coffee in bed since . . . wait, actually, no one had *ever* brought her coffee in bed. Other than the room-service waiters at hotels.

She picked up the mug and breathed in the hot, warm, earthy coffee smell.

"Now. How do you feel about breakfast?"

She looked up from her mug. Was this a trick question?

"I have very strong, positive feelings about breakfast at any given moment. Why . . . why do you ask?"

He walked toward the bedroom door.

"Wait here."

Seconds later, he was back with a tray in his hands. Okay, no, it wasn't a tray, it was a cookie sheet, but did she care about that? Not in the slightest. He set the cookie sheet/tray on her knees, and on it was a plate with a pile of golden scrambled eggs, three pieces of bacon, and two slices of generously buttered toast. Oh, and a knife and fork, and a little pot of jam. A little pot of jam? Now she knew this must be a dream.

"This looks amazing," she said, because that's what you say in dreams to people who bring you freshly made breakfast. "Did you make all of this?"

He smiled that same proud smile from when she'd complimented his risotto the night before. Apparently, no matter how good of a cook you were, you liked it when people told you your food was good. Now that she knew that, she'd tell him constantly.

"I did. I hope you like scrambled eggs. I wasn't sure. I know you like pancakes, but . . ."

Luckily, she was a fan of all breakfast foods.

"I love scrambled eggs. I love all of this."

She could never let Courtney know he'd made her breakfast *twice*. Oh shit, and he'd made her dinner last night, too. Courtney had such inane ways of judging relationships, but convincing her that it was just that Carlos loved to cook would be a losing battle.

He got back in the bed next to her, his own plate in his hands.

"You haven't even tried it yet. How do you know you love it?"

She picked up her fork and took a bite of eggs. Delicate and creamy, they were everything she wanted scrambled eggs to be.

"Now I've tried it and I know I love it. Satisfied?"

He nodded.

"Very much so."

Far too quickly, she'd finished all of her food and lay back down in bed.

"Oh my God, I'm so full I'm going to die."

He was still chewing on his last piece of bacon.

"Maybe you shouldn't have eaten so fast, hmmm?"

She pulled the blankets over her head.

"I worked up an appetite. I was hungry!" she said to the underside of his comforter.

He pushed his plate down to the foot of the bed and put his head under the blankets to join her.

"What did you say?"

They were almost nose to nose, tucked underneath his warm heavy blankets. It felt like they were in a cocoon together. She could happily stay like this with him all day.

"I said I worked up an appetite for all that food."

He put his hand on her knee and ran it up and down the side of her body. She'd kept the sheet wrapped around herself as she ate, but now her whole body was available to him again.

"You sure did. Why do you think I woke up early to make you breakfast? I thought you might be hungry."

"Mmmm, thank you for that." His hand kept moving up her body. She turned over onto her

253

back, and he pushed her legs open. "What time is it? When do you have to be at work?"

He kissed her neck.

"Um. I think about seven thirty? I know how you feel about waking up early, but I thought the coffee and breakfast would help?"

Her eyes popped open and she pulled the covers down.

"Seven thirty in the *morning?*" She looked around the room, not seeing a clock anywhere that would confirm his statement. But then, why would he lie about that? "You woke me up at seven a.m.?"

He dropped kisses along her shoulder.

"I know, I know, I'm so sorry. But I was awake. And hungry. And I thought you might want some eggs . . ." he kissed her cheek, "and bacon . . ." he kissed her other cheek, "and strawberry jam . . ." he kissed her mouth. He made kissing into an art form. Never rushed, never impatient, no matter how fast and eager and forceful he was.

"Hmmmm. I guess you're going to have to find a way to make my hour of lost sleep up to me. Do you have any idea of how you're going to do that?"

She could feel him smile against her skin.

"Oh, I have some ideas."

Later, when he was frantically getting dressed to go to work, he stopped just as he'd buckled his belt.

"Oh, hey, are you free Saturday night?"

She picked up her jeans from the floor and pulled her phone out of the pocket.

"Let me check. Why, what's up?"

She scrolled through her calendar—birthday party Friday night, and ugh, a wedding shower with Dana on Saturday afternoon, but nothing Saturday night.

"Yeah, I'm free. Are you sure you don't mean Saturday afternoon? If you can give me a good excuse to get out of this wedding shower I have to go to, I'll love you forever."

Ooops. She turned to pull her jeans on and decided to pretend she'd never said that. Luckily, it didn't seem like Carlos had heard anything past "free."

"It's no big deal, but my buddy Drew and his fiancée, Alexa, will be in town, and I'm going to have dinner with them that night, if you want to join us."

Wait, what? He wanted her to meet his friend and his friend's fiancée? Part of the whole reason she had wanted to stay away from relationships was so she wouldn't have to hang out with people's annoying friends when she didn't want to. The last time she'd done that, she was with Fisher and his friends at Dodger Stadium, and the whole world knew how that one had ended.

Why hadn't she waited to see what he'd had in mind *before* saying she was free? She could have used the wedding shower to get out of this. It would have been the only good thing a wedding shower had ever done for the world!

"If you have work to do or whatever, it's cool." Carlos was digging through his sock drawer. "But Drew and Alexa are fun, and I think you'd like them."

He didn't seem to really care whether she went or not. That made her feel better. Maybe he was just inviting her so he'd have some company around his smug couple friends when they started talking about countertops or wedding flowers or the adorable bed-and-breakfast they'd stayed in on their last romantic getaway.

"Okay, sure," she said. "Just let me know when and where."

He had met *her* friends, after all.

"Will do!" he said as he put his watch on. They walked out of his house together, and he kissed her at the bottom of the steps. "I might just make it to work on time. See you Saturday."

She kissed him back.

"See you Saturday!"

What had she gotten herself into?

"So *this* is the new house!" Drew said, standing at Carlos's front door on Saturday afternoon. "I can't believe you bought a house without consulting me."

Carlos waved Drew into the house.

"Please, you would have been useless during the entire process. The only reason I managed to actually find a house to buy was because I didn't have you around trying to convince me that I needed an in-house sauna or man cave or granite countertops or whatever thing it is they sell you on those house shows you like to watch."

Drew walked in the house and nodded as he looked around.

"You know, I've gotten Alexa hooked on those things, too? Sometimes on Saturdays she's all ready to go to the farmers' market and brunch and yoga and whatever else and, like, four hours later we're still on the couch deep into a house-shopping marathon. It's fantastic."

Carlos rolled his eyes. Then he looked at Drew's face. Damn it, the guy looked so fucking happy he could barely even make fun of him.

"I'll give you the grand tour as long as you don't tell me anything more about those shows. The house is pretty small, and I haven't done half the things I've wanted to do with it, but if you tell me that I need a double sink or recessed lighting or any of that bullshit, I'm kicking you out."

Drew accepted the beer Carlos handed him and took a long swig.

"I'm already a fan of this TV. Does it swivel so you can watch it both in the kitchen and from the couch?"

Carlos nodded and patted the top of the TV.

"It sure does. It makes me happy every day."

After a walk around the house, where Drew asked a surprising amount of questions about the heated floors in the bathroom and the kitchen, they ended up on the couch in the living room with the game on.

"Oh, hey, how's Jessie doing?"

Carlos automatically reached for his phone to check to see if anyone from the family had called him. Nothing.

"She's hanging in there. Her blood pressure is still high, and I'm still constantly worried about it, but her doctor doesn't seem to be. She's still only thirty-three weeks. I think my mom and aunt are saying rosaries every day about it. Hell, I should, too."

Drew patted him on the shoulder.

"She'll be okay, man. I'm sure her doctor is doing everything she should be."

She probably was, but that didn't make him any less terrified.

"Yeah. It's just that this time of year. I think everyone in my family gets pretty paranoid about health stuff. Me included."

Ever since Nik had brought it up, he'd been thinking about talking to Angela about their dad. Nik was probably right that Angie was the only person who knew what it was like to lose their dad. Maybe sharing that grief with her would help them both.

But he wasn't sure he was ready to do that. He'd spent almost five years trying to beat back his grief; the idea of welcoming it in felt obscene.

Carlos got up to get them chips and salsa and more beer. Drew immediately grabbed a chip, but hesitated before dipping it into the salsa. Carlos rolled his eyes.

"Oh my God, you haven't even been gone a year. I didn't forget you're scared of spicy food."

"I was just checking! I wasn't sure you stocked Drew-style salsa anymore."

Carlos leaned back against the couch cushions. Nik was right about this couch; it was pretty magical.

"I don't. I bought this just for you. Be honored. I wouldn't buy this bullshit for just anyone."

Drew put his hand over his heart.

"I am, man. I am."

At the next commercial break, Drew cleared his throat.

"Um, actually. Speaking of. There was something I wanted to ask you."

Speaking of what? Carlos raised his eyebrows at him.

"I'm flattered, but I don't think I'm ready to get married any time soon."

Drew threw a chip at him.

"Fuck you. I'm taken, remember?"

"Yeah, yeah, I remember," Carlos said.

"Anyway. I was going to say that if it wasn't for you, I probably never would have figured my shit out, and well, will you be my best man?"

Damn it. Carlos hadn't planned on getting emotional today, but he was surprisingly touched by this.

"Oh shit, man, of course I will."

"Thanks." Drew let out a deep breath. "I was going to ask when you were up in Berkeley for the engagement party, but you'd just found out about Jessie at that point and there was a lot going on. Just make sure your speech isn't too wild—my grandma is going to be there."

Carlos grinned.

"Oh, my speech is going to be fantastic." Carlos rubbed his hands together and reached for the good salsa. "This is going to be fun. Do you guys have a wedding date yet?"

Drew shook his head.

"Not yet—we're working on it. Probably sometime next summer. Hell, I'd do it tomorrow if I could. But you'll be the first to know as soon as we have a date. You better lock down that entire week for me."

Carlos laughed.

"You got it. I'm just trying to imagine what I would have thought if someone told me at this time last year that you'd be telling me a year later you'd be ready to get married 'tomorrow.' I would probably fall over in shock."

Drew picked up the empty salsa bowl and walked into the kitchen to refill it.

"You probably would have. Hell, I definitely would have. What can I say, sometimes when it hits, it hits."

At the next commercial break, Drew said—oh so casually—"Hey, so what's going on with this Dodgers-game girl? What's she like? We are going to get to meet her tonight, aren't we?"

Carlos rolled his eyes. Drew was doing that "we" thing that couples always did. Had he turned into one of those people already?

"Yes, 'we' are. Lucky for you, she was dying for an excuse to get out of some wedding shower she was supposed to go to, so you're it." Well, that was sort of true. Maybe that would stop Drew from trying to turn tonight's dinner into a whole couples' thing. "Don't make this into a big thing. I'm not ready to get married to her tomorrow."

"Okay, okay, it's not a big thing, I heard you the first time."

The smirk on Drew's face made Carlos pretty sure he hadn't heard him at all.

Dinner with Carlos, his friend, and his friend's probably perfect fiancée was the last thing Nik wanted to do. The one good thing about Fisher had been that all of his friends were so annoying that she'd made fun of them to their faces constantly without them even realizing it. She probably couldn't pull that off with Carlos's friends.

Also, she had no fucking idea what she should wear. Everyone at the shower was in cute little floral dresses, and she hadn't worn a cute little floral dress since she was seven years old. Her concession had been not wearing black to the shower in the first place. But tonight she wanted to not fit in a little less aggressively.

She stared into her closet for a full five minutes before she gave up and called Dana.

"Okay, I went to that boring shower with you; now you have to pay me back by getting me out of this dinner tonight."

"Why don't you want to go?" Dana asked. Nik could tell by her regular breathing that she was running. It was good that she liked Dana so much—otherwise she'd hate her for being able to have a regular conversation during exercise.

"He's not even my boyfriend. Why do I need to meet his friends? Plus, what if they hate me?"

They probably would hate her. They would think she was too mean or sarcastic or abrasive for Carlos.

"Why'd you tell him you would go, then?" Dana asked. "You usually don't say yes to things you don't want to do."

Maybe she should wear that leather motorcycle jacket again? She liked that jacket. It made her feel like a badass.

It would make her feel like a very sweaty badass tonight; it was well over eighty degrees outside. She put the jacket back in her closet with a sigh.

"That's not true. I do things I don't want to do all the time. I went to that stupid shower today with you, didn't I?"

Dana's loud huff from a normal person running would have just meant they were out of breath, but not from Dana.

"Courtney and I don't count. No really, why did you say yes?"

Nik sighed.

"He asked if I was free for dinner—was I supposed to lie? And he'd just . . ." No, she shouldn't tell Dana about Carlos making her breakfast. She wasn't Courtney, but she'd still react to that. "Plus, you guys have met him. It felt churlish to say no to meeting his friends."

"Okay, then you have to go. But they'll like you! We liked Carlos, didn't we? And Courtney and I are a pretty tough crowd when it comes to men. Wear that navy blue striped dress you wore to my birthday party. And do not wear those booties I know you're already thinking about wearing. They look like clown shoes."

She put the booties back into her closet.

"I hate you. You're the worst. I'll wear some sandals or something."

"I hate you, too," Dana said. "Now I've got to go. I'm about to meet my running partner."

Nik stopped halfway through picking up her silver sandals. They made her legs look great.

"Haven't you been running this whole time?"

"Just a mile, running to meet her." Nik had never said "just" and "a mile" about running in her life. "Okay, talk later! Let me know how it goes!"

Dinner was at Café Stella, one of her favorite restaurants in Silver Lake and one that had the advantage of being so close to her apartment she could walk there, even in her hot silver sandals. She told people she loved it despite how trendy and Instagrammable it was, but she had been known to post a few Instagrams from it herself. She saw Carlos when she walked in, but he was too busy talking to the two people on the other side of the table to notice her walking toward them.

Ugh, why was she so nervous about this?

"Hi," she said, when she was standing right next to the table.

"Hey!" Carlos jumped out of his chair and kissed her on the cheek. "I didn't even see you come in." They sat down, and she did a double take when she saw the woman across the table from her.

"Nik, these are my friends Drew and Alexa. Drew and Alexa, meet Nik."

Carlos had *not* told her that Alexa was black. From everything that he'd told her about Drew, mild salsa and all, it would never have occurred to her that he'd be engaged to a black woman.

And . . . judging by the quickly masked look of surprise on Alexa's face, Alexa hadn't known *she* was black. She hadn't thought to have the "did you tell your friends I'm black?" conversation with Carlos—she assumed that because he was Latino she didn't have to. Which was probably partly true; she hadn't been worried that his friends were racist. But if Alexa had been the white woman that she'd expected her to be, that look of surprise on her face would have been a hell of a lot more stressful. Instead, she felt some of her anxiety about this evening drain away.

"It's so nice to meet you both. I've heard a lot about you," she said. *Except that Alexa is black.*

"Same here," Drew said. "I, um, saw your claim to fame on SportsCenter before I even knew Carlos was there."

Alexa nudged him, none too subtly.

"What Drew meant to say right there was that—"

Nik laughed.

"I appreciate that, but it's okay. Three weeks ago, bringing that up would have made me 'accidentally' spill my drink on anyone who did it, but I'm not as sensitive about it anymore."

"So, Nik," Alexa said, "Carlos tells us you're a writer? What kind of stuff do you write?"

She wasn't as sensitive about the proposal any-more, but she was still glad Alexa changed the subject.

"A combination of investigative journalism and celebrity profiles. Getting to do a profile of Ivy Robinson in the middle of working on a story about foster kids was a real pick-me-up, let me tell you."

"The profile in *Vanity Fair*? You wrote that story?" Nik nodded and Alexa's eyes lit up. "That was such a fun read! My girlfriends and I kept texting each other quotes from it."

There was nothing like a pure spontaneous compliment to make you like someone.

"Thanks so much. I had a lot of fun writing it. I'm glad it came through for the reader. And . . . I think Carlos said you work for the mayor of Berkeley?"

Alexa nodded.

"Chief of staff."

"Wow, big job. How do you like it?"

Her wide smile said it all.

"I love it. Sometimes I hate it, obviously, and sometimes it drives me up a wall. But even in some of those times, I love it."

They talked about both of their jobs for a while, while the guys talked about doctor stuff, until the waitress interrupted.

"Have you guys had a chance to look at the drink menu?" she asked.

Both Nik and Alexa shook their heads; they had been too busy talking.

While Alexa looked at the drink menu, Nik looked around and smiled despite herself. The sunset through the glass roof of the restaurant tinted the sky a soft pink. There were plants growing everywhere and lights hanging from ropes overhead. Even she had to admit that it was stupidly romantic. Carlos reached over and took her hand under the table. The restaurant must be getting to him, too. She smiled at him.

"I'll have a glass of the sparkling rosé," Alexa said.

Carlos squeezed her hand. Nik looked down at her menu so she wouldn't giggle.

"Um, I'll have one of those, too, please," she said. He squeezed her hand harder and she squeezed back.

They switched their conversation to the food menu and the four of them hotly debated whether to get fries or mashed potatoes with their steaks (they decided on both).

After they ordered food, Alexa brought the conversation back to Nik's job.

"I loved all the stuff about Ivy's stylist in that piece. My best friend is a stylist in the Bay Area, and obviously that isn't as high profile a job as it is around here, but it was still such a great read for her, especially since Ivy's stylist is another black woman."

She still could not believe Carlos hadn't told her that Alexa was black.

"That's so interesting that your friend is a stylist. I hadn't really realized there were stylists outside of the celebrity centers of New York and L.A. But of course there are plenty of people who live elsewhere who need to get dressed, too. I guess I'm so stuck in this world I've gotten myopic about it."

Carlos tapped her on the hand that was just reaching for her wine.

"Excuse me. I hate to interrupt. But what the hell is a stylist?"

The rest of the table burst out laughing, even Drew. Carlos immediately turned on him.

"Oh, so this is something *you* know? You leave L.A. and now you're an expert?"

Nik was still laughing, more at the look on his face than anything else.

"I don't know why Drew knows it, but honestly, this isn't the kind of thing most people know unless you pay a lot of attention to celebrities, which, for good or bad, I do. A stylist is basically someone to help you get dressed, which sounds stupid, but for celebrities, it's totally necessary. And honestly, whenever I talk to one, I wish I had one myself."

Alexa nodded.

"Yeah, that's exactly what Maddie does. She has some local minor celebrities in her client list, but more of her clients are just really busy women who have to look polished, but don't have the time or inclination to figure out how to do it themselves. Using people like her has become more common, especially for women who aren't sample size, whether they're petite or plus-size or tall or anything else where shopping for clothes is a lot more of a pain. I'm just grateful she's my best friend and she helps me for free. I wouldn't be able to afford her on my salary. And I'll tell you how Drew knows what a stylist is—because Maddie told him he was no longer allowed to go out in public with me if he kept wearing those busted old canvas sneakers he loved so much, that's how."

Carlos's laugh boomed across the restaurant.

"You mean someone actually managed to get him to get rid of those things? I'd been trying for years! I'm convinced of the utility of stylists now—no need to say anything else."

While they were still waiting for their food, Nik got up to go to the bathroom and Alexa joined her. When they were washing their hands afterward, Nik looked at Alexa in the mirror, and the two glasses of sparkling wine on an almost empty stomach eliminated her filter.

"Okay, I just have to say. Carlos did *not* tell me that you were black."

Alexa dropped her hands on the counter.

"Neither of them told me you were black!

What is wrong with them? I know Drew saw you on that video, so he definitely knew. I never saw it, though—I don't pay attention when he's watching most things on ESPN, except when Serena is playing. When you sat down, I almost killed them both."

Nik handed her a paper towel.

"I thought you looked surprised when I sat down."

Someone else walked into the bathroom, and Alexa lowered her voice.

"Pleasantly surprised, obviously, but I mean come on." She held open the door for Nik on the way out of the bathroom. "But hey, Carlos is great, so now I'm even happier for him."

Nik decided to ignore that comment. She knew that she and Carlos were on the same page, and if his friends wanted to do some kind of "we want everyone to find the happiness that we've found!!!" thing that newly engaged couples did, he would have to be the one to burst their bubble, not her.

After dinner, dessert, and a few after-dinner drinks, the four of them hugged good-bye.

"Well, that was a lot better than I thought it would be," Nik said when she got into Carlos's car.

Oops. She hadn't meant to say that out loud.

"What do you mean? You didn't think you were going to like my friends?"

She dodged that question.

"You didn't tell me Alexa is black!"

He froze, halfway through backing out of his parking spot.

"Seriously? I didn't?" He laughed. "I was just going to say that I'm sure I told you that, but then, I'm sure that's the kind of thing you'd remember."

She looked at him sideways, her eyebrows sky-high.

"You're absolutely right; I would have."

He shook his head as he drove the short distance to her apartment.

"I can't believe that. I'm sorry." He put his hand on her knee and smiled at her. "I guess I'm going to have to find a way to make that up to you, aren't I?"

She smiled back at him.

"Well, I did have plenty of rosé this evening."

Chapter Fifteen

• • • • • •

Wednesday night after work, Carlos drove straight to Angela's apartment. The last time he was there he'd noticed that her cheap IKEA bookshelf was falling apart, so he'd bought her a new good one. He called when he was outside of her house.

"Hey!" she said when she answered the phone. "Did those million messages in the family group text drive you as crazy as it did me?"

He laughed and got out of the car.

"Oh my God, Angie—I checked my phone after a few hours of seeing patients and panicked because I had thirty-five new messages, but they were just Mom, Tia Eva, and Jessie all talking about Popsicles? What was even happening there?"

Angela sighed.

"I know! I'm sure Jessie's going stir-crazy, but that made even me want to yell at her."

Carlos popped open his trunk.

"Please tell her not to do that again. I know you'll get mad at me if I say it. But also, come open the door. I'm here."

He hung up the phone and lifted the box with her new bookshelf in it out of his trunk. He was at the front door of her building just as she opened it.

"What are you doing here? You didn't tell me you were coming over tonight."

He walked past her to the elevator.

"Do you have a hot date? I hope so."

She rolled her eyes as they got in the elevator.

"No, but good try. Just making dinner and getting some work done tonight. What's in that box?"

He followed her out of the elevator to her apartment.

"A new bookshelf. That old one of yours has got to go, and I knew if you bought yourself one you'd just make me put it together anyway, so I figured I'd do it on my own schedule."

"You bought me a bookshelf?" She opened the door for him. The smell of garlic wafted toward him. "And you're putting it together for me tonight? What did I do to deserve this?"

He set the box down on her living room floor and pulled it open.

"Probably very little. Where's that toolbox I bought you?"

She went to her hall closet and took the toolbox off of a shelf there. When he opened it, he was thrilled to see that things were all in the wrong places. She must have actually used it since the last time he was here.

"Do you want a beer? I have wine, but you always get all fussy about my wine, so I'm not even going to offer it to you this time."

He definitely couldn't have rosé around his sister.

"Yes, please." He slid all of the shelves out of the box and glanced at the instruction manual. This shouldn't take too long.

"Here." She handed him a beer and looked over the pile of wood and wood-like materials on her living room floor. "This looks like it'll be bigger and less flimsy than the one I had. Thanks, Carlos."

"No problem." He opened the little bag of screws and reached for a screwdriver. He should have bought Angie an electric screwdriver along with this tool kit. Oh well, now he knew what he'd get her for Christmas. "Are you still in the middle of cooking, or can you hang out and talk to me while I do this?"

She sat down on her easy chair and set a glass of wine on the table next to her.

"I put a roast chicken in the oven like thirty minutes ago, so I have plenty of time. If you want dinner to reward you after you're done, I'll have plenty of food once it's done cooking."

He screwed the side of the bookshelf to the bottom and grinned at her.

"Oooh, are you making those crispy potatoes to go along with it? I love those things. I could eat a million of them."

She shook her head and sighed. "Unfortunately, I am. I guess I won't have any potatoes left over for lunch tomorrow."

He picked up the other side and fitted a screw into the bottom of the bookcase.

"You definitely won't. You'll barely have enough for yourself."

She took a sip of her wine and watched him for a few minutes.

"Come on, you can tell me about your new girlfriend. I know you have one; I can sense it. I promise I won't tell Mama if you tell me!"

Of course. He should have known that as soon as she got him alone she would quiz him about that.

"God, no. Don't worry, if there's ever anything to tell you about in that category—which there won't be for a long time—I'll tell you first."

She moved to join him on the floor and picked up the bag of screws.

"You've just seemed much more relaxed over the past few weeks. It's nice."

"Mmmhmmm." He had been more relaxed over the past few weeks, come to think about it. But that was just because he'd been settling in at work.

He reached his palm out for another screw, and she handed it to him.

"You don't have any snacks or anything? I'm getting hungry, smelling that chicken cooking and knowing we won't get to eat for, like, thirty more minutes."

She shook her head and closed her eyes.

"You storm into my house without warning, take over my living room, claim all of my potatoes, and now you're demanding a snack?" She stood up. "Next time I'm not answering my phone when you call."

The emptiest of empty threats. He kept screwing the back of the bookshelf in while she rummaged around the kitchen.

"I was wondering," he said, his eyes focused on the bookshelf pieces. "What did you do with the money from Dad's life insurance?"

From the corner of his eye, he saw her walk back into the room, but he didn't look up.

"That trip," she said after a long pause. She sat down on the couch in front of him. "Remember that trip I took with Jessie to Italy a year later? That's what I spent it on."

He stopped pretending he was still occupied with the bookshelf and looked up at her, but she was looking down at her lap.

"I felt like I should spend it on my student loans or a down payment or something, but after you bought that car, I kind of felt free to do what I really wanted to do with it."

He hadn't told anyone in his family that was how he'd bought his car.

"Wait," he said. "How did you know that I used mine to buy the car?"

She rolled her eyes at him.

"Carlos. I'm not an idiot. And I know you better than anyone. Do you think I thought you got a sudden raise or something?"

She had a good point.

"Anyway, your trip," he said.

She nodded.

"I'd always wanted to go to Italy, ever since he bought me *A Room with a View* when I was a kid. Dad always made fun of me for how obsessed I was with that book and with the idea of going to Italy someday. 'Mexico isn't good enough for you?' he would say. But he took me to see the movie when there was a showing of it on the big screen at the ArcLight that time and out to Italian food afterward. And at Christmas he would always slip me little things about Italy, like cookbooks or Italian language books, stuff like that."

Her voice caught, and she stopped for a second.

"Anyway, I did use some of the money to pay off my credit card debt. But the rest paid for tickets for me and Jessie to fly to Rome and train tickets to Florence and Venice." She laughed.

"Jessie got so mad at me for insisting on paying for her, but I told her that Dad would flip out if I went alone, and he would want her to go with me—all of which she knew was totally true."

He shook his head.

"I thought you guys went because Jessie got that promotion."

She looked at the framed picture on the wall of her and Jessie on a balcony with Italy in the background.

"That's what we told Mama and Tia Eva. We knew I would get lectures from them if we told them the truth. Jessie did get that promotion. But it came well after I'd already booked our tickets. Our excuse before it happened was going to be that one of us had had a terrible breakup, but we hadn't decided who yet."

He shook his head.

"I'm not sure if that would have worked as well with them."

She leaned back against the couch and laughed.

"It definitely wouldn't have."

He reached for the bookshelf pieces again.

"So um," he said as he lined up the little wooden dowels. "About Friday."

She slowly straightened up.

"What about Friday?" Her voice was soft, gentle. It made him concentrate hard on inserting the dowels into the sides of the bookshelf, so he wouldn't have to look at her as he talked.

"I don't know if you have any plans. But I thought it might be nice if we could do something together that day. And maybe . . ." For some terrible reason, his voice caught. "Maybe talk about Dad."

She sat down next to him and put both arms around him. He abandoned the bookshelf and hugged his little sister close.

"I would love that," she said. "I would love that a lot."

He wiped his eyes and hoped she didn't notice. "So would I."

Nik got a text from Carlos on her way into Natalie's Gym on Thursday night.

What're you up to on Saturday? Want to help me make enchiladas? I'm making a huge batch so Jessie can have some for her freezer, but I promise we'll get to eat some of our labor.

She had no idea how to make enchiladas, but she had no doubt Carlos would tell her exactly what to do. And she knew the result would be delicious, if he was in charge.

What time and what should I bring?

She asked the person at the front desk where she could find Natalie, and was directed to an office in the back.

4ish. Bring some beer, no offense to rosé.

"Hi." Nik poked her head into Natalie's office. "Do you have a second?"

She'd thought for the past few weeks about Carlos's suggestion to write a piece about Natalie's Gym and had decided he might be right. A gym in L.A. that had a sliding scale was unusual in the first place, and one that was as positive about all kinds of bodies as Natalie's was like a unicorn. A ton of women's magazines would jump at a story about a woman-owned gym in L.A., especially with someone as perky and photogenic as Natalie at the heart of it.

Natalie looked up and smiled at her.

"Nik! Of course. Hi!" How was Natalie's hair always so perfect? This woman worked out for a living, and yet she had a perfect swinging blond ponytail.

"Hi. I wanted to ask you if you were open to me writing a story about you and your gym."

Natalie's smile faded. She stared blankly at her and didn't say anything. So Nik kept talking.

"I've written for the *L.A.* and *New York Times*, *Variety*, *GQ*, the *New Yorker*, and a lot more. You can look me up to check out my work to make sure I'm legit. This isn't why I started coming to your gym—I started for very different reasons—but it's pretty rare to find a place that promotes feminism, actually practices being inclusive, and is accessible to women of so many different backgrounds and socioeconomic classes. So I want to write about it."

Natalie still didn't say anything. Uh-oh. Nik

didn't really want to write this story without Natalie's cooperation and permission.

"Yes." Natalie nodded, but still wasn't smiling. "Okay. Email me and we can schedule a time to talk in the next few weeks. Does that work for you?"

Nik took the card Natalie handed to her and gave her one of her own.

"Absolutely. Thanks so much, and I'll be in touch. See you in there."

Natalie nodded and turned back to her computer.

Nik left Natalie's office and walked into the locker room to change for class. Natalie hadn't seemed happy about the idea of Nik writing about the gym, even though this was only a good thing for her business. This piece was either going to be a disaster or more interesting than she thought.

At the bar after class, as soon as they got their drinks, Courtney zeroed in on Dana.

"Okay, spill it."

Dana's eyes widened.

"Spill what? What are you talking about?"

Nik was equally confused.

"Yeah, spill what?" she asked Courtney.

Courtney glared at Nik.

"Not you too. Are you too busy with your new man to see what's right in front of your face?"

She gestured at Dana.

"This one is over here smiling like there's no tomorrow, beaming at her phone when she thinks we don't see her, AND when I stopped by her house the other day to drop off cupcakes, she had a huge vase of gorgeous peonies in her bedroom and she said she had to go for a run as soon as I looked at them."

Oooh. Nik looked at Dana, who had a very happy, and very guilty, look on her face.

Courtney banged her hand on the table.

"Who." BANG. "Is." BANG. "The New Woman?" BANG. BANG. BANG.

By this time the whole bar was looking at them, and Dana, shaking with laughter, had her face in her hands. Finally she sat up.

"Okay. Courtney's right. I didn't tell you guys because . . ." She sighed. "I didn't tell you guys because The New Woman is Natalie. And since we're still all in the class with her for another week, I thought—"

Nik was glad her glass wasn't in her hand, or she would have dropped it.

"Natalie, our Natalie? Natalie from the gym? Tall? Blond? HOT? That Natalie?" she asked.

Courtney was still staring dumbfounded at Dana.

"That Natalie," Dana said. "Anyway, it's still pretty new—I asked her a question after class a few weeks ago, and one thing led to another and we became running partners."

That's not how "one thing led to another" was supposed to end.

"And then?" Nik asked.

"And one day, we got back to my place after a run, and I invited her inside for some vitamin water, and then . . ."

Courtney leapt across the table to throw her arms around Dana.

"I'm so mad at you for keeping this a secret from us," she said, while hugging her tightly.

Nik shook her head. "Now I'm going to have to put a long disclaimer on my story about the gym—I can't even believe this." She tried to frown, but Dana was grinning so hard it was impossible not to grin back at her.

"Don't get too excited, you guys," Dana said. "Again, it's only been a few weeks, but things are good so far."

Nik sat back and smiled.

"Now who's mad at me for signing all of us up for self-defense classes, huh? You two will never be able to argue with me ever again."

They both threw ice at her.

Chapter Sixteen

• • • • • •

Nik pulled up to Carlos's house late Saturday afternoon, with a six-pack of beer in her hand and her old Stanford T-shirt on. She had a feeling that enchilada making was a messy endeavor.

"Hey! Come on in." Carlos wrapped his arms around her and held on tight.

"Everything okay?" she asked.

He nodded and kissed her hair.

"It's been a kind of emotional week, that's all. Glad you're here."

She pulled his head down to her and kissed him.

"I'm glad to be here."

They stood like that for a while, until he kissed the top of her head and pulled away.

"Okay. Let's get cooking."

They walked together into the kitchen, which looked prepared for battle. There were packs of tortillas stacked in one corner, bags of dried chilies in another, aluminum baking pans all over the kitchen table, and many other ingredients that she didn't recognize lined up on the counter. Her eyes widened.

"You ready for this?" Carlos surveyed the kitchen and rubbed his hands together.

She wasn't totally sure, but she nodded anyway.

"The first thing we have to do is to make the sauces," he said.

Sauces, plural. This dude didn't play around. She handed him the six-pack, and he took two beers out of it and put the rest in the fridge.

"Excellent. Let me get you started and I can pull out some snacks for us."

Soon, she was standing over the sink, pulling the papery skins off what seemed like hundreds of tomatillos. He was standing next to her, quartering onions, and lining them up on a big cookie sheet with garlic and a variety of green peppers.

It felt peaceful, standing there and cooking with him. Some game was on the TV, but on low, so it was perfect background noise. They weren't talking, but the silence between them felt easy. She could feel him smiling next to her.

When she was done, she washed and dried the weirdly shaped little fruits and lined them up in even rows on the cookie sheet.

"Perfect." He'd moved on to shredding the pot full of beef. It smelled amazing. She opened her mouth and he slid a piece between her lips.

"Oh my God, that's good," she said.

"Now I know that you are sincere when you say that in bed, because you say it just like that."

She smirked at him.

"Or I could be lying both times."

He shook his head.

"Impossible. I know how good that meat is. If I'm cocky about anything, it's my enchiladas."

She shook her head as she washed her hands.

" 'If he's cocky about anything,' he says."

He laughed and picked up the two cookie sheets full of vegetables.

"Open the oven so I can get these inside?"

Once the vegetables were broiling, she turned to him.

"What's next?"

He nodded at the other side of the stove.

"We need to get the chilies stemmed and seeded, and then soak them long enough so they soften. Put those on, and pull the chilies apart over the garbage can so the seeds come out, pull the stems off, then drop the pieces in that big pot."

She opened the bags of chilies as he carefully transferred all of the shredded beef from the cutting board to a big bowl. Once the bags were all open, she ripped each dried chili open with her fingers, and let the dry seeds rain out into the garbage can. Some of the seeds kind of stuck to the inside of the chilies, so she scraped them out with a fingernail before tossing the chili pieces into the pot on the stove.

"Beef enchiladas and chicken enchiladas . . .

there are no vegetarians in your family, I take it?"

Carlos opened the oven again and took the sheet pans of vegetables out.

"God, no. They would probably all flip out if I brought over vegetarian enchiladas. Which is a shame, because I make some really good ones with cheese and onions in the same kind of red chile sauce we're making now. I just save those for parties with my friends instead of my family; even my carnivore friends happily eat them."

She rubbed her fingernail against a stubborn seed to loosen it from the pepper.

"That sounds delicious. I'd eat those in a second."

Carlos tipped all of the vegetables into a big pitcher.

"Excellent, you might just get the opportunity some time."

He stuck a bunch of cilantro leaves and a hand-held blender inside the pitcher, and in about thirty seconds the roasted vegetables had become a fragrant olive-green sauce.

"See?" He turned to her for the first time in a while. "Now the tomatillo sauce is all . . . oh my God, what are you doing?"

She stopped, just as she'd pulled the stem off another dried chili.

"What? Isn't this what you told me to do?"

She had no idea why he was looking at her with that appalled look on his face.

He crossed the kitchen and picked up a box that had been sitting next to the bags of chilies.

"Gloves! Nik! Holy shit, you've been touching all of those chilies with your bare hands. Did I forget to tell you to put gloves on? Oh no."

She had no idea what he was talking about.

"What do gloves have to do with anything?"

He took her by the waist and pulled her over to the sink.

"You were touching dried hot chilies—and their seeds—with your bare hands. Your fingers are going to be on fire soon." He turned on the water and handed her the bottle of dish soap.

Oh.

Oooooh.

She poured the soap over her hands and scrubbed them with his sponge.

"I'm going to say something I don't normally say out loud, and especially not to men. I am an idiot."

He laughed but still looked concerned.

"I refuse to agree with that statement on the grounds that it may cause you to murder me."

She laughed.

"No, it's not your fault." She felt really stupid. "The box was sitting right there. I should have paid attention." She wiggled her nose. "It's okay. You don't have to stand over me and supervise my hand washing. Move on to your next task."

He picked up the box of surgical gloves and pulled a pair on.

"Okay, just keep washing your hands for a few more minutes while I work on these chilies."

She nodded. She reached up to scratch her nose, but caught herself just in time.

For the next few minutes he pulled the chilies open—taking a lot less care to remove all of the seeds than she had—while she scrubbed her hands. Finally, she turned off the water and turned to him.

"I think my hands are all right. But the thing is that my nose . . ."

He dropped a dried chili into the pot, with his latex-encased hands, and picked up another.

"Okay great, we must have caught it in time. Pull some gloves on and let's go."

She couldn't stand it anymore.

"I will in one second, but the thing is that my nose is on fire."

He dropped the chili and turned to her.

"What did you say?"

She grabbed his hand. It was getting worse by the second.

"My nose is on fire! My face! My face is on fire!"

He slowly looked up at her. Her face felt like it was bright red. How had it gotten so hot so fast? She wanted to submerge her head in a cold bathtub. Or a lake. Or maybe the ocean would help. No, too much salt.

"Your face. Oh shit. You touched your face, didn't you?"

She threw her hands in the air.

"Who cares, what does it matter? I mean, I guess I did, but I don't remember doing it, but also it's kind of moot right now because my face is on fire! What do we do to make this stop?"

She knew she wasn't being rational, but she didn't care. Because her face was on fire and getting hotter by the second.

Carlos opened the fridge and muttered to himself as he looked through it.

"Milk is good for capsaicin burns, but it's not like you can sit there with your nose in a bowl of milk, hmmmm."

He was being altogether too calm about this. What the fuck was he talking about, "capsaicin." This was not the time for fancy medical words. Had he not noticed that her FACE WAS ON FIRE?

"Carlos!"

"Sorry, sorry. What about this?" He took a tub of sour cream out of the fridge.

She took it from him.

"What do you mean 'what about this?' What's this going to do?" Why the hell was she even asking questions? She would literally do anything right now to make this stop.

He took the lid off of the tub of sour cream.

"Put it all over your face."

She narrowed her eyes at him, but scooped a big dollop out of the tub with her fingers anyway.

"Are you sure about this?"

He nodded.

"Of course I'm sure; I'm a doctor, aren't I? Smear a big layer of sour cream everywhere it hurts."

How the hell had she gotten herself here? This morning, she was waking up in her nice, normal bed in her nice, normal apartment in Silver Lake, and just a few hours later, a man was standing in front of her ordering her to smear sour cream all over her face. And the worst part was, she was going to do it.

"Fine, but if this doesn't work, I'm going to kill you and bury your body far, far away."

He nodded.

"You have my permission."

She patted the sour cream all over her nostrils, cheeks, and upper lip. It felt so soothing that she immediately applied more.

"There," he said. "Does that feel better?"

She dug her fingers back into the tub for more.

"God, yes. I'm not sure if it feels better because it's cold or if there's more to it, but I don't care right now—all that matters is that it feels better. Put the rest back in the fridge so that if it's the cold, I can put more on when this stuff warms up." She took a deep breath as the heat finally started to recede. "Please. I meant to say please, right there."

He grinned and put the tub back in the fridge. She turned to the sink and washed her hands to get the sour cream off, and then immediately took two surgical gloves from the box and put them on. After this experience, she wanted to wear them everywhere. She could be like one of those never nudes, except just for her hands. Who knew when hot chilies could attack you? Better to be prepared. People might think she was a lunatic, but those would just be uninformed people who had never experienced what she'd just experienced.

Carlos put his arm around her.

"Are you feeling better?" he asked. "It seems like the sour cream is helping?"

She turned to face him.

"Yeah, I think so. I feel like I'm cooling—"

Carlos burst out laughing.

"You . . . oh my god . . . the . . . your face!"

He was laughing so hard he bent over. She put her gloved hands on her hips while she waited for him to calm down from laughing at, not with, her. It wasn't her fault that his fucking chilies set her face on fire.

"It's just . . . you just . . ." He was laughing too hard to talk. Finally, he grabbed her by the hand and pulled her out of the kitchen and into the hallway that led to his bedroom.

"Where are you taking me? Are you trying to take me to bed?" She gestured to her face, which she knew from experience was set in a death glare. "Does this look like my 'I want to have sex' face?"

He stopped in the hallway and doubled over again, before he pulled himself together and dragged her into the bathroom.

"That! Look at that!" He pushed her in front of the mirror.

She'd been so distracted by gratitude for her face feeling better, that she'd sort of forgotten that she had *smeared sour cream all over her face.*

"Oh my God."

Carlos was shaking with laughter behind her.

"I know!"

"I look . . . I look like a drunken clown."

Carlos pointed at her. "You said it! I didn't! I did not say that! Remember, I did not say that!"

"Oh my God." She turned to Carlos, who started laughing again as soon as she turned around. She grinned, felt the drying sour cream crack as her face moved, and giggled at the ridiculous sensation. Soon, she was laughing so hard she could barely breathe.

She held up her gloved hands and laughed even harder.

"I'm sorry for laughing at you!" Carlos said, while still laughing at her. But she couldn't really blame him. "Does it still hurt? Do you need more sour cream?"

She shook her head, unable to talk. Eventually, she took a deep breath to answer him.

"More sour cream for my face, you mean? What do you think I am, a baked potato? Are you going to give me some butter and salt next?"

That destroyed both of them. Soon, they were both sitting on his bathroom floor, shaking with laughter and holding each other upright. Tears were streaming down her face, driving paths through the tacky sour cream, and that made her laugh even harder.

Finally, her laughter subsided.

"I'm sorry I yelled at you for laughing at me. And, you know, just in general."

He rested his arm around her shoulders.

"That's okay. Your face was on fire. I feel like you're allowed to yell when your face is on fire."

She took a deep breath.

"Oh my God, I feel like I've been exercising; my abs hurt from laughing that much."

He ran his hands through her hair.

"God, the last time I laughed that much was . . ." He paused for a while. "I can't even remember the last time I laughed that much. That felt pretty good."

She smiled up at him.

"Well, that makes it almost worth setting my face on fire, then." He opened his mouth, and she lifted her index finger and shook it at him. "I said *almost* worth it. Don't get any funny ideas."

He laughed.

"Okay, I have a confession to make."

Oh no. It was never good news when a man said that to you.

"What is it?"

He took a deep breath.

"I had no idea if the sour cream would work. When I said I was sure, what I meant was that I seriously couldn't think of anything else."

She punched him on the arm, and he fell back against the bathroom floor with a grin on his face.

"You asshole. I thought this was going to be a real confession. I'm very angry at you for making me smear sour cream on my face on a lark, but it worked so I can't really be mad at you, which makes me even madder."

He stood and offered her his hand to pull her up off of the floor.

"I know, it's a real conundrum, isn't it? Ready to attack these enchiladas again? This time with gloves on?"

She nodded.

"You know what they say. No glove, no love."

He groaned and pushed her ahead of him back into the kitchen.

• • •

An hour later, Carlos looked around his kitchen, satisfied. Nik was covering the last of the six trays of enchiladas with aluminum foil; soon they'd all go in the oven. She'd offered to wash the dishes, but he'd thought it would be cruel to let her wash the pot that the enchilada sauce had cooked in—those were the chilies that had attacked her, after all. So instead he was standing at the stove, elbow deep in soap bubbles, as he scrubbed all of his pans clean.

"Don't you have a dishwasher?" she asked him.

He nodded.

"Yeah, why?"

She looked at him like he'd lost his mind.

"Because you're scouring your pots like that by hand—why don't you just put them in the dishwasher?"

He rinsed the second to last pot and put it in his dish drainer.

"No child of Susana Ibarra would put pots in a dishwasher. Look, it took me until after med school to not completely wash my dishes before putting them in the dishwasher, okay? I have heard people say that they put pots in the dishwasher, in the same way I've heard people say they didn't have student loans or they drove to the Westside without traffic or they got a dirt-cheap plane ticket to Europe. All of those things seem imaginary to me, just in the same way putting my pots in the dishwasher would be."

She wet a paper towel and wiped down his counters.

"I get it. Some things, we just can't fight."

When the pots were done, he slid the first two trays into the oven and looked over at Nik.

"While we wait, why don't we . . ." Oh no. She still had sour cream on her face, but now it was dry and crusty. "Why don't we . . ." He couldn't laugh at her again; she'd kill him this time.

"Why don't we what?" She moved over to him and put her hand on his. Just then, a big flake of sour cream fell off of her face and onto the floor.

That did it. He leaned against the sink, laughing so hard he couldn't stand up straight.

"It's still . . ." He took a deep breath so he could talk. "It's still there! The sour cream! It's just all white and flaky now! You look like you have a skin disease!"

She didn't laugh. She just stared at him, until he got spooked and quieted down. Shit, he'd really pissed her off this time.

Finally, she moved closer to him.

"Carlos?" she asked.

"Yeah?" Oh no.

"Do you think I'm sexy?" And with that, she took the edge of the sheet of sour cream on her face and peeled it off in a big strip.

They laughed even harder this time than last time. Every time they would quiet down for a second, she would rub at her face and more disgusting white sour cream flakes would come off, and they'd both start back up again.

While they were still gasping with laughter, he heard the jingle of his ringtone. He pulled his phone out of his pocket. Jessie, probably calling to check on the status of her enchiladas.

"Hey, Jess!" he said, with laughter still in his voice. "Don't worry, they're in the oven. I'll bring them over for your nice big freezer tom—"

"Carlos, I'm at the hospital. They're saying I have to have the baby now. I'm scared."

"What?" He'd never heard this panicked tone in Jessie's voice before. "Back up, tell me what's going on."

He moved out of the kitchen into the living room.

"I took my blood pressure today, and it was high, so Jon and I came to the hospital. But I thought it would be okay, because that's happened a few times in the last few weeks and they just gave me a few more tests and sent me home." He could hear the tears in her voice. "But this time, after the other tests, they all looked really worried. Right now they're deciding if they're going to induce me or if I need to have an emergency C-section."

At that she broke down.

"I didn't want to have a C-section. I really wanted to . . . I had my birth plan ready so early. I knew just what I wanted to do . . . and I'm only thirty-four weeks; it's too early. What if there's something wrong with my baby?"

It broke his heart to hear Jessie cry like this. He wanted to cry just listening to her. Nik had come over to him, and without thinking, he reached for her hand. She wrapped her other arm around his waist.

"Jessie, where's Jon? Where's your mom? I'm coming. I'll be there as fast as I can get there, okay?"

Nik squeezed his hand and tried to pull away, but he wouldn't let her.

"Jon's here. He's calling his parents. I haven't called Mom yet; I wanted to call you first."

He nodded. The tension that had left his shoulders in the past two hours all fell back on them.

"Okay. Call your mom now. I'm on my way, okay? You or Jon call me if anything happens before I get there. I love you."

She sniffed and took a breath.

"I love you, too. See you soon."

When he hung up the phone, Nik put her arms around him. He sat down and pulled her onto his lap. He buried his head in her chest. Neither of them spoke.

Finally, he lifted his head.

"She sounded so scared. I've never heard Jessie sound scared before about anything." He pulled Nik closer. "I have to go now."

She nodded.

"I know."

But he sat there with his arms around her for a minute, her head in his chest, his nose in her hair. It was so hard to let go, but he did.

"Go, they need you," she said.

He walked into his bedroom to throw on a clean shirt and grab a hoodie. He came back out and sat at the table while he put his shoes on. Nik stood next to him and stroked his hair while he tied his shoes.

When he stood up and saw the kitchen, he put his head in his hands.

"Oh shit. What am I going to do about the enchiladas?"

She shook her head.

"Don't worry about that. I'll stay here and deal with them. Just give me whatever instructions you need to."

He hugged her.

"Oh, thank you so much." He checked the timer. "Okay, those are done in thirty minutes. When you take those out, the chicken ones cook for only twenty, with five minutes with the aluminum foil off at the end." He stepped back. "Are you sure? You don't have to do this, I can just . . ." She put her finger on his mouth to stop him from talking anymore.

"I'm sure. Go to the hospital. Keep me posted about Jessie?"

He kissed her hard on the mouth as an answer.

Chapter Seventeen

• • • • • •

On his way up to the maternity floor, Carlos wondered if anyone else in his family had gotten to the hospital yet. Probably not, but Tia Eva and his mom must be right behind him. He'd talked to Angela in the car on the way there, but she was on her way from Santa Monica, so it could take her God only knew how long to get there.

He quickened his pace as he got closer to Jessie's room. What if she wasn't there? What if she was already in surgery and hadn't had time to tell him? The room door was closed, and he knocked only once before opening it.

"Jessie!" She was on the bed, Jon sitting next to her and holding her hand.

"Thought you might be done with me already, huh?" she said. But she said it with a crack in her voice.

He made it to her bed in three steps so he could hug her.

"No, asshole, I thought you might already be in surgery, that's all." He stood back. "What's the plan? How are you?"

She took a deep breath and closed her eyes.

"The doctor said they're going to do a C-section. Soon," Jon said. He squeezed Jessie's hand. "It's going to be okay. They do these all the time here."

Carlos took her other hand.

"They do, I promise. I work here, remember? Would I work at a place where I'd worry about my cousin having surgery? Hell no. You and the baby will be great. I promise."

She nodded without opening her eyes.

"Thirty-four weeks is a pretty scary time to do this. My poor little girl. I thought I could hold on at least another month for her."

Carlos put his finger under Jessie's chin until she opened her eyes and looked at him.

"Jess. Jessica. Do not blame yourself. This isn't your fault. You have done everything right. *Everything.* You came to the hospital today because you just wanted to double-check, even though you thought it was fine—that was you making all of the right decisions to keep your little girl as healthy as she can possibly be. Doing this C-section, even though it's something you never wanted, is you making another choice for your little girl, okay? This hospital has a great NICU, and you're in really good hands. I promise."

She nodded as tears slid down her face.

"You'll stay? Until she's out? Until it's all done?"

He gripped her hand.

"You're going to have to send me away—that's how long I'm going to stay."

The door banged open, and his mother and aunt stormed into the room.

"Jessica!" He stood back to allow his aunt to throw her arms around Jessie. "Mommy will take care of everything."

He and Jon locked eyes. He barely managed to not laugh out loud. Leave it to Tia Eva to give them some levity.

It was only about ten minutes later when the doctors came into the room to prep Jessie for the surgery and kicked everyone but Jon out. They all filed into the nearest waiting room. Thank God his mom was here to calm Tia Eva down. He put his arms around his mom for a minute. She hated hospitals.

"Anyone want anything while we wait?" he asked them. "I can go to the cafeteria to get us something to eat or drink."

"Oh, I couldn't eat anything!" Tia Eva said.

His mom smiled at him. They both knew she'd want something as soon as he left.

"I'm sure Tia won't be able to eat anything, but why don't you bring us back some coffee and maybe some cookies or something like that? We might be here for a while. Coffee might be good. Don't you think, Carlos?"

"Great idea, Mama," he said, and walked out

of the waiting room before Tia Eva thought of something she might want.

On his way down in the elevator, he pulled his phone out of his pocket. Shit, he'd forgotten to charge it last night, and now he was down to three percent battery. Did he still have that charger in his office? He hoped so, or else this was going to be a very long night.

He had texts from many of his family members, but he ignored them all and clicked on the text from Nik.

How's Jessie? How are you?

He sighed. He wished he was back at his house with her, laughing and eating enchiladas. He could really use one of her hugs right now.

She's about to have an emergency c-section. I got to talk to her for a little bit. She's anxious and scared but powering through. I'm in the waiting room with my mom and aunt for the foreseeable future, just escaped to the cafeteria for drinks and snacks.

The elevator doors opened, and he walked into the cafeteria. All hospital cafeterias were terrible in their own ways. His, like many newer hospitals, had been trying to do a healthy food push, which meant that the food was no longer terrible junk food, but terrible healthy food.

Is Angie there yet? That'll help, right?

He filled up three coffee cups, one with a ton of milk and sugar for his aunt and two others with decreasing amounts of both for his mom and himself. He found a stack of oatmeal raisin cookies and grabbed as many as he could carry. He texted Nik when he was in line to pay.

Not yet, she's on her way from a meeting on the westside so it could be a while.

Oh shit, he needed to let Angie know about the C-section as soon as possible. But his battery was almost gone, and he did not want to tell her with his mom and aunt right there. He could run to his office right now, but Tia Eva was probably upstairs even more worried than he was. He needed to get back there. And he couldn't text Angie about this from his almost dead phone—she'd freak out when she couldn't get in touch with him.

Nik already knew what was going on. Could she call Angela?

No, he didn't want that. He liked to keep his personal life and his family strictly separate. And plus, Angela would go crazy with the whole "girlfriend" thing then.

But this was an emergency, and he didn't seem to have a better option.

Can I ask you a huge favor? Can you call my sister and let her know Jessie's in surgery now for a c-section? Long story but she doesn't know yet and my battery is almost out. I might have a charger somewhere, but I should let her know asap.

He stared at his phone until she texted him

back. Luckily, there were a number of people ahead of him in line. Saturday early evenings were busy times in hospital cafeterias.

Of course, just text me her number.

He sent Angie's number to Nik and walked back to the elevator balancing all of his beverages and food.

Nik checked the timer on her phone. Five more minutes before she needed to take the enchiladas out of the oven. She had a minute to call Angela before the timer went off.

The problem was that the thought of calling Angela freaked her out. Would his sister be mad about her having this news when actual family didn't? Nik wouldn't blame her if she did. Also, she had no idea what Carlos had told Angela about her, if anything. She knew that Carlos and his sister were really close, but she didn't know if they talked about stuff like this. At the bar after the baseball game, Angela had seemed relaxed and funny, just like Carlos . . . but it could be a different story if she knew Nik was sleeping with her brother.

"Oh my God, just call her already," she said out loud to Carlos's sliding glass window. The window didn't respond.

She cold-called people all the time—it was literally part of her job—and yet she was frozen with her finger over the phone.

307

She sighed and hit call. Maybe Angela wouldn't pick up? Most people didn't pick up calls from numbers they didn't know. Maybe she could just leave Angela a message. She obviously wouldn't call back, and then—

"Hello? Hello, this is Angela, who's this? Is it the hospital?"

Nik cleared her throat.

"Hi, Angela. Um, no, not the hospital. This is Nik. We met at Dodger Stadium?"

Oh Lord, she was doing that uptalk thing that she always instructed younger women against doing. Come on, Nikole. Get it together.

"Oh. Hi, Nik. Uh . . ."

Right, she should get on with it.

"Carlos asked me to call you. He's at the hospital and his battery is almost dead, but he knew you'd want an update."

"Oh." That was a weird "Oh," right? Maybe. It sounded more like an "ooooh." But she'd only met Angela once—that might just be how she talked. "Thanks for calling. What's going on with Jessie?"

"Carlos said they just brought Jessie in to get an emergency C-section, and that your mom and your aunt are both there at the hospital with him."

Angela let out a deep breath.

"Oh no. I know she was trying so hard to avoid a C-section. She must be so scared."

Nik nodded as she stared through the window.

One of Carlos's neighbors, an older man with big glasses and a cane whom she'd seen a few times before, walked by and waved at her. She waved back.

"She talked to Carlos when they first told her it was a possibility, and I think she was pretty worried. I know Carlos got to the hospital in time to see her before the surgery, and I'm sure that helped."

Nik's timer went off, and she pushed buttons on her phone madly to make it stop making noise.

"What was that?" Angela asked.

"Oh, I'm at Carlos's house. We were making enchiladas for Jessie when he got the call, so I stayed here to let them finish in the oven. That was just my timer."

Why was she babbling? She could have just said that was her phone timer and let it alone.

"Oh." *That* "Oh" had definitely been more . . . smug? Hmmm. "Okay. Is there anything else he said to tell me?"

Nik wedged the phone between her shoulder and ear and put oven mitts on. She didn't need to burn her hands, too.

"That's everything I know. I hope you get there soon, and I hope all goes well with your cousin."

Nik opened the oven and carefully took out the trays of enchiladas.

"Thanks, Nik. And thanks for calling."

"Bye, Angie."

Oh shit. She'd slipped and called his sister Angie. That's what Carlos always called her, and so that's how Nik thought of her, but she'd very clearly introduced herself as Angela when they'd met.

Well, now his sister probably hated her.

Or maybe his sister barely gave her a second thought, since her mind was kind of occupied with her cousin undergoing emergency surgery at that exact moment? Yes, that was more likely. Way to make everything about yourself, Nikole.

She slid the remaining two trays of enchiladas into the oven. Cooking and agonizing over whether people were mad at her. This was definitely not how she usually spent Saturday nights.

She picked up her bag from where she'd dropped it by the door and brought it over to Carlos's couch. Thank goodness she'd brought her laptop with her; at least she could get some work done while she waited to hear what was going on with Jessie and her baby.

She set her laptop on the coffee table, opened it, and instead of getting work done, mindlessly scrolled through her various social media news feeds for way too long. No, this wasn't helpful. She stood up and walked back into the kitchen. Maybe she needed a snack. Oh God, yes, a snack sounded like a great idea. And Carlos had tortilla chips, how perfect. Something she could stress-eat for hours as she got more and more tense, just what she needed.

Shit, the enchiladas. She'd put the second round in the oven right after getting off the phone with Angela, but she hadn't set her timer. Carlos had said twenty minutes, but she had no idea how long they'd already been in there. Five minutes, ten? She could check them, but she didn't have a clue what enchiladas would look like after five minutes versus after ten versus after fifteen, so that would be no help. She set her timer for fifteen minutes and crossed her fingers.

You guys, I'm freaking out—I'm at Carlos's house and he left in a rush because his cousin is going to have an emergency c-section, and I stayed here to babysit the enchiladas we were making her, and I may have ruined them. That was a slight overstatement, but that's how it felt to her, okay? Now I'm sitting here waiting to hear any news and stress eating chips.

That reminded her. She got up and went to the fridge and got the jar of salsa.

It must have been an emergency, who the fuck would leave you in charge of food in the oven?

Thanks, Courtney. Always there with a kind word.

No, but seriously, of course you're freaking out, that's stressful. Do you know what's going on? Do they need cupcakes? I'm just packing up the shop—we were open late tonight, I have some left over.

Ooh, cupcakes were a great idea. Not for Carlos, for herself.

I desperately want all of your cupcakes, but I feel like they strike the wrong note when no one knows what's going to happen. Like, "here's some cupcakes to celebrate this stressful emergency!" you know? He texted me after he got to the hospital and said they were bringing her in for surgery, but that's all I know.

She wanted to text him again, but she had no idea if his phone had power yet. And even if it did, he was probably busy with his family; he probably didn't want to hear from her. She reached for another chip just as Dana texted.

Oh no, Nik! Poor Carlos and his poor cousin. Do you need anything?

Did she need anything? Yes, lots of things: Carlos to be on the couch next to her; his cousin—who she'd never met, but felt a kinship to because of their shared love for serial killer books—to be okay; his cousin's baby to be okay; his sister to not hate her for calling her Angie; to know what to do right now; cupcakes. Dana couldn't get her any of those things, though.

No, I'm okay. I have my laptop here, I'll be fine. Just worried, that's all.

Both of her friends texted back in quick succession.

312

Okay, keep us posted. We're here if you need anything!

Let me know if you need bourbon, or change your mind about cupcakes, or if you need anything else.

She spent the next thirty minutes trying to find something to occupy her mind: she finished cleaning the kitchen; she tried and failed to edit the story she'd been working on that day; she took the enchiladas out of the oven; she thought about snooping in his medicine cabinet—it was really the perfect opportunity to do some snooping when he wasn't around to catch her—but she didn't have the heart to do it. Everywhere she went, she kept her phone in her pocket, but he never texted.

She felt so helpless. She kept remembering that look on his face when he'd answered the phone and heard his cousin crying, and how when he'd gotten off the phone, he hadn't said a word but had held on to her so tightly. She wanted to do something, anything, to fix this, to make him feel better, but there was nothing she could do.

Finally, she texted him out of sheer anxiety.

Any news? How are you doing?

He texted back right away. He must have found a charger.

Starving. Wish I had some of those enchiladas we made. No news yet but it should be soon—c-sections don't take all that long. I might start freaking out if we don't hear something soon, actually.

"Might" start freaking out—she was pretty sure he was already freaked out and just trying to keep it together.

Keep me posted, okay? If you have time.

She opened a cabinet door in the kitchen to grab the aluminum foil to cover the enchilada pans, and next to it, she saw a stack of paper plates and plastic cutlery.

Should she . . . ?

No, that was ridiculous.

But Carlos and his whole family were all at the hospital. And they were starving. And all the food was right there. And the hospital was only about fifteen minutes away. And this was the one thing she could do to help.

She wrapped a pan in aluminum foil and put it in a grocery bag, stacked the paper plates and plastic forks in another, and was in her car three minutes later.

The entire way to the hospital, she kept thinking about turning around. He probably didn't want her there. If they were really hungry, they could probably get food from the cafeteria or something, couldn't they? But she kept thinking about his last text and the look on his face when he'd hung up the phone and the sound of his cousin crying on the phone to him, so she kept going.

She parked in the hospital parking garage and carefully lifted the bag full of still warm enchiladas out of the back seat of her car. Then she stopped, put everything down, and put lipstick on before she picked it all back up again. She carried everything into the hospital and asked the way to the maternity ward.

"Are you family?" the woman at the front desk asked her.

"No . . . but a family friend," she said. That was only sort of a lie, right? She lifted the bags she was carrying. "I'm bringing food to the family. She's in an emergency C-section now, and the family is all in the waiting room."

She really hoped the woman didn't ask her Jessie's last name, because she'd just realized she didn't know it.

"Oh, that's great. It's the seventh floor. Go on up. Turn left. You won't be able to miss the waiting room."

She was right; she couldn't miss it. She could hear them talking as she approached the waiting room. That must be a good sign. If anything bad had happened, they'd all be pretty quiet.

This was a terrible idea. Why hadn't she texted Courtney and Dana when she'd thought of it? They would have told her it was a terrible idea. This is what happens when you don't ask your friends for advice—you make stupid decisions.

She could still turn around and go back.

Maybe she should still turn around and go back?

She straightened her shoulders and walked in.

"Nik!" Carlos stood up when he saw Nik walk through the door. What the hell was she doing there?

She had two big grocery bags in her hand and a very tentative smile on her face. He didn't meet her eyes.

"I thought you guys might be hungry, so I brought some enchiladas over."

Did she think that's what he was asking for when he texted her that he wished he'd had some of the enchiladas? Because, wow, that had not been what he meant.

He tried to smile and took the bags from her. Now he had to introduce her to his mother. He hadn't introduced a woman to his mother since he was in his early twenties.

"Mama, Tia Eva, this is my friend Nik. She was helping me make enchiladas for Jessie when I got Jessie's call, so, um . . ." He looked down at the bags. "I hope you're as hungry as I am."

He opened the bags and set out the food, all without looking at Nik. His stomach rumbled when he unwrapped the tight aluminum foil from the baking pans.

"Nikole, did you say? It's nice to meet you," his mother said. Nik handed him the paper plates, and he dished up enchiladas for his mom.

"It's nice to meet you, too," Nik said.

"How do you and Carlos know each other?" Tia Eva asked her.

Oh shit. How were they supposed to answer this?

"Through me," Angela said from behind them. "Thanks for bringing over the food, Nik!"

Thank God for Angela. And this had the benefit of even being sort of true. As Angie hugged Nik, she stared right at him. Her smile was very smug. Damn it.

"It was no problem at all," Nik said. "But um, I should go, I don't want to intrude, I know this is family time. I'll just talk to you later and you can let me know how everything goes, okay?"

"Oh no, you can't go now!" His mom picked up a paper plate. "You have to stay and eat enchiladas with us after making all that effort." She scooped two enchiladas onto Nik's plate and handed it to her without waiting for a response.

Nik glanced at Carlos and shrugged. He turned away to dish up his own plate. Maybe her feelings were hurt that he hadn't been thrilled when she walked in, but it was her own fault for showing up without checking with him first. She went to sit on the other side of the room with her food.

Angela looked at him, at Nik sitting alone, and back at him with a glare. *Fine.* He made a plate for himself and sat down next to Nik. He wasn't sure what to say to her, not with his mom and aunt right across the room and his sister . . . oh wow, his sister sat down right next to him.

"They could have been a little spicier, you know, Carlos," his mom said. "What kinds of chilies did you use? You should have added hotter ones in there. You're too used to cooking for," she glanced in Nik's direction, "your friends, not your family."

He and Nik looked at each other for a split second with laughter in their eyes, and both immediately looked away. He could only imagine how long she'd have had to keep the sour cream on her face if he'd used hotter chilies.

"No, Mama—I usually make it spicier, but I toned down the spice in these because I was making them for Jessie for after the baby, and I know a lot of breastfeeding mothers like to avoid food that's too spicy. It can upset the baby's stomach."

His aunt made a hand motion like she was batting the whole idea of what he'd said out of the room.

"*Our* babies don't get their stomachs upset by spicy food. You're listening to too many of those other doctors. I'm sure Jessie isn't worried about that."

Carlos knew there was no point in responding to that one.

"Where did you get the meat?" his aunt asked. "It's good, but you probably paid too much for it, in one of those fancy grocery stories you go to over there."

"I got it at El Rancho market, Tia Eva."

Tia Eva took another bite and changed the subject. Carlos tried not to smile.

Soon, his mom and aunt were in a deep discussion about the woman who used to live across the street from them with her children.

"I'm sorry," Nik said under her breath to him. "I wasn't thinking. I was just worried about everything, but I shouldn't have just shown up here. I'll go as soon as I finish my food."

He shrugged.

"Now that you're here, you might as well stay for a little while."

She scooped some enchilada onto her fork.

"Well, I don't know what your mom and aunt were complaining about: these are the best enchiladas I've ever had."

He grinned at her. It always thrilled him when she complimented his cooking; he couldn't help it.

"I'm glad you liked them, especially after what they did to you. And I feel better, now that I got some food in me. I was so stressed before you got here—*my* blood pressure was probably sky-high."

She looked at him sideways.

"Hmm, you know one way to find out how high your blood pressure is? Going to the doctor."

Did she really need to bring that up right now? With his sister right there? He looked away.

She nudged him with her knee.

"I'm sorry. You left me such a perfect opening there, but I should have resisted. This isn't the time for that. Forget I said anything and have another enchilada."

He shook his head and smiled, despite himself. He nudged her with his knee back.

"I can't stand you. Did you know that?"

She grinned at him. "I know."

He touched her hand for a second. He couldn't help it. Even though he hated that she'd come, he felt better with her here next to him. He sighed.

"Sorry if I seem on edge, I'm just so worried. I'm five minutes away from charging in there and waving my badge around and demanding answers." He paused. "That *might* get me fired, but I'd probably get the answers first."

She laughed.

"Yeah, maybe don't do that. At least, not just yet."

She took his empty plate and Angela's and got up to toss them away. While she was gone, Angie leaned over to him.

"I knew it," she said.

He didn't have time to respond before Nik sat back down.

She sat closer to him this time, so close that her shoulder was touching his. Every part of him wanted to put his arm around her, but instead he moved his legs so he was touching hers. She smiled but didn't look at him.

They sat like that in silence for a few minutes, until Angela leaned over.

"Carlos, I'm going crazy here. Is it supposed to take this long? Do you think something is wrong?"

He opened his mouth to answer, when Jon burst into the room.

"Everyone is okay!" he said, with a huge smile on his face.

The whole room was on their feet. Nik put her hand on his arm.

"Jessica? The baby?" Tia Eva asked, her voice wavering.

"Jessie is fine and the baby is, too!" he said. Tears started running down his face.

Oh thank God.

"When can we see them?" he asked Jon. "Everything's fine? Really?"

Tia Eva was sobbing into Jon's arms. He looked up from her and nodded at Carlos.

"Really. They're both hooked up to a few machines, and the baby's going to have to stay in the hospital for a week or so, they think, but the doctors say she'll be all right. I'm not sure when you can see them, but sometime tonight. I've got to get back to them right away, but I wanted to tell you all the good news."

Carlos's hand somehow made its way into Nik's. She squeezed hard, and he squeezed back.

"What's her name?" His mom asked, just as Jon was about to leave the room. "Jessie said you hadn't decided yet."

He smiled.

"I think she wanted to be the one to tell you guys. I don't want to spoil that for her. Just a little while longer."

And before anyone else could ask him a question, he raced back down the hall.

Carlos pulled Nik and Angela together into a hug and buried his head in Nik's shoulder.

"They're going to be all right!" That was all he could say, over and over.

When he finally let them go, he realized his face was wet.

"I don't even know why I'm crying," Nik said. "I don't even like babies."

He and Angela both laughed as the tears streamed from their eyes.

Carlos wiped his eyes with his sleeve, and then went over to hug his mom and his aunt.

After a few minutes, he came back to Nik. She'd found a box of tissues. She took a few and handed the box to Angela, who brought them over to their mom and aunt.

"Oh thank God," he said. "I'm so relieved. I'm so happy."

He gave her another enormous hug.

"I don't even know Jessie," she said. "I don't know why I'm crying."

He grinned.

"You probably got some chili in your eye; don't worry about it."

She laughed between her tears.

"That must be it." She pulled away and wiped her eyes again. "I should go now, though. I don't want to be in the way. This is a family thing."

Carlos shook his head.

"Oh no you don't. You can't leave now. Wait at least until we find out if we can see Jessie."

Carlos sat back down and threw his arms around both Angela and Nik. Luckily, he was pretty sure his mom and aunt were too distracted by their discussion of what the baby name could be to notice.

Finally, Jon bounced back into the room.

"You can all see Jessie, but only for a few minutes, okay? The baby is in the NICU. I'm going back to her, but I'll take you to Jessie first."

"Jessica!" Tia Eva raced into the room and threw her arms around Jessie. "I was so worried. I love you so much."

Well, that did it. The whole room was crying again. Including both him and Jon.

When it was his turn to give Jessie a hug, he pulled Nik along with him.

"This is Nik. She's the one who recommended all of those creepy books I bought you that you

323

loved. She dropped by to bring food for all of us while we were waiting, and I made her stay so she could meet you."

Jessie was glowing, despite the tears still streaming down her face. She reached out to grab Nik's hand.

"Nik, it's so nice to meet you. Those books kept me from going crazy over the past five weeks, I can't thank you enough."

Nik smiled back at her.

"I was happy to help. And I'm so happy that everything went well today."

Jessie beamed at her.

"Me too. We still have a bumpy road ahead. She'll be in the NICU for a while, and I'm"— more tears spilled from her eyes, and Carlos put his hand on her shoulder—"worried, but the doctors seem very optimistic, so I'm going to be optimistic, too."

"What is her NAME?" his mom said from the other side of the room.

Jessie smiled. He and Nik stepped back so everyone could see her.

"Her name." Jessie looked at her mom and smiled. "Her name is Eva Jane. After her two grandmothers."

Tia Eva charged the bed and would have tackled Jessie with her hug if Carlos hadn't intervened.

Chapter Eighteen

· · · · · ·

As soon as Carlos walked inside his house, he fell down onto his couch and tugged Nik down with him.

"I am so damn tired," he said.

He buried his head in the curve of her neck and finally let his face relax.

"I could not be happier right now to be here on the couch with you. I managed to keep it together around my family for most of the night, and now I need to let myself fall apart for, like, thirty seconds."

She wrapped her arms around him. He breathed in her smell, her warmth, her presence. They lay there in silence for a long time.

She kissed him on the cheek.

"Hey. I'm really sorry that I showed up at the hospital without checking with you. I think I made something already stressful for you harder. I feel really bad about that."

He'd already forgotten that he'd been irritated when Nik walked in. So much had happened tonight.

"No, it's okay," he said. "I was surprised when

you showed up, but I think having you—and the enchiladas—there made it easier on everyone. Plus, my mom hates hospitals and getting to criticize my cooking helped take her mind off of things."

She ran her fingers slowly through his hair and he closed his eyes. He wished he could stay like this forever.

"When my dad died . . . my mom was at the hospital with him by herself. She'd called both me and Angie, but neither of us got there in time. It was pretty hard on her. I don't think she's set foot in a hospital since. I could tell she was having a tough time there tonight, especially since we were all so worried." He bent down and kissed her hand. "The enchiladas helped. Thank you."

She squeezed his hand.

"Did you . . . how was yesterday?"

He pushed her hair back from her face and smiled at her. Of course she'd remembered.

"I spent the evening with Angie. She said Mama likes to spend the day at church. Angie usually spends it with friends or Jessie. The first year Angie asked me if I wanted to meet up with her, but I told her I had to work. Which was true, but I'd switched with someone to make sure I was working all day that day." He ran his finger down her cheek. "But yesterday the two of us ate a lot of tacos and drank some of Dad's favorite beer, and just . . . talked." He never would have spent the anniversary of his dad's death with Angela if it hadn't been for Nik. He was so glad he had. "Thanks for . . . well, thanks."

She smiled up at him.

"You're welcome."

He leaned forward the few inches between them and kissed her. It had been so hard to not kiss her in the hospital. She kissed him back hard. They dove into each other like they were parched, like it had been just weeks and not hours since they'd last kissed, like she'd wanted to kiss him in these last few hours as much as he'd wanted to kiss her.

He started to pull off her shirt, then stopped and sat up.

"Come to bed. Please?"

She stood up and reached her hand out to him.

Once in his bedroom, he wasted no time in undressing her. She stood there and let him unbutton her shirt, pull off her tank top, unzip her jeans and pull them down to the floor, until she was in only a matching set of a hot pink bra and underwear.

"Where did this come from?" he asked her, as he ran his finger over the lace on the bra.

She smiled and reached for him, but he stepped away. He wanted to concentrate on her first.

"I bought it last week," she said. "I thought you might like it."

He touched the lace at her hip and ran his finger

underneath it. He kept going until she gasped. He liked it when she made that noise.

"Lie down," he said. She obeyed him at once.

"Open your legs." He knelt on the bed in between her legs and stroked her underwear again, first on the outside, and then on the inside.

"You were right. I do like these. I like them a lot. But it's time for them to go." He grabbed them from each side and pulled them off her body. She looked down at him. She was already breathing hard. So was he.

He bent his head down to where the underwear had been.

"Let's see how much you like something now."

By her gasps and screams and fingernails in his back, she liked that a lot, too.

"You have *got* to get those clothes off," she said afterward, as he crawled over her body.

"I had to wait! You would have drawn blood otherwise. Take pity on a poor man."

She inspected her fingernails and laughed.

"I'll cut them before next time." She lay there and watched him as he jumped off the bed, threw his clothes off, and rolled a condom on.

He climbed back on top of her and paused.

"We need to get this off, as much as I love it." He unsnapped her bra and threw it aside. "Ahhh, that's better." He caressed her breasts, and she moaned and closed her eyes. He slid inside of her while her eyes were still closed, and she smiled and clenched around him as their bodies came together.

Afterward, he collapsed on top of her, his head nestled in the hollow between her breasts.

"Mmmm. You know what?" he asked her.

"What?"

"You taste like chilies."

They both laughed until they cried. He fell asleep, still with a smile on his face.

Carlos woke up the next morning, Nik's head on his chest, her curls tickling his nose. He looked down at her and smiled. He was so happy to have her with him. He wished she could be with him all the time. His life was so much better with her in it.

"Holy shit." He sat bolt upright, and she groaned and rolled onto his pillow.

"What? Do you have to be at the hospital?"

He shook his head and stared at her.

"I'm in love with you! I love you!"

He hadn't meant for this to happen. He'd just thought they were going along, having great sex and hanging out a lot, too, sure, but that it was all just fun. But along the way, he'd fallen in love with this smart, abrasive, caring, hilarious woman.

Now she sat up.

"What? You what?"

He turned to face her. How had he not realized this was happening? She was still half asleep, her

329

hair was standing up straight, and she had that scowl on her face that she always had first thing in the morning. He loved her so much.

"I was just lying here awake and thinking about yesterday, and how happy I was that you were at the hospital, and how happy I was to wake up in bed with you, and how happy I always am with you. And I realized I love you."

Sure, he hadn't meant for this to happen, but he was so glad it had. They would be perfect together. They were *already* perfect together. They got along so well; they laughed together so much; they'd understood each other from the very beginning. Her friends liked him; his friends like her. Hell, his family even liked her after last night. The timing was all wrong, but that didn't matter. This was going to be so great.

She rubbed her eyes and wrapped the sheet tighter around her body.

"Are you sure you're awake? You had a pretty stressful day yesterday. If this is you talking in your sleep or the end of a dream or something, it's okay, I won't be mad. Go back to sleep and we can pretend this never happened."

That was the weirdest reaction to an "I love you" that he'd ever heard of.

"I don't want to pretend this never happened! I'm in love with you!"

"Oh my God, will you stop saying that?" She looked terrified. Why did she look like that?

"Really? That's your reaction?" he asked her.

She shook her head.

"I'm sorry. I didn't mean it like that; it's just you woke me up with this and I'm so confused."

He got out of bed.

"Okay. Let me go make us some coffee. I'll be back."

He pulled sweatpants on and went into the kitchen. Had he been dreaming? Was this just him being emotional after last night and making some big declaration for no reason?

No. This wasn't that. He loved her. If the emotions of last night had made him realize it earlier, fine, but it would have come out at some point anyway.

Had he measured the right amount of coffee into the filter? He'd been so busy thinking about Nik that he couldn't tell. He dumped it all out into a bowl and measured it again and put all of it, plus two more scoops, back into the machine.

When he went back into the bedroom Nik had put on yoga pants and his old UCLA T-shirt. She was sitting on the edge of the bed. He handed her coffee and sat down next to her.

"I thought about this when I was making the coffee, and the thing is, I love you."

She wrapped her hands around her coffee cup and let out a deep breath.

"Okay. What do you mean you love me? That doesn't make sense. We haven't even known each other for that long. You told me you didn't want a relationship!"

He took a gulp of his way too hot coffee and winced.

"That's all true. Well, except that it does make sense, it makes perfect sense to me. Also, we've known each other long enough to know how we feel about each other. We've seen each other in some serious ups and some pretty bad downs. When I'm having a hard time, you're the perfect person to have around, because you're warm and comforting, but you're also honest with me, even when you're saying something I don't necessarily want to hear. And you know exactly when and how to make me laugh."

He took another sip of coffee. It was still too hot.

"And, I did say I didn't want a relationship. But you know what?" He made a wide gesture around the two of them. "This is a relationship! We see each other at least twice a week. You wake up here in my bed and you stay here and hang out with me instead of racing home. We text all the time. You helped me make food for my cousin. I met your friends; you met my friends. You met my family!"

She blew on the top of the coffee but didn't take a sip.

"I know, but that all doesn't mean we're in a relationship. It just means that we're good friends. Good friends, who also sometimes have sex."

He raised his eyebrows.

"Sometimes?"

She rolled her eyes.

"More than sometimes, but you know what I mean!" She finally took a sip of her coffee. He watched her face while she drank it. He loved that way she always closed her eyes and smiled at the first sip of coffee every morning. How had it taken him this long to realize that he loved her? Sure, it had only been six weeks, but now that he realized it, he knew he'd felt this way for a while.

"I do know what you mean, but I have plenty of good friends—even good female friends—and I don't feel about them the way I feel about you, sex or no sex."

She raised her mug to her mouth again but lowered it without drinking any.

"I just . . . I thought we were both clear about what we wanted here. I was having a great time—I *am* having a great time with you. I just didn't expect this today. Or ever."

He set his mug down on his bedside table and took her hand.

"Look. I didn't intend for this to happen, but it did. Can we talk about what happens next?"

She didn't let go of his hand, but she didn't exactly hold on to it, either.

"I don't really know what you want me to say.

I was happy going along the way we had been going."

He nodded.

"So was I. I'm happy to keep going along the way we've been going, too."

She narrowed her eyes at him.

"I think there's a 'but' at the end of that sentence."

He couldn't help but laugh at the skeptical look on her face. She always read him so well. That was another reason he loved her.

"Fine, you're right. I'm happy to keep going along the way we've been going, *but* I'm in love with you. I get if you're not ready to say it back right now, but I can't pretend that's not how I feel."

She let go of his hand. Fuck.

"Carlos." She started with his name. That was never a good sign. "I like you so much, and we've had a great time together, but this isn't what I want." He tried to break in, but she stopped him. "That you say you love me . . . it changes things. It changes everything."

Why was she acting like this? What was wrong with her?

"Why do you say that it changes everything? It doesn't have to! And if it changes things, can't it change them for the better?"

She shook her head.

"No. No, it can't change things for the better. It

never does. It'll mean you'll want more from me, things I'm not prepared to give you, and it'll ruin everything good about what we had." She put her coffee cup down. "Don't you think this was just an endorphin high or something from last night? You can say yes. I won't get mad. I'm pretty sure you'll be relieved in a day or so that I didn't take you seriously about this."

He stood up. He couldn't believe what he was hearing.

"No, I won't. I won't be glad you didn't take me seriously. This isn't an endorphin high, and I don't want to keep fucking doing what we had been doing. I'm in love with you, Nik! We have something special here, and I know you know it, too. In the short time you and I have known each other, we've been there for each other in all the ways that count. I've told you things about my life and my work and my family that I've never told anyone else."

He looked at her, sitting at the end of his bed staring down into her coffee cup instead of looking at him. He was suddenly furious.

"Does that even matter to you? Or is it just that you're good at asking questions, so you used me as journalism practice, to get me to spill all of my secrets? Did you think you'd won something when you got me to talk to you about my dad's death? 'Stupid Carlos, he doesn't realize I don't give a fuck about him. I'm just taking notes on what technique worked this time.' Was that it?"

She stood up to face him. At least now she was looking at him.

"Or is it just that you get off on getting men to fall in love with you and then rejecting them? Five months for Fisher, what's it been, six, seven weeks for me? Was I your new record? I bet you're thrilled now. Are you going to go celebrate tonight? Another guy that the great Nik Paterson couldn't care less about fell in love with her; where's the confetti?"

"No, Carlos, what a shitty thing to say. You know that wasn't it. You know I really do care about you."

He turned his back on her and grabbed a shirt out of his dresser.

"That's bullshit. I tell you I love you, and you tell me you *care* about me."

He pulled the shirt on as he walked out of his bedroom. He grabbed his keys off of his coffee table.

"Are you seriously going to leave right now while we're still in the middle of this?" she said from the hallway.

He didn't look at her as he slid on the shoes next to his front door.

"We're not in the middle of this anymore. We're done with this. Isn't that what you've been telling me? I can't believe you met my family. I wish you hadn't bothered to come to the hospital last night. If you really cared about me, you wouldn't have wasted my time. Fuck caring about me."

He saw her flinch right before he slammed the door.

Chapter Nineteen

• • • • • •

Nik stood in Carlos's living room and stared at the front door. What the hell had just happened?

Her bag was on the floor by the couch. She dug through it for her phone.

Where are you guys? I think Carlos and I just broke up?

As she waited for Courtney or Dana to text back, she collected her stuff from throughout his house: her oversized Stanford hoodie that she'd left here a few weeks ago in his closet, her bobby pins on the nightstand, a travel-sized bottle of her conditioner in his shower. As she walked around and tossed her things in her bag, she got more and more angry. What the fuck was wrong with him, springing "I love you" on her like that and then getting mad at her for not falling all over herself being thrilled about it?

Trust her to get involved with the kind of guy who was so full of himself he imagined his love was God's gift to any woman.

Oh shit. At the shop and I can't leave. Come here? I have bourbon in the back.

Nik put her shoes on and grabbed her keys out of her bag.

Be there in 15 min.

She'd known from the beginning that he was arrogant and thought he knew everything, but she'd let herself ignore that because he was so much fun. She never should have dated him in the first place.

It took more like thirty minutes to get to Cupcake Park, given the vicissitudes of L.A. traffic and parking. Thirty minutes of listening to her most angry music on repeat and fantasizing about hitting cars with baseball bats. So when she walked up to the shop and was faced with a line out the door, she almost pushed herself through the crowd of chattering, happy people like a battering ram.

Luckily, she came to her senses before she ruined her friend's business. She turned around and went through the alley and in the back door. She couldn't help but think about when Carlos had rescued them when Courtney had her cupcake crisis . . . and about everything that happened later that night. Damn him.

She went through the kitchen and into the shop.

"Hey," she said to Courtney, as she popped up behind her. Courtney jumped and spun around.

"Holy shit, you scared me to death. I was wondering if you were stuck in this line."

Nik shook her head.

"I saw it and came through the back door. But this is amazing, look at all of the people here, and it's only nine a.m."

Courtney nodded and loaded half a dozen confetti cupcakes into a box.

"I know, it was like this yesterday, too. The *L.A. Times* did a piece on the shop this week, *and* someone on the Food Network came by this week and Instagrammed all the cupcakes she bought, so people are going wild."

How had she missed all of this? She'd known everything that had happened with Courtney's shop for the past year, and she'd missed an article in the *Times*?

"This is so awesome, Courtney!" she said, and hugged her friend. "You're a hit!"

Courtney hugged her back, but quickly turned back to her cupcakes.

"It's great for business. I just hope we don't screw it up. I made triple the cupcakes this morning, with more flavors than we usually have most days because I thought it would be like this today and I wanted to make sure to capitalize on this. Keep your fingers crossed."

Nik held up her crossed fingers as they walked into the back room.

"Dana texted that she's on her way," Courtney said. "Tell her to come through the back. I'm going to take some more cupcakes out front, and I'll shoot back in here as soon as I can take a break, okay? Don't say *anything* until I get here."

Nik sat down on one of the chairs at Courtney's worktable. She glared at the tray of spicy chocolate cupcakes and took a lime coconut off of the tray next to it.

Suddenly all of her anger left her, and she just felt sad. Another depressing end to a relationship. And this one felt worse than any ending had since Justin. She had really *liked* Carlos. Damn it.

Dana walked in five minutes later, still wearing her running clothes.

"Hey, there you are. It's a mob scene out there."

"Hey!" Nik stood up to hug her, sweaty running clothes and all. "How are things with Natalie?"

Dana beamed.

"Great. I was just finishing a workout with her at the gym when I got your text." Dana looked at her. "We can talk about that later, though. Are you okay?"

Nik shook her head.

"I'm not great."

Dana pulled her in close.

"Oh, honey, what happened?"

Nik let herself be comforted by Dana's tight hug for a few moments.

"I can't tell you anything until Courtney gets back here, because she'll—"

"Destroy both of you, yes." Courtney walked back into the kitchen with three cups of coffee on a tray and set them on the table. She opened a cabinet, reached into the back, and pulled out a bottle of bourbon, and poured a tot into each of their cups.

"Okay. My staff can hold down the fort for a little while. What did he do, and how painful will it be when I kill him?"

Nik took a swig of coffee and winced. That was a lot more bourbon than she'd expected.

"He told me he loved me. And when I didn't say it back, he was furious, said I used him up and discarded him like I do every man I date, and stormed out of his house. You know, garden-variety Nik breakup." She sighed and reached for her drink again.

Courtney shook her head and poured more bourbon into Nik's cup.

"Okay, obviously we hate him now, but I'm going to need you to back up here. He told you he loved you? Did you see this coming? Did you . . . were you glad that he said it? How did he make you feel like shit? What happened in between the 'I love you' and the storming out of the house part? I feel like we're missing a lot here."

Nik glanced down at herself and realized she was still wearing Carlos's old UCLA T-shirt. She reached for another cupcake.

"No, I didn't see it coming! It came out of nowhere first thing this morning. And no, of course I wasn't glad he said it! You guys know how I feel about 'I love you's!' I don't get this.

I was so happy with the way things were, and he had to fuck it all up."

"Did you . . . tell him that?" Dana asked.

She shrugged. So fucking what if she had?

"More or less. We had a deal! We talked about this! He said he didn't want anything serious. I relied on that! And then he springs this 'I love you' bullshit on me this morning."

Dana narrowed her eyes.

"When you say 'more or less,' what exactly do you mean? What did you say to him?"

Oh God. Now Dana, the romantic, was going to get all upset on Carlos's behalf, she just knew it.

"I told him that he was probably just feeling emotional because of last night. Oh!" She just realized she'd texted them about Jessie but had never given them the update. "The baby was born last night. She and Jessie are both okay."

"Oh, that's so great!" Dana said. "But wait. You told him that he was just being emotional? Didn't you think that would upset him?"

Well, yes, *now* she did.

"I didn't think about that before I said it! Look, I was kind of flustered when he sprang this on me, okay? It was first thing in the morning— everyone *knows* I'm not at my best first thing in the morning anyway. I was exhausted because we were at the hospital for hours last night, we got back to his house super late, and then—"

Courtney broke in.

"Wait a second. You were at the hospital with him? When did that happen? How?"

So much had happened in the past twenty-four hours.

"It's a long story, but like I texted you guys, I'd been at his house helping him make enchiladas for his cousin, and . . ." She saw Dana and Courtney exchange a glance and stopped. "What? What does that look mean?"

"Nothing," Courtney said. "Go on. You were helping him cook enchiladas for his pregnant cousin, and?"

She knew it didn't mean "nothing," but she went on anyway.

"And we had just put the first batch in the oven when he got the call from his cousin in the hospital. So he raced there, and I stayed back to finish baking them."

Why were they making her go through this whole timeline? They knew this part already; she'd texted them last night. She'd also told them the important part, which was that Carlos had ruined everything.

"But how did you get from there to the hospital?" Courtney asked.

"I texted him to check in and see how he and his family were doing, and he said they were all stressed and hungry, so I packed up one of the pans of enchiladas with some paper plates and took them over there, which meant that I was there when they found out that Jessie and the baby were both okay. We were all so relieved."

She'd been so happy just last night, of course it all had to come crashing down this morning.

Courtney and Dana exchanged those annoying looks again. Why were they looking at her—and each other—like that?

"You brought them food to the hospital. Did he ask you to bring it, or . . ." Dana raised her eyebrows.

She shook her head.

"No, and that's the other thing! When I walked into the waiting room, he didn't seem happy that I was there at ALL. He barely looked at me, and his sister had to jump in to answer the 'How do you two know each other?' question from his mom." She'd thought he'd gotten over that. She'd thought in the end he was happy to have her there. And she'd been so happy to be there, to share that experience with Carlos and his family. That's why what he'd said this morning had felt like such a slap in the face. "I tried to leave after dropping off the food, because it didn't seem like he wanted me there, but his mom insisted that I stay and eat. But obviously I shouldn't have gone: this morning, one of his comebacks to me saying that I thought this was just a casual thing was 'You met my family!' like that automatically made us married or something." She refused to let herself cry. "And he said he wished I hadn't come.

"Anyway," she said, before either of them could say anything comforting. That would just put her over the edge. "Why is it so weird that I brought them food to the hospital?"

Dana put her hand on her arm.

"It just . . . that doesn't seem like you, that's all."

Nik shook Dana's hand off and took a huge bite of her cupcake. She tried to calm down as she chewed. It didn't work.

"That's a pretty mean thing for one of my best friends to say about me. You don't think I'd bring food for you in the hospital if you were sitting there waiting for a family member?"

Dana reached for her arm again.

"Of course you would. That's my point. You would for me, you would for Courtney, you would for probably a handful of other people, but that's it. I love you with my whole heart, Nik, but you don't do favors for people you don't care about. I can't picture you doing something like that for any of the guys you've dated in the last five years. The rest, you'd absolutely contribute to flowers or food or whatever, if someone else organized it, but a hospital visit? No, come on."

Nik sat and thought about that. Okay, she had a point there.

"Even if that's true, what does it matter? I'm not saying I don't care about him. I *told* him I cared about him! But when I told him that, he

346

acted like I'd told him his food was just as good as the food from Taco Bell or something. I said I was happy to keep going the way we'd been going, and we could just pretend he'd never said 'I love you.' "

"What did he say when you said that?" Courtney asked.

Nik put her head in her hands.

"He got really mad. Why do people think 'I love you' is the only meaningful thing you can say to a person? Why did he have to say he loved me?"

"Nik." Courtney's voice was gentle, which meant she was about to say something bad. "Why does it scare you so much for someone to say they love you?"

She shook her head.

"It doesn't scare me! I just know from experience that that's when everything gets bad, that's all."

Dana sighed.

"Justin really did a number on you, didn't he? Just because he was an asshole doesn't mean they're all going to be like that."

She leaned her head on Dana's shoulder and thought about denying that this had anything to do with Justin, but what was the point? Courtney got up and fetched the bourbon bottle and poured more into all of their coffee cups. Nik took a sip and sighed.

"I don't think about him that much anymore, except for that time I profiled the quarterback of his favorite team for *GQ* and pictured his face when he'd see my byline. Well, and those times when I have low moments and I hear his voice in my head. But Justin, in his terrible way, did me a favor. First, he made me feel like there was something wrong with my writing, then he made me feel like there was something wrong with me for loving writing and my career. But the end result of all of that was that he made me sure that I don't ever want to let anyone make me feel that bad ever again."

Courtney pushed her chair around the table so the three of them were all shoulder to shoulder.

"I know, honey," Dana said. "But that doesn't mean you have to close yourself off to everyone forever. You are great at being strong, and there's no one else that either of us would have on our side in a fight. But it's okay to be vulnerable with more people than just the two of us, you know? Letting yourself have feelings for people is scary, I know it is, but you can't go through life with most people at arm's length. Not everyone is going to be like Justin."

Nik buried her head in Dana's shoulder.

"I know," she said. "But—counterpoint: what if I don't *want* to be vulnerable with people other than you guys?"

Dana and Courtney didn't even respond to that.

Nik sighed.

"I hate this. This is all Fisher's fault. If he hadn't done that stupid proposal in the first place, none of this would have ever happened, and I never would have even met Carlos."

"Would you really want that?" Courtney asked.

"Yes! Okay, fine, no. I just wish Carlos had listened to me!" Nik said. "Okay, maybe telling him he was being emotional was a shitty thing to say, but I didn't know how to react and I didn't want this to ruin everything, but everything is ruined anyway."

She put her head down on the table. Dana and Courtney immediately put their arms around her.

"I'm so mad at him for how mean he was to me this morning, but I hate that I hurt his feelings. See, this is another reason why I never should have dated him in the first place. I should have stuck to my streak of dating guys I couldn't care less about. When I do that and we break up, I feel fine! Look at Fisher—did I care if I hurt his feelings? Not really! I need to find another Fisher."

"No you don't," Dana and Courtney said in unison.

She shook her head.

"There must be something wrong with me. Here I have this great, smart, kind, hot man telling me he loves me, and I recoil. Everything was so great, and now it's over, and he thinks I'm an unfeeling asshole. Maybe I am."

Courtney got up and grabbed a box of tissues out of a cabinet and brought them over to her. She sat up and took a handful.

"Okay, first of all, if he thinks that, Carlos doesn't know you at all. You are loving and kind and funny and the best damn cheerleader anyone has ever had."

Damn it, now Courtney was going to make her cry even more.

"Second, there's nothing wrong with you. I'm not saying that you're perfect, but who is? It's okay to not react perfectly all the time; it's okay to say no to people; it's okay even to not love someone back."

Nik wiped her eyes and nodded.

"What if I want to be perfect though?"

Dana laughed.

"As my mother would say, it's nice to want things."

All three of them laughed.

"Your mom *would* say that," Nik said. "Have you told her about Natalie yet?"

Dana shook her head. "It's only been a little while. I just told you guys! But . . ." she smiled. "Hopefully soon."

Nik reached for her now cold bourbon and coffee drink and drained the cup.

"I've got to try to make a bourbon and coffee

350

cupcake," Courtney said. "Oh fuck. Speaking of cupcakes, I have to get back out there."

Nik stood up.

"Give me an apron, I'll help. You don't want people complaining on Yelp about your long, slow line."

Courtney tossed an apron to her from the closet.

"Good, you owe me for all the cupcakes you just ate."

Carlos forced himself to turn off the shower. Usually when he took a shower it helped him figure out the answer to whatever he was stressed about, but this shower had just made everything worse. As soon as he stepped inside, he saw the empty space where Nik's bottle of conditioner used to be. She really had made sure to take every reminder of her existence out of his house, hadn't she? Not that he could forget her.

Nor could he forget how ashamed of himself he was. He was thirty-four, not fourteen; he was a little too old to storm out of his house full of righteous anger. Granted, he was still furious at Nik for the way she'd reacted this morning, but he was probably just as mad at himself for blowing up at her.

Maybe he'd been naive, but he hadn't expected her reaction this morning at all. It wasn't that he was so arrogant he thought any woman who was lucky enough for him to fall in love with her should be overjoyed . . . okay, fine, a *little* part of him may have thought that. He'd always just figured that when he got ready to seriously date someone, finding the someone would be the easy part.

Maybe she was right. Maybe he wasn't in love with her after all. Maybe this was just a momentary feeling, because of all of the emotion from last night and then all of the sex they'd had afterward. Maybe he could just . . .

He put his jeans on and sighed. Bullshit. He knew he loved her; he knew it to his core. He loved her for her kindness, her ability to laugh both at him and at herself, and her intelligence. But most of all, he loved her for that feeling he had when he sat next to her on his couch in silence or woke up next to her in bed, that feeling of peace and happiness. That he was with someone who understood him and everything about him. That everything was right with the world.

He sat down on his bed to put his shoes on. He had to pick up Angela, go to the hospital with her to check in on Jessie and the baby, and potentially throw his weight around if anything wasn't perfect. What he wanted to do was to go for a long run or play basketball all afternoon with people he didn't like or drive his car really fast along winding roads for three hours. Anything to not have to think or talk to people.

"Hey!" Angela hugged him when she got in his

car, and he hugged her back. Great, now he felt like an asshole for being so grumpy about this visit.

"Hey. Have you talked to Jessie today? I texted her this morning, but she hadn't seen the doctor yet."

"Yeah." Angela settled back into the car. "That's what she told me, too. She sounded anxious about the baby. I think it's killing her that she can't be there with her the whole time."

One of Angie's feet tapped against the passenger-side door. It was a nervous habit she'd had since she was little. It drove him crazy, but he forced himself not to yell at her to stop.

"Of course it is. It'll be easier once she can move around more."

"The baby is going to be okay, right? They weren't just saying that last night?"

He nodded. There were no guarantees, but everything he'd heard last night had satisfied him.

"Nothing is certain, but let's put it this way: if I'd been really worried, I would have been at the hospital and inside that NICU by dawn."

Angie stopped tapping her foot.

"Okay, that does make me feel better." She turned and looked behind her. "No Nik? Where is she?"

Damn it. Of course Angie would do this today.

"No, she had work to do." He sped up as he got

onto the freeway. Maybe she would be distracted by him driving too fast and would abandon this line of questioning.

"I'm happy for you, you know," she said. "So happy that I'm not even going to gloat about how I've known for weeks there was something going on there."

He should have known that nothing could distract Angie when she got going.

"Nothing's going on there. She was just at my house when I got Jessie's call and the enchiladas were still in the oven, so she said she'd stay to finish them. And then when she checked in to see how things were going, I said we were all hungry, so she brought them over, that's all." He shrugged. "No big deal."

Angela had a big grin on her face. It made him want to throw things.

"Mmmmhmm. Any girl you're dating who I get to meet is a big deal."

He cut around another car in the fast lane and gritted his teeth. Did Angie really have to do this right now?

"You'd already met Nik. You met her at the exact same time I did." Thank God the hospital exit was in only three miles.

"You know that doesn't count. You don't bring girls around the family; we both know that. And Nik met everyone who matters last night, so I'm just saying, it sounds serious."

He shook his head.

"It's not serious. Last night was an emergency; don't think too much of it." Oh God, this was going to be a disaster. Everyone was going to keep asking him about Nik for months, and he would have to be reminded about how he'd felt this morning over and over again.

"Oh, please with that 'it's not serious' bullshit. I was sitting right there when she brought up you going to the doctor, and if that doesn't say serious, I don't know what does. Don't worry, I won't say anything to Mama. She already called me this morning to ask what I knew about her, but I didn't say much. Mama was so happy that you'd found a nice girl who takes care of you. She said she'd be happier if she were a Mexican girl, but at this point she'd take anything, and I told her that—"

He couldn't take this anymore.

"We broke up, okay? We broke up this morning. I told her I loved her; she didn't feel the same way; we broke up. She's the first person in years that I've talked to about Dad, which probably should have been my sign that I was falling in love with her, but I didn't realize it until this morning. But it doesn't matter, because we broke up."

He didn't look in Angie's direction. He didn't want to see the look of sympathy he knew was on her face.

"Oh, Carlos. I'm so sorry."

He shrugged.

"It's probably for the best. I can't date anyone seriously now. You guys need me. I should have never gotten involved so closely with her as it was."

Angie turned her whole body toward him.

"What are you talking about? Who needs you?"

He glanced at her. Why was she playing dumb?

"The family. You, Mama, Tia Eva, even Jessie sometimes, though she has Jon for most things. Who would put together your bookshelf or change your light bulbs on those high ceilings of yours or go shopping with Mama or answer all of your phone calls? I don't have time to do all of those things and get involved with someone. I shouldn't have let myself get so close to Nik in the first place."

He looked at Angela, expecting her to be nodding at all of this. Instead, she was looking at him like he had two heads.

"Carlos. Are you really trying to tell me that you think you can't date someone seriously because you have to be free to put together book-shelves for me on a moment's notice?"

He shook his head.

"Not just that, it's a lot of things—you know that. Dad's gone, so I need to—"

She cut him off.

"That's the stupidest thing I've ever heard.

356

I know I'm your little sister, but I'm a grown woman. I can put together my own bookshelves or pay someone else to do it. Mama is not a little old lady. She doesn't need someone to go to the grocery store with her. She goes with you because she likes to spend time with you. We don't need you to put your life on hold to take care of us. We can take care of ourselves. I'm pretty sure I speak for Mama—and Jessie and Tia Eva—when I say that we want you to be happy, not spending all of your leisure time doing errands for us."

Angie clearly didn't understand.

"I know you can take care of yourselves. That's not the point. What if I fell in love with some woman, and I was with her when there was an emergency? I would never forgive myself if I wasn't there for someone in the family when they needed me."

Angie put her hand over his.

"But there would be nothing to forgive. You and I both weren't there when Dad died, and I hate that, too. But it was no one's fault, and you can't spend your life trying to make sure something like that doesn't happen again."

He pulled off the freeway and made the turn toward the hospital.

"This isn't about Dad! It's just that I'm a doctor, and—"

Angie talked over him.

"Plus, you *did* fall in love with a woman, and

you *were* with her last night when there was an emergency, and what happened? She sent you off to the hospital to take care of your family, and then she showed up a few hours later because she thought you needed her. Which you did. You don't always have to be the hero, Carlos, and you definitely don't need to be my dad. It's okay to just be my brother."

Finally, he exploded.

"Angela, can we please stop talking about this? You've made your point: you don't need me, I'm wasting my life, et cetera, et cetera. I get it—enough. Can we please just concentrate on Jessie and little Eva today?"

Angie nodded. She was silent until they got out of the car in the hospital parking garage.

"I'm sorry if I made things worse. That's not what I meant to do."

He pulled her hair.

"No, I'm sorry for getting mad."

She gave him a one-armed hug.

"You know I'm here if you ever want to talk, right?"

He nodded as they got in the elevator.

"I know. Thanks. Now, let's go see our new little cousin."

Chapter Twenty

● ● ● ● ● ●

The sparkly sign in front of Natalie's Gym was the first thing to make Nik smile in days.

She never should have gone out with Carlos in the first place. After everything with Fisher, she should have kept her distance from Carlos and all other men for at least several months, if not years. And now she'd spent the last three days inside her apartment with too many pints of ice cream, trying and failing to concentrate on her work instead of how much she missed Carlos.

She was even doing that thing where she caught herself checking her phone every time it buzzed, hoping it was him. She hated doing that thing. She'd always felt scornful toward the kind of woman who would do that thing. Why was she such a bitch? Now she felt sympathy for those women and even shittier about herself right now.

And the buzz from her phone was never him. She hadn't heard a single thing from Carlos since he'd slammed that door on Sunday morning.

Enough wallowing. She'd finally pinned Natalie down for an interview time for her story about the gym, thank goodness. She was looking forward to talking to Natalie, if only to get her mind off of herself for once this week.

She still felt lucky that Natalie had even agreed to the interview. Between her hesitation when Nik had brought it up and her slow response to Nik's emails about scheduling a time, it was clear that she was reluctant about this story for some reason.

She walked into the gym and knocked on Natalie's open door.

"Hi!" Natalie said. "Come on in." She was smiling, but Nik could see her hands trembling. She couldn't tell if it was because Natalie was just nervous about being interviewed in general—lots of people were like that—or if there was something specific that she was anxious about. Either way, Nik knew she had to have a gentle approach in this interview.

"Hi!" Nik echoed her. "Does this time still work?"

Natalie nodded and waved her inside.

"Yes, sure, of course. Close the door so we can talk. I told Jamila I'll be busy for the next hour and to only interrupt if it's an emergency."

"Great." Nik sat down, took out her phone and recorder, and flicked them both to record. She always had a duplicate now, just in case. "Before we start, I want to make sure that it's okay that I record our conversation so that I can make sure to be accurate when I write about this."

Natalie glanced down at the recording devices and swallowed hard.

"Sure, yes, of course."

Nik took her notebook out of her bag but didn't open it yet.

"You know, Natalie," she said, "you don't know me that well. So it makes sense that you wouldn't really trust me yet." Natalie tried to cut in, but she kept talking. "It's okay, it doesn't hurt my feelings that you don't trust me. A lot of people have reasons not to trust writers or strangers or anyone at all. I can tell that you're nervous about this interview. Lots of people don't like being interviewed—it's normal to be anxious. But please know I'm not trying to trick you or do some gotcha piece about your gym or anything like that. I'm not that kind of person, and I'm not that kind of writer."

Natalie looked straight at Nik the whole time she was talking. When she stopped, Natalie slowly lowered her hands onto the table.

"I know," she said. "I mean, I knew all of that, about you. Mostly because of Dana, but it still helps to have you say it."

"Good." Nik smiled back at her. "Speaking of Dana, if there's anything you say to me today that you want to be off the record, please know that I wouldn't tell her about it."

Natalie's smile was faint, but it was there.

"Thank you for saying that."

Nik opened her notebook to her list of questions.

"Why don't we get started? I stumbled upon your gym kind of accidentally—I was searching for a self-defense class to take with my girlfriends, and your Punch Like a Girl series happened to start just a few days later, so I booked it on an impulse. I'd never even heard of your gym before, but it already has a very loyal clientele. Where did you get the idea to start this gym? How long have you been around?"

Natalie's smile was stronger now.

"Just over a year. I know it's pretty young for a gym, but I feel like I managed to tap into a need that was out there—a place for women of all kinds to feel supported and comfortable within their own skin, but more than just that, a place that could make all of us feel stronger, both inside and outside, and allow us to face our fears. A lot of people are afraid of the gym, and I hate that. I wanted this to be a place that people would look forward to going to, where people could be excited about working out and exercising, without the fear and shame and ridicule."

She'd gotten more animated and comfortable as she talked, and Nik hoped she stayed like that.

"Well, at least from my point of view, as someone who has always hated gyms, you've succeeded," Nik said. "Why don't we back up a little—how long had you wanted to open a gym? Have you worked at gyms in the past?"

"Oh God, I feel like I've spent my life in gyms," Natalie said. "I was a cheerleader in college, which meant I worked out a ton."

Nik laughed.

"Of course you were a cheerleader in college. I should have known." She paused. "That's a compliment of your teaching style, by the way. I've never had someone cheer me on so well for anything."

Natalie's cheeks got bright red, but she looked pleased. She was more relaxed now. Maybe it had been just nerves about being interviewed.

"That's so good to hear. Thank you. And then I graduated from college during a time when it was impossible to find a job. I was a math major." Nik managed to keep her face from looking surprised, but barely. And then she wanted to smack herself. Why was she still underestimating this woman, just because of what she looked like? "And I was looking for jobs in business or consulting or even teaching, and there was nothing. So to pay my rent, I got a job working at the front desk of the gym near me. After a while, I got curious about what the personal trainers did, so I started asking one of them a bunch of questions about her job: how she got it, what the certification was like, all that stuff. And eventually, I took the plunge."

As Natalie told her all about her personal

363

training certification she seemed to be getting more relaxed.

"I was one of the top trainers by the time I left. My parents kept asking me if I was going to get a different job, go corporate, maybe go to business school. But I really loved my job. And I was good at it."

Nik nodded.

"I bet you were. I've had trainers before, and none of them were even half as good as one of your classes." It helped to flatter sources during interviews, but this had the benefit of being true. "Why did you leave the gym?"

Natalie turned to her glass of green juice again, but not before Nik saw that her eyes had filled with tears.

"I got married. One of my clients." She shrugged. She still looked down at her juice. "Such a cliché, I know."

Nik shrugged along with her.

"Clichés wouldn't be clichés if they didn't happen all the time." Of course the whole problem was the husband. "So . . . why did you leave the gym after getting married? Did you decide to go to grad school after all?"

She shook her head. She still had tears in her eyes, but she was looking straight ahead now.

"No. My husband didn't think it was appropriate for me to keep working as a trainer after we were married. He said there would be too much touching other people; he knew I was bi, and he said he didn't have a problem with it, but it meant that working with women was a problem for him, too. So I quit." Nik raised her eyebrows but didn't ask a question. Natalie answered it anyway. "I know what you're going to say. Before I met him, I would have said the same thing. I didn't . . . by the time we were married, he'd convinced me of a lot of things. He said my job now was to take care of our house and him and that he'd take care of supporting me. I thought that was so sweet."

Sweet was one word for that.

"When did you stop thinking it was sweet?" she asked.

Natalie put her hand over her eyes for a second. She put it down and sat up straighter.

"I'm sorry. I don't usually talk about this."

Nik reached across the table and touched her hand.

"No need to apologize. You're doing great, so great."

Natalie smiled faintly.

"You sound like me when you say that."

Nik squeezed her hand, then let go.

"What can I say? I learned from the best."

Natalie's smile got a little bigger and then faded.

"What did you ask? When did I stop thinking it was sweet? It took a while." She shook her head. "That's not true. I don't think I ever thought it was sweet. But somehow I'd stopped trusting myself and my feelings."

Nik let out a deep breath. That sounded all too familiar.

"When I told him I missed the gym, he yelled at me for being ungrateful, and I thought he was right. But I really hated not having my own money. We had a joint bank account, and whenever I bought anything, he asked me a million questions about it, so eventually I just stopped buying things other than groceries. Sometimes I would get cash back and hide the cash."

Natalie picked up a piece of paper from her desk, crumpled it into a ball, and straightened it out.

"But I thought all of that was normal and showed how much he loved me. There are all of those commercials and things in women's magazines about hiding things you buy from your husband. They always make it seem like a thing all women do, that it's a joke we're all in together. So I didn't think having to sneak around to buy new sports bras was a big deal."

She sighed and took a deep breath. Nik thought about all of the articles and ads she'd seen that had made that exact joke. Good God, sometimes it felt like all of society was complicit in trying to make life harder for women.

"Even when he made it harder and harder for me to see my friends, I thought it was normal.

People didn't see their friends that much after they got married, right? He said people who loved each other shouldn't have anything to hide from each other, so he should be able to read all of my emails and texts. So I stopped texting my friends very much. I didn't really see them much, either. Sometimes I would sneak out and get coffee with my best friend, Kiki. But I just thought he was acting like that because he loved me so much."

How could anyone ever trust someone again after someone they loved had made them feel so isolated and doubt their own instincts?

She certainly never had. Well, she'd started to trust Carlos, but that had been a mistake.

"I've had a lot of therapy since that time, and now I know there is such a thing as 'emotional abuse.' But I'd never heard that term then. So when my friends and family told me there was something wrong, it would just make me frustrated and mad at them. He never hit me; everything was fine! How could they think I was one of those poor, beaten-down, abused women? That wasn't me. Didn't they know me?"

Tears poured down Natalie's face.

Nik pulled a packet of tissues out of her bag—she always came prepared with them for interviews, just in case—and handed a stack to Natalie. Natalie took a deep breath and started again.

"I wasn't abused. It was just that my husband loved me more than anyone had ever loved me, and he wanted all of me. And if he got mad at me sometimes because he wanted fish for dinner and I'd made chicken, or if I went to the wrong gas station to fill up gas for his car, or when I miscarried but didn't lose the pregnancy weight right away, it was only because he wanted me to be perfect. He wanted me to be the best I could be; that was all."

Now Nik wasn't sure if she wanted to cry or if she wanted to take her new punching skills on the road and knock this man into oblivion. Maybe both.

"How did you realize what was going on? How did you decide to get out?"

Natalie looked down at her desk for a long moment.

"I wish I could say it was one thing, but it wasn't. The first time I remember consciously thinking 'This is not the life I want' was when I went running one day soon after he'd told me to lose weight after the miscarriage. All I wanted was to stay home under the covers, but I knew he would know if I didn't exercise—we both had those fitness bracelet things, and he could see my activity all day. It made me feel like I was constantly being spied on." She looked down at her bare wrist. "I guess I was. So I went running because I had to, and I hated every second. I hadn't talked to my family or any of my friends in months, so I didn't know where to turn."

Nik hated Natalie's husband, all men, and all of society for making Natalie feel like a relationship like the one she'd been in was normal.

"About a month after the miscarriage, I went to my doctor. The whole point of the visit was to see when I could start trying to get pregnant again. But when I was sitting there waiting for her, I realized that the idea of getting pregnant and having his baby and that baby tying me to him and that life forever made me feel panicky. I got up and left, and I told him the doctor said we shouldn't try for a few more months. A few days later, I logged in to an old email account that I'd had from before I got married, one that he didn't know I had. And that day I emailed Kiki and my mom. I didn't say anything, really, just hi, and asked how they were doing, stuff like that. They both responded right away, and I started emailing them more and more. And one day, I went for a run with Kiki. I didn't quite tell her everything, but I told her a lot."

God bless Kiki. She had to remember to give Courtney and Dana extra-big hugs the next time she saw them.

"How did you get out?"

Natalie pulled another tissue out of the packet.

"After weeks of emails, Mom ended one of hers with something like 'What do you think about coming home to visit? I have to drive down that way for work next week, and I can pick you up?' I said yes right away, and I told her that I'd meet her at Kiki's office. I spent the next six days terrified he'd see that email somehow or suspect something, but he didn't. That morning, I left my phone at home under the couch cushions and I took a taxi to Kiki's office. I took that fucking fitness bracelet off in the taxi and left it deep in the back seat, and I've never worn one since. When I got there and saw Kiki and my mom, that's when I really broke down for the first time."

Nik wished Kiki and Natalie's mom were there so she could hug them, too.

Natalie opened a drawer and pulled out two bottles of water.

"Want one? I'm thirsty after all of this crying." Nik took one and took a long sip. After that story, she would have even taken green juice.

"I guess that got kind of far away from why I started this gym. Except that I can't really tell one part of it without telling the whole of it. I lived with my parents for a while afterward—working at a local gym, getting more comfortable with myself, and going to lots of therapy. I let all of the money from my divorce settlement sit in the bank. Luckily for me, my mom is a lawyer and called in a favor with one of her divorce lawyer friends who took my case."

Nik smiled.

"Good job, Mom. Okay, let's go back to my initial question: where did you get the idea to start this gym?"

Natalie grinned at her.

"One day, I had an appointment with a client, and she came in spitting mad. She'd been on the treadmill before meeting me, and the guy next to her started lecturing her about her form. She was a marathon runner, mind you. And I thought of how great it could be if we had a gym for women of all shapes and sizes, where we could learn about our bodies and how strong we are without having to be on display to men while we did it. A place for all women: black and white; gay and straight; Latina and Asian; cis and trans; athletes and couch potatoes; and everything in between. And then I thought about the money I had in the bank. And after about a year of research and planning, Natalie's Gym was born."

This story was going to be so good. Her editor at *O* magazine was going to love it.

"What about the boxing classes? Did you teach those before? Did you always know you wanted them when you decided to start the gym?"

Natalie nodded.

"I never taught them before coming here, but I took them at a few different gyms after the breakup and really loved them. They were one of the first things I knew I wanted at this place."

"What was your goal in teaching these classes? Why were they important to you?"

Natalie made a fist, flexed her hand, and made a fist again.

"Women who know how to fight hold themselves differently. I've seen that in the women who've taught me, in the women who've taken my classes, and especially in myself. You walk into any situation with an attitude that you've got this, you can defend yourself, you are strong. My marriage sapped me of a lot of my strength, and what made it worse were the constant messages I got from society that women are weak, women should be afraid, women should settle for whatever they can get. And I want the women who walk into this gym to know that women have power and agency and deserve great things in life."

"Amen," Nik said.

Natalie high-fived her.

"And it starts so young!" she said. "I really want to do a program for teenage girls. They need more things to counteract the messages that they get that there's something wrong with being a girl, that they should hide the things about themselves that make them unique and fun and strong." She grinned. "That's why I called the class 'Punch Like a Girl'—there's this constant message that to do anything like a girl is weak. I wanted to turn that on its head."

Carlos's teen clinic would probably be really into the idea of partnering with Natalie's Gym on a program like that, especially after things he'd told her about some of his patients and the abuse that they'd suffered.

She tried to shake off thoughts of him, but it was impossible. She had to ask Natalie the question she'd been wondering the entire time they'd been talking.

"This is a personal question, and I understand if you don't want to answer, especially since Dana is my friend. But how did you learn to trust people again after what happened to you?"

Natalie shook her head slowly.

"It was really hard. I beat myself up for a while after my marriage ended. I blamed myself for trusting my ex, for letting him control me, for giving in to everything. I didn't trust my own judgment for a long time. The whole time I was researching the idea for this gym, I kept second-guessing myself, thinking it was a terrible idea. But I was right; I did have a good idea, and even just doing all of that research was me learning to trust myself. Once I learned to trust myself, my instincts, and my emotions, trusting other people was a lot easier."

Nik drove home a few hours later, after lots of time hanging around the gym, and even taking one of those cycling classes that she always mocked Dana for loving. She couldn't stop thinking about everything that Natalie had said, but especially that last part. Did she trust herself? With her work, definitely. With anything else? She had no idea.

Chapter Twenty-one

• • • • • •

When Carlos's phone rang on the way home from the hospital on Saturday night, he grabbed for it.

Drew. Not Nik. Why did he keep doing this to himself? She wasn't going to call him. Not after what he'd said to her.

He sighed and answered the phone.

"Hey, man, what's up?"

"Hey," Drew said. "How's the baby?"

He'd texted Drew right before he had left the hospital on the night the baby was born but hadn't talked to him since. He hadn't really been in the mood to hear stories of relationship bliss. And he really hadn't wanted to deal with telling him about Nik. But he couldn't avoid his best friend forever.

"Still in the NICU, but doing pretty well. I'm on the way home from the hospital right now, just spent a few hours hanging out with her and Jessie." Jessie had been released on Wednesday. Her blood pressure wasn't quite normal, but it was getting lower every day. But little Eva still had at least another few days in the hospital so her tiny lungs could improve and she could gain weight.

"I'm on my way *to* the hospital. I'm on call and just got called back in. How's Jessie?"

"She got released on Wednesday, but she's only left the hospital to sleep. She's at Eva's side all day. But all of the signs are good. Such a relief."

"Great. I bet Jessie won't relax until Eva's at home, though."

He thought of Jessie's anxious face and how Jon kept trying to force her to eat.

"Not one bit."

Drew coughed.

"So I have some news."

Uh-oh. That could be anything.

"Okay . . ."

Drew laughed.

"You sound so suspicious. We have a wedding date! Mark it on your calendar in bright red, et cetera."

A wedding date, of course. He should have expected that.

"Great, when is it?"

Drew laughed.

"Here's the thing: it's in October."

He counted the months in his head.

"This October? Four months from now October?" He grinned. "Wait. Do you have *other* news to tell me?"

"What do you . . . oh God, no, Alexa isn't pregnant! We're moving fast, but not that fast.

Our favorite venue had a cancellation, and after Alexa had pulled some strings to get us to the top of the waiting list, we couldn't say no. Alexa's already been frantically looking for wedding dresses with her friend Maddie. And apparently, I need to start frantically doing something—I'm just not sure what that something is. So I figured I'd call you, because you're really good at telling me what to do."

Carlos laughed. He was indeed really good at telling Drew what to do.

"You finally acknowledge this now. You spent years complaining about it."

"Look, I always did what you said . . . eventually. Anyway, I think we need to find tuxes or something? You want to come up again some weekend soon and we can sort that out?"

Carlos got off the freeway exit for his house. A trip up to the Bay Area sounded like the break from his life that he needed.

"As soon as the baby's at home with Jessie and Jon, I'll drive up there. I was just thinking that I needed a long solo drive."

"Perfect. Tux shopping sounds basically terrible, but at least we'll get a fun weekend out of it. Oh, and please text me how to spell Nik's name so we don't get it wrong on the invite."

Shit. He couldn't dodge this one.

"Actually . . . you don't need to know how to spell her name. We broke up."

He heard a horn honk at the other end of the line.

"What? I almost ran a red light. When? What happened?"

It felt so depressing to say it out loud, but he had no real choice.

"Last weekend. Sunday morning, the day after Jessie had the baby. We were at the hospital together . . . long story, it's not important. Anyway, I told her I was in love with her and . . . it didn't go well."

"Catch me up here: you're in love with her? I thought you gave me some bullshit about how it wasn't serious."

He sighed.

"I guess you realized that was bullshit sooner than I did. But it doesn't matter; she doesn't feel the same way."

He'd only told this terrible story twice and he was already sick of it.

"Oof. She was at the hospital when Jessie had the baby? So she met your family?"

Thanks, Drew, for narrowing in on one of his sore spots.

"Unfortunately. Get this—she sent cupcakes to Jessie at the hospital on Monday."

He had been both touched and furious when he'd walked into Jessie's hospital room on Monday to see that Cupcake Park box. He knew, even before Jessie had told him, that they'd come from Nik.

"That was so nice of her," Drew said. "I bet you wanted to smash every single one of those cupcakes with the bottom of your foot."

"I wanted to throw them out the fucking window."

He heard the noises from the other end of the phone that signaled that Drew had driven into the parking garage.

"Do you have to go?"

"Nah, I have at least three or four more minutes," Drew said. "The staff parking is way on the top floors. It'll take a while to get up there. What do you mean it didn't go well? I'm guessing she didn't say it back?"

Carlos pulled up in front of his house and turned off his car, but he didn't bother to go inside yet.

"Not only did she not say it back, she said it would be better if we could pretend I'd never said it, which wasn't exactly the reaction I'd hoped for. So I got mad, said some not great stuff to her, left the house, and drove away." He sighed. "You don't have to tell me that I didn't handle it well. I already know that."

He looked out the window while he was talking. Damn, he really needed to mow his lawn.

"Have you talked to her since?" Drew asked.

Carlos sighed again.

"No. I want to, but I don't know what to say. I don't know if there's anything I can say."

He'd thought about texting her, especially after Jessie got those cupcakes. He'd wanted to say thank you and to apologize for being such an ass. Mostly the latter. But after he'd seen all of those texts from Fisher after *their* dramatic breakup, he sort of felt like he should avoid texting her anything. He didn't want to be that guy.

"Hmmmm," Drew said. Carlos heard him get out of his car. "I can think of a few things. I seem to remember a certain conversation last year right around this time . . ."

"That was different—you hadn't told Alexa how you felt," Carlos said. He should have known Drew would throw his own advice back in his face.

He'd be lying, though, if he tried to pretend that the only reason that he hadn't texted Nik was because of Fisher's crazy texts. The real reason was: what if it didn't make any difference?

He'd obviously sprung the whole thing on her too fast, which had been a big part of the reason everything escalated like it did. He should have done it all so differently. He's already thought of at least five or six better ways he should have told her. He wanted another chance to talk to her about everything. About them. But it all still felt so tender. He wasn't ready for her to reject him again.

"I know, I know. Sorry, forget my advice. What

I should have said was, that fucking sucks; do you want to come up here this weekend and get really drunk with me? We can pick out some incredibly ugly tuxes for the wedding if you want."

Carlos laughed.

"Alexa would skin me alive. And really, man, thanks. I would, if the baby wasn't still in the hospital. But as soon as she's home, I'm on my way. I'll keep you posted."

A weekend getting drunk with Drew sounded like exactly what he needed.

"Awesome, I'm looking forward to it. Okay, now I really do have to go."

"Tell Alexa I said hi."

He hung up the phone and got out of his car. Talking to Drew had helped in some ways and made it worse in others. He was so happy about marrying Alexa in just a few months that it made the breakup feel even worse.

Oh well. He walked up his front steps and unlocked his door. Drew couldn't sit around in his underwear on his couch and eat pizza and drink beer all night like he could. Who had it better, huh?

He tried not to answer that.

Nik jumped at the noise outside on Monday afternoon. Did people *really* need to set fireworks off in the middle of the afternoon? The Fourth of July wasn't even for a few days. The amateur fireworks got earlier every damn year. She stood up to get some water and realized she couldn't remember the last time she'd left the house. Oh right, for her last self-defense class. Four days ago. She'd been buried in work all week—or as her friends claimed when they tried to get her to go out to brunch that weekend and she'd refused, she had buried herself in work.

At least she'd been able to concentrate on work again. It was a relief to dive headfirst into a story and not let herself think about Carlos, and what he was probably doing right now, and how much she missed him, and why she hadn't heard a single thing from him in the eight days since he'd slammed his front door. The thing was, as soon as she stopped working, those things were all she could think about.

She looked down at herself and winced. She was wearing the same leggings she'd been wearing for days and a threadbare tank top. And she desperately needed a shower.

Twenty minutes later, she left her house, showered; in a mostly clean pair of jeans, a gray T-shirt, and her biggest pair of sunglasses; and with her hair in a topknot. See, she could act like a human being. Sort of.

She walked the mile to the coffee shop while she listened to the audiobook of her latest true crime book. She wished she could tell Carlos to get it for Jessie.

She still wasn't sure if she'd done the right thing when she'd sent Jessie cupcakes. But she'd been a few hospital rooms away when Jessie had had her baby. She'd cried along with Carlos's whole family when Eva was born, and she'd seen the tiny baby just hours later. It still hurt, more than she wanted to acknowledge, that Carlos had said it was a waste for her to meet his family, after everything they'd shared that night. But it felt wrong to pretend none of that had happened, that she didn't care, just because she and Carlos were over. So she'd sent the cupcakes, the ones that Carlos had told her that Jessie and her husband had particularly liked. None of the spicy chocolate ones.

She thought about sitting down to drink her large iced coffee at the coffee shop, but she hadn't brought a book or her laptop, and she didn't feel like staring at the tiny bright screen of her phone. She wandered down the street and half-heartedly glanced into boutiques, but she wasn't really in the mood for shopping. After a few blocks, she turned around and walked home.

She was still in the world of the murderous cult as she approached her building. It wasn't until she was halfway up the steps that she saw someone standing by the front door.

Fisher. Fisher was standing by the front door.

"What the fuck are you doing here?" she said to him. She backed away to stand on the sidewalk.

She didn't want to talk to him in the shadows of her building. He followed her.

"Hi, Nik." He put his hand on her waist. She immediately stepped away. "I've missed you."

Was he fucking kidding her?

"I haven't missed you. What are you doing here?"

He tossed his hair back and smiled.

"I should have expected that from you. You're always making little jokes, aren't you? I hoped I'd get a warmer greeting, though, after everything we were to each other."

"You hoped you'd get a warmer greeting?" She had actually dated this guy. For months, even. What in God's name had she been thinking? "After those texts you sent me? You can go straight to hell."

He smiled his gleaming white smile at her and tried to put his arm around her. She stepped away again, but he followed.

"Look, I know we both got a little heated after the Dodgers game, and I'm sorry if I said anything to upset you, but—"

"*If?* Was that supposed to be an apology?"

The smile was still plastered on his face. How had she ever found him attractive?

"Look, can we go somewhere a little more private and talk?" He looked around at the people driving and walking by them and grimaced. "Upstairs, maybe?"

She tossed the rest of her iced coffee into the trash can at the curb.

"No. Say what you have to say to me here. You seem to like having important conversations in public. Why stop now?"

He sighed.

"Just keep your voice down, okay? I got a lot of bad publicity last time. I don't want to have to deal with that again."

Well, now she'd have to turn up the volume.

"Bad publicity last time . . . I can't even believe you. Spit it out, Fisher. What are you doing here? I thought you got the message that I didn't want to see or talk to you anymore."

Finally his smile dropped away, and he moved closer to her. She backed away again.

"Look, Nik. Haven't you realized by now what a mistake you made? We had a good thing going. Mutually beneficial, isn't that what they call it? Good for you for many reasons, and quite frankly, it was good for me to be seen with you. People had this impression of me that I was shallow and only good for the dumb-guy parts, and no one would even send me the good scripts."

For good reason. The dude had a great body but couldn't act his way out of a paper bag.

"But more than once," he continued, "directors would talk to you at parties, and then they would see me with you and they would be a lot nicer to me. And my agent told me people said they thought there must be more to me if I was dating someone smart and interesting and urban like you."

Urban. She wondered if Fisher's agent had really said that or if that was Fisher's translation from "black." At least now she knew where the out-of-the-blue proposal had come from.

"So you proposed to me, in public, without talking to me about it first, because you thought it would help you get ahead in your career?"

He nodded eagerly.

"It would have! I still don't understand why you said no. It would have been great for you, too." He waved his arm up and down her body. "I mean, look at you. People who look like you don't usually get to go to the places I would take you. You had so many more opportunities, dating a person like me." He smacked her butt.

Without even thinking about it, she took a step back, shifted her weight onto her back heel, pulled her fist back, and punched Fisher right in the face.

"Oh wow. It really does hurt your hand," she said as Fisher writhed on the ground at her feet.

A woman walking with a baby stroller stopped next to them.

"That was amazing!" she said. "How did you learn to punch like that?"

Nik shook out her fingers. The pain was worth it. She grinned at the woman.

"Natalie's Gym, over on Larchmont. It's fantastic; you should take one of her classes!"

The woman rocked the stroller back and forth with her foot while she took out her phone and made a note.

"Natalie's Gym. Thank you! Great job." She started to walk away with the baby, and then turned back and looked down at Fisher, who was still on the ground. "I bet you've had that coming to you for years!" She waved good-bye to Nik as she walked off.

Nik looked down at Fisher.

"Stop moaning. You're fine; you're not even bleeding."

He struggled to his feet and glared at her.

"My face is my most precious commodity, next to my body. I can't believe this." He turned his back on her and walked to his car. "I should call the police on you."

"What, and tell them you got punched by a girl?"

Nik laughed all the way up to her apartment. She kept replaying the scene in her mind where she'd punched Fisher, and it made her happier every time.

She unlocked her front door and dug around in her freezer until she found a bag of frozen vegetables for her knuckles. Just think, less than two months ago she'd been so freaked out by Fisher's texts that she'd had to have Carlos search her apartment, and now, she'd knocked him to the ground all by herself. Carlos would love this story so much.

Shit. She couldn't tell Carlos.

She sank down on the couch and put her head in her hands.

She had plenty of people to tell who would be excited for her. Courtney and Dana would crack up. Natalie would be thrilled. So why did it hurt so much that she couldn't tell Carlos?

Because Carlos would have been so proud. He was the only one who knew how far she'd come. He'd seen her that night; he'd been worried about her; he'd cheered her decision to go to Natalie's class. Courtney and Dana had guessed, and Natalie had helped, but Carlos *knew.* He'd been so ready to protect her, but she'd protected herself.

He would have loved that. He would have been so happy for her and impressed that she'd stood up for herself. That's what was so great about Carlos, damn it. Why did he have to go and ruin everything?

Courtney and Dana had said that she needed to learn how to be vulnerable, but she'd been vulnerable with Carlos in a way she hadn't been with any guy in years. She'd let him know how scared she was that first night they'd gone out, when she'd let him search her apartment. She'd told him what Justin had said about her writing and how it still made her insecure sometimes. She'd cried with him when the baby was born. Maybe none of those things would be a big deal for someone else, but they were for her.

Ugh, why was she back to thinking about Carlos? She went to the kitchen to pour herself a drink. She deserved one for her triumph.

Maybe not rosé—she wasn't going to let Carlos's jokes about it ruin her favorite wine forever, but why push herself right now? She made a gin and tonic and brought it back over to the couch.

"Cheers!" She lifted the glass with her unbruised hand. It had been so great to watch Fisher fall to the ground. She took a sip of her drink, thought of the bruise that was probably already marring his perfect face, and smiled. God bless that woman in the stroller.

She took out her phone to text her girlfriends.

Fisher was waiting in front of my building when I got home today, and long story short, I punched him in the face.

Mere seconds later, Dana texted back.

!!!!!!!!!!!!!!!

And then like twenty of the fist-in-the-air and fireworks emojis.

Courtney screeched in.

WHAT

OMG

TELL US EVERYTHING

Nik grinned and relaxed into her couch cushions. Who needed Carlos when you had girlfriends?

She texted them the whole story—one-handed—and then, halfway through her gin and tonic, she fell asleep on the couch. She woke up two hours later from a dream about Carlos high-fiving her. When she realized it was just a dream, she started to cry.

Should she text him and tell him what happened? God knows she wanted to. But he was probably still pretty mad at her.

And if he wasn't? Texting him wasn't fair to him. He deserved more than she could give him—than she knew how to give him.

Instead, she texted a picture of her raw knuckles to her friends. Their responses made her smile through her tears.

Chapter Twenty-two

● ● ● ● ● ●

Carlos sat at his desk and stared at his phone. His meeting had been canceled at the last minute. That unfortunately gave him time to make that phone call he'd been avoiding all week.

All week? He'd avoided making that call for the past five years.

He picked up the phone.

"Yes, hi. I'd like to schedule an appointment with Dr. Guerriero? Just a physical. Yes, Carlos Ibarra." He swallowed hard, as the person on the other end took his insurance information. "I totally understand if you can't get me in for a while—oh, you have a cancellation tomorrow? I don't know if . . ." He took a deep breath. "What time tomorrow?"

He hung up the phone and stared out the window. Tomorrow. Damn it.

No, tomorrow was too soon. He should call back to reschedule. He picked up the phone.

"Dr. Ibarra?" One of the nurses poked her head into his office, and he put the phone down again. "There's someone at the front desk to see you. She says she's your cousin?"

He stood up. If Jessie had left the NICU to come over to his office to see him, it was either really good or really bad news.

"I'll be right there."

He almost ran down the hall.

"Jessie?" He poked his head into the waiting room. The huge smile on her face answered his question. She ran over to him, and he threw open the door so she could follow him back to his office. But the door was barely shut before she threw her arms around him.

"We get to take her home today! Yesterday they said maybe, but I was too scared to tell anyone. Last night I couldn't sleep, partly because of the fireworks going on all night, but mostly because I was just praying that I would have my baby at home with me by tonight. And my prayers were answered. Just a few hours for them to do all of the paperwork and to give us all of her instructions. Oh, Carlos! I get to take my baby home!"

He hugged her tight and pulled her down the hall to his office. Once the door was closed, he hugged her again.

"I didn't think she'd be able to go home this early. You've got a fighter on your hands. When they told me you were here to see me, I . . ." He wiped his eyes. "Anyway, this is wonderful. I'm so happy for you and for Eva, who won the mom lottery." He took a step back and handed her the

392

tissue box on his desk. "Where's Jon? Do you need help getting Eva home?"

Jessie took a handful of tissues and shook her head.

"He's upstairs with Eva. I've barely stopped crying since the doctors told us she could go home today."

Carlos gently pushed her down in one of the chairs in front of his desk and sat next to her.

"And you, you're okay?" He shook his head. "No, you don't have to tell me. I'm your cousin, not your doctor."

She leaned over to hug him.

"Just for that, I'll tell you that my blood pressure is almost normal. And I can even fit into some of my pre-pregnancy shoes now. Not clothes, let's not be ambitious, but I was getting very nervous I'd never be able to wear those Tory Burch flats again, so that was a tiny relief."

His office phone rang and he ignored it.

"I don't know who Tory is, but if that's a relief to you, it is to me, too. Do you need anything? Food, diapers, a crib, bottles, anything?"

She laughed, even though tears were still trickling down her face.

"Don't forget, you already brought me those enchiladas. We've already defrosted one pan and have been eating them all week. And I think my mom has spent all day every day since Eva was born cooking for her little namesake; my freezer is going to be filled to bursting soon. I don't even know what else we need. I'm mad at myself for not letting my friends push the date of my shower up. I thought it was tempting fate, if you can believe that. Thank God someone already bought us the bassinet so she has somewhere to sleep."

He made a mental note to buy whatever was the most expensive thing on the registry. Okay, okay, maybe Angela was right; he could pull back a little. The second most expensive thing.

She stood up.

"I should go. I probably have to sign a bunch of stuff, and I can't wait to get our little girl out of this hospital, even though I'm sort of terrified to pull her away from the people taking care of her."

Carlos put his hand on her shoulder.

"You and Jon, *you* are the people taking care of her. And you'll do a wonderful job, I promise."

She punched his arm.

"Damn you, Carlos. I *just* stopped crying, and now you've got to get me started again?"

She leaned in for a hug, and he kissed her on the forehead.

"I'm so happy for you, Jessie. And I can't wait to spoil little Eva rotten."

She opened his office door.

"I can't wait for that, either. Oh, and you thanked your friend Nik for me for the cupcakes, right? Tell her I said that was so thoughtful. I want to send her a thank-you card, but this week has just been . . ."

He had not thanked Nik on Jessie's behalf, no.

"Don't worry about it. You've been kind of preoccupied this week; she understands." He was sure Nik *did* understand, so that wasn't exactly a lie. "Go back upstairs to your baby. Call me if you have any questions at all, okay?"

Right, right, she was his cousin, not his patient. This shit was hard.

"Actually, you should probably call the NICU and not me, they know this stuff better than I do. But let me know if you need anything at all, okay?"

She nodded.

"I will. Have I ever told you how glad I am that you're my cousin?"

He grinned.

"I'm not sure, refresh my memory about why? You had at least ten or fifteen reasons, correct? Can you list them for me?"

She walked into the hallway.

"Never, you're cocky enough as it is."

She disappeared toward the elevators with another wave over her shoulder, and he went laughing back to his desk.

Maybe he *should* text Nik to thank her for the cupcakes. He couldn't keep pretending to Jessie that he'd done that without actually doing it, right?

And wouldn't Nik want to know that Eva was okay and was getting to go home from the hospital? She'd been there the night Eva was born; she'd cried along with everyone else. Shouldn't he let her know?

He laughed at himself. That was a pretext, and he knew it. He didn't need to thank Nik; he needed to apologize to Nik. He hated what he'd said to her that awful morning, he hated the memory of the hurt look on her face when he'd walked out of his house, and he hated that she'd remember him like that. Even if she didn't love him back, he didn't want her to hate him.

An email was probably the way to do this, not a text. A text felt too immediate. Like he'd be expecting a response.

He scrolled back through his work emails until he found her email address.

To: Nikole@NikoleDPaterson.com
From: Carlos_Ibarra@
          eastsidemedicalcenter.com
Subject: cupcakes

Jessie wanted me to make sure to thank you for the cupcakes. They made her so happy. She appreciated it a lot. So did I. She's doing a lot better and Eva is, too—they're taking her home from the hospital today.

I'm sorry for what I said that morning
and how I acted. I can't apologize
enough.
You don't have to respond to this.

Carlos

That seemed so blunt and inarticulate, but at least it was all true.

He pressed send.

Nik pulled into the grocery store parking lot at ten on Friday night. It was her favorite time to go to the grocery store, and she hadn't been able to go on a Friday night in a while. The place was almost empty, the employees were in party moods, and the other people who were there on Friday nights were always buying huge bags of chips and cartons of cheap beer, which always made Nik so happy she wasn't going to their terrible parties.

As she walked inside, a bleary-eyed man carrying a huge bag of diapers almost knocked into her on his way out.

"Sorry!" he shouted. Then he walked into the parking lot right into the path of a car that braked just in time. Poor guy probably hadn't slept in a week.

That made her think of Jessie and Jon, and baby Eva. And Carlos.

She'd barely been able to think about anything else since she'd gotten Carlos's email the day before. She'd written and deleted about five responses until she'd finally given up.

She walked through the store, still thinking about the email. She stopped in the baked goods aisle and stared at four shelves full of different gluten-free flours without really seeing them. She wanted so much to respond, but she had no idea what to say.

She shook her head to try to clear her mind. Thinking like this was not going to help. And for God's sake, especially not in the grocery store. She had a list, remember? And—she finally realized what she was staring at—sorghum flour was not on it. She pushed her cart until she found olive oil and checked it off her list.

She sped through the store, grabbing bananas, granola, bread, tomatoes, bacon. Oh good, she could make herself a BLT when she got home tonight. People always said it was a bad idea to go to the grocery store while hungry, but she always made herself delicious meals when she got home from the grocery store on those Friday nights.

She made her way to the dairy aisle to stock up on yogurt. When she saw the big tubs of sour cream, she laughed out loud, startling the employee stocking the dairy case. She didn't think she would ever be able to see sour cream without remembering when she'd spackled her face with it after she'd set herself on fire with chilies. And when she laughed so hard with Carlos about it that they'd ended up sitting on the bathroom floor in tears. She grabbed six containers of yogurt, still with a smile on her face.

Would she always think about Carlos whenever she saw sour cream? She hoped so, despite everything. Seeing that sour cream made her think of how happy she'd been around him, at every moment. It made her think of how proud he was of all of her accomplishments, from writing for the *New Yorker* to signing up for boxing class. It made her think of how he'd dropped everything to help her, more than once, and how happy she was to be able to help him the night Eva was born. She never wanted to stop thinking about him.

Wait.

Holy shit.

Oh no.

WAS THIS WHAT LOVE WAS?

Being happy when you thought about someone; wanting to never stop thinking about them, even when you were fighting; having every damn thing in the grocery store remind you of them, from diapers to sour cream; wanting to be a better writer and friend and person because of how they were and how they made you feel; wanting to be with them, all the time, even though you kept fighting it.

Motherfucker.

She was in love with him.

Now what?

She walked to the register like she was in a dream. She didn't know how to do this. How did a person even handle this sort of thing?

She didn't like this; she didn't like it at all. She felt gooey and vulnerable and helpless. She didn't like feeling any of those things. If this was what Natalie had meant by trusting herself and her emotions, she wasn't a fan of it at all.

When she'd been with Justin, she'd felt anxious and needy and constantly on edge, like she had to prove herself all the time. Thinking about him had never made her feel happy like thinking about Carlos did. She knew Carlos loved her— as difficult and prickly and loud as she was—just for being her. And she loved him for being the funny, kind, warm person he was. She loved him so much.

Oh no, this was awful.

She preferred her comfortable, easy, safe flings with guys she didn't care about to all of these terrible feelings. Her first instinct was to get in her car, get on the freeway going east, and just keep driving.

Yes, that was a good idea. She should drive until she hit the desert and then stay there. That way, she would never have to deal with this and maybe eventually it would go away.

She stuck her credit card in the stupid card

reader that beeped at her like she'd done something wrong and thought hard about that plan. She could go right now. These bananas and that granola, plus the bottled water that she'd bought weeks ago and had been too lazy to take out of her trunk, all of that could last her a few weeks, right? Not that she would have any way of knowing. She hadn't driven to the desert or slept outside since . . . okay, it was definitely within the last ten years—she'd be fine.

She pushed her cart to her car and loaded her groceries into the trunk. What all did she need, anyway? Food, water, a bucket of some sort? There must be an REI that was open late nearby somewhere where she could buy one and a flashlight and an emergency sleeping bag that would become an actual cocoon for her so she didn't have to deal with how she'd fucked everything up.

She sat in her car but didn't turn it on.

She put her head down on her steering wheel. And, oops, she honked the horn with her nose. She sat up with a jerk and waved an apology to the dog in the car facing hers. It still barked at her.

Maybe driving to the desert in the middle of the night in July wasn't the best idea she'd ever had, but the alternative was to actually think about this, and how she didn't know how to do this, and what if his email had meant he was apologizing for saying he loved her because he hadn't actually meant it, and how she didn't know what she would do if she never saw him again, and the desert sounded better than all of that.

The Vons parking lot was no place to figure this out. Maybe . . . maybe Carlos would be waiting on her doorstep this time. Yes, she would go home, and he'd be waiting for her there. She would leap into his arms and say she loved him and that she was sorry for everything, and he would say he'd never stopped loving her, and they'd go upstairs and have lots of sex, and everything would be perfect.

She started her car and raced home, convinced more and more every moment that that was what was going to happen. It made perfect sense. He had sent that email so she would be ready to leap into his arms when he showed up! Which she would!

She pulled into the parking lot behind her building and walked around to the front with her groceries, ready to pretend to be surprised as soon as she saw him.

But no one was there.

Fuck.

Did this mean she was going to have to figure out how to fix this herself?

She walked into her apartment and put her entire grocery bag in her refrigerator, too tired and confused to unload it.

She pulled out her phone to text Courtney and Dana. But what was she going to say to them? "I just realized I'm in love with Carlos and don't know what to do"? She already knew what they would tell her to do.

TELL HIM—that's what they would say. Courtney would use all caps; Dana wouldn't but would use exclamation points, but the message would remain the same.

But didn't they know how hard it would be to tell him something like that?

Yeah, they'd been her friends for fifteen years. She was pretty sure they knew. But they would tell her to do it anyway. The assholes.

When she realized that she was cursing at her friends because of their imaginary conversation with her, she knew she'd gone fully around the bend. Okay, tonight she was going to make no impulsive decisions, neither driving to the desert nor texting anyone would happen. She turned off her phone and went straight to bed. Maybe in the morning she would be over this love nonsense.

She woke up the next morning after ten full hours of sleep and stumbled to the kitchen to make coffee. She opened the refrigerator to get milk and did a double take at the full grocery bag stuffed onto the middle shelf of her refrigerator.

"Why the fuck did I do that? Was I drunk last night?"

Oh. It all came back to her now. Way worse than drunk.

The coffee pot beeped at her, and she poured herself a cup and drank about half of it like a very hot tequila shot.

She sat down and stared into her coffee mug for five full minutes. Then she took out her phone to text her friends.

I realized I'm in love with Carlos and I don't know what to do.

She sat there, staring at her phone, waiting for their responses.

OMG. This is so exciting! I knew it! You've got to tell him!

That was Dana, of course. Wait a minute, what did she mean, she knew it?

FINALLY. But why are you telling us, tell HIM.

"Finally" was not the response she had expected to get.

Why are you guys acting like this is old news? I just realized it last night and I almost had a breakdown in the Vons parking lot!

She poured another mug full of coffee. What had she been thinking last night, granola? All she wanted right now was a doughnut.

Oh, honey, we've known this for weeks, but it doesn't matter that you're late to the party. All that matters is that you got here at all. Right, Dana?

Right! Go get him!

She hated them so much.

"Go get him!" they said. Like that was easy. Like she knew how to do something like that. Like she wasn't terrified to do it.

She finished her cup of coffee and poured another one. Then she picked up her phone and scrolled back through her call log until she found the number. She took a deep breath.

"Hi, Angela? Hi, this is Nik. We, um. We met at the Dodgers game, and . . . yeah, that Nik. I need a favor."

Chapter Twenty-three

• • • • • •

Carlos didn't think he'd ever get Angela to leave Jessie's side. They'd been there for the past four hours, and the way Angie looked at Eva, it seemed like they'd be there for another four hours, minimum. The original plan had been for Angie to go today and for him to go tomorrow, but Angie had called him that morning and said Jessie wanted to see them both today, since her mom was coming over tomorrow. He didn't quite understand the logic there, but he chalked it up to hormones and went along with it.

Plus, it wasn't like he had anything better to do.

"Hey, man," he said to Jon when Jessie and Angie were giggling about something in the corner, Eva sound asleep on Jon's chest. "I'm sorry we've been here for so long. I'm sure you two wanted to be alone with your baby more in these first few weeks."

Jon laughed.

"Thanks, but I've known my wife's family long enough to know that there isn't going to be a day in the next month, minimum, when we'll be alone with our baby. And you know what, that's fine with me. These past few months have been so stressful, and now we have this tiny baby who we are responsible for, and I'm grateful for every bit of help from everyone in your family, because I sure as hell don't know what I'm doing." He looked down at his daughter on his chest and then back up at Carlos. "I'm glad she has you guys. Come over anytime."

Carlos patted him on the shoulder, realizing just in time to do it softly enough so he wouldn't wake the baby.

"We're going to be over so often that you're going to get sick of us. I already adore my new little cousin."

Jon stroked Eva's mass of dark hair.

"Anytime you want to come entertain her late at night so we can sleep, just let us know."

Angela stood up and interrupted their laughter.

"Hey, Carlos, you ready to go? We should probably give Jessie and Jon some time alone with their baby."

He stood up too.

"I was just saying that to Jon." He rubbed Eva's little head as a good-bye and hugged Jessie.

"I thought you were trying to get us to move in," he said to Angie once they'd gotten in the car.

"Oh." She looked out the passenger window. "I just thought Jessie needed some company, that's all." She turned to look at him. "Was that all right? You didn't have plans tonight, did you?"

On a Saturday night? Of course he didn't have plans. The person that he'd had plans with for most of the Saturday nights this summer clearly never wanted to see him again. She hadn't even replied to his email.

Sure, he'd said she didn't have to, but he'd still really wanted her to reply.

"No," was all he said. He didn't want to sound too bitter. "I was happy to stay there as long as they needed us."

Angie let out a relieved sigh.

"Oh good, that's okay then."

He dropped her off at her apartment, then drove the short distance to his house. His only plan on this Saturday night was to watch the Dodgers game from the couch. Whatever snack he ate along with it would have to be low in cholesterol, after what his doctor had said on Friday, but he could handle that.

He unlocked his front door and stepped inside.

What the hell?

There were blue and white streamers, Dodger pennants, and boxes of Cracker Jack everywhere. And standing directly across from him, wearing a blue and white baseball T-shirt and jeans, was Nik.

"Hi," she said.

"Nik." My God, it was so good to see her. He

wanted to cross the room in one leap and embrace her. He wanted to tell her how much he'd missed her. He wanted to tell her how much he loved her, still. Wait, no, that's what started all the problems in the first place. He dropped his keys on the table by the door and didn't move. "Hi."

"Hi," she said again and smiled. "I, um. I got your email. I know you said I didn't have to respond, but I have something to . . . I want to . . ." She shook her head. "Hold on."

She pulled aside the blue tarp that had been covering his TV, and he looked at the brightly lit screen.

CARLOS
I LOVE YOU
NIK

"I wanted an actual JumboTron," she said, "But it would have been really hard to get one of those inside your house, so I decided to work with what I had: a laptop hooked up to a TV and terrible graphic design skills."

He took a step toward her. He kept looking from her to the screen and back to her.

"Is this for real?" he said.

She rolled her eyes at him.

"You know me too well to ask me that, come on. Would I, Nikole Paterson, do something like this as a joke?"

He shook his head and took another step toward her.

"You wouldn't, but I had to make sure. And I wanted you to say it out loud."

She looked straight into his eyes.

"Carlos. I love you. I'm in love with you. I realized it in the sour cream aisle at Vons last night. Isn't that a ridiculous place to realize you're in love with someone? Well, that's how it happened to me. I saw the sour cream, and I laughed, and I thought about you, and I thought about how happy you make me and how much I missed you, and then I realized what all of those feelings meant, and then I felt like a fool for letting you go." Tears were streaming down her face by that point. He wiped them away with his thumb. "So I thought I should tell you, and I'm sorry—I'm so sorry—that I didn't realize it earlier, and that I was so skittish and scared when you said you loved me."

He pulled her into his arms. He couldn't remember the last time he'd been this happy.

"Oh, Nik."

She pulled back.

"Wait, wait, let me finish. I've spent so long being afraid of love, because the last time I was in love, the man I loved only loved one part of me, but not all of me, and I thought love meant having to sacrifice a part of yourself. But then I was with you, and you loved every part of me, even the parts I don't like. And that scared me more, because I thought there must be some trick and that I couldn't let myself believe it or I'd fall into the trap. But finally I realized it wasn't a trap."

He held her face in his hands and kissed her.

She kissed him back with so much joy and sincerity and love that he almost started crying. He pulled her down onto his couch and kept his arms around her.

"I missed you so much," he said. "I kept wanting to call you, to say you were right and to just pretend I didn't love you, just so I would have you in my life again, but I couldn't bring myself to do it."

She wiped her eyes.

"If you had, it probably would have crushed me. I would have pretended it hadn't, gone along with it, and we would have done this same stupid thing for like another year or two before I finally admitted to myself how much I loved you. So it's a good thing you didn't."

She kissed him again.

"How's Eva?" she asked.

"Tiny. Beautiful. Perfect," he said. "Jessie and Jon are exhausted but so happy and totally in love with their daughter. Thanks again for the cupcakes. Jessie really did tell me to say that; it wasn't just an excuse to email you."

She smiled.

"I wondered. And sort of hoped." She took a deep breath. "Carlos, I'm still not sure if I know how to love someone, and I really don't know if I know how to let myself be loved, so I hope you'll be patient with me as I figure out how to do this. But I really love you so I hope you will be."

"I will be as patient as you need me to, but I think you know how to love someone a lot better than you think," he said.

She smiled at him and kissed him again.

"I really hope so," she said. "I missed you so much, too. I kept trying to deny to myself how much I missed you, and how much a part of my life you'd become, and how important you were to me. And then when I realized it, it terrified me. I was so scared to feel this way. If we're being honest, which I hope . . ." she paused and closed her eyes for a moment. "Sorry, I just . . ." He ran his fingers through her curls and waited for her to collect herself. She leaned her head on his shoulder for a second, sat up straight and started again. "If we're being honest, which I hope we can always be to each other, I'm still scared to feel this way." She laughed. "As if you hadn't already noticed that."

He kissed her cheek. He'd noticed. But he'd also noticed that, despite her fear, she was still here. Sitting next to him.

"And then I was scared that you wouldn't still feel the same way. That I'd been right the first time, that it was all because of emotion and adrenaline and you'd realized you were better off without me."

"You weren't right the first time," he said. "Even though I tried to convince myself you were."

"Thank God for that," she said.

"Thank God for that sour cream," he said. "I can't believe I'm going to have to be in debt to sour cream for the rest of my life. We can't tell anyone that part of the story, it isn't romantic at all. It couldn't have been something sexier?"

"Like what? Eggplant? Hot dogs? Bananas?"

He laughed and pulled her against him.

"I was thinking, I don't know, chilies, or bacon, or even your favorite rosé. But for this"—he gestured to the TV, the decorations, to Nik—"for you? I'd take anything."

"See? That was so . . ." She beamed at him, as tears ran down her face. "You're much better at this romance stuff than I am."

He wiped the tears away with his thumb and kissed her again.

"You're doing great," he said.

He looked around his house with a grin.

"I can't believe this," he said. "I'm so happy you're here."

"Good," she said. "Because I can't believe I pulled this all together at the last minute today, so you'd better appreciate it."

And then he realized something.

"ANGELA."

She leaned back against the couch cushions and laughed.

"Angela, indeed. She gave me the key and kept you away until I was all ready for you. I had to make my case to her first, though. Let me tell you, she was very suspicious when I called her this morning."

That's why they'd stayed at Jessie's for so long.

"I bet she was. But she always liked you. Plus, she knew you were the reason I finally went to the doctor."

She sat up with a jerk.

"You went to the doctor? Really?"

He gave her a tentative smile.

"I went yesterday."

She threw her arms around him.

"Oh, Carlos, I know how hard that must have been for you. I'm so proud of you!"

He buried his nose in her hair. That coconut smell made him so happy.

"It was really hard. But I did it. And I'm okay. My cholesterol is a little high, but not anything my doctor is super worried about, so I'll cut back the red meat and add more leafy greens and I should be able to manage it."

She ran her hands through his hair.

"I am so glad to hear that. Oh! I have some news, too."

He pulled back and looked at her, and she smiled.

"I punched Fisher in the face."

He jumped up from the couch.

"You what? Oh my God." He picked her up and swung her in a circle. "You are a superhero. What the fuck did that bastard do this time? I can't wait to hear everything."

She held up her hand and wiggled her fingers.

"He went down like a ton of bricks, it was amazing. My knuckles are still a little raw. I'm so sad you weren't there to see it, but luckily, plenty of people walking and driving down my street did. He was so mad about that. It was so great."

He sat back on the couch and pulled her down next to him.

"I love you so much."

She beamed at him.

"I know."

About the Author

Jasmine Guillory is a graduate of Wellesley College and Stanford Law School. She is a Bay Area native who lives in Oakland, California. She has towering stacks of books in her living room, a cake recipe for every occasion, and upwards of fifty lipsticks. Visit her online at jasmineguillory .com and twitter.com/thebestjasmine.

Center Point Large Print
600 Brooks Road / PO Box 1
Thorndike, ME 04986-0001 USA

(207) 568-3717

US & Canada:
1 800 929-9108
www.centerpointlargeprint.com